D1826750

THE RETREAT

KAY JAYBEE

Published by Xcite Books Ltd – 2013
ISBN 9781909520813

Copyright © Kay Jaybee 2013

All rights reserved. No part of this book may be
reproduced, stored in a retrieval system, or
transmitted in any form or by any means, electronic,
electrostatic, magnetic tape, mechanical,
photocopying, recording or otherwise, without the
written permission of the publishers: Xcite Books,
Suite 11769, 2nd Floor, 145-157 St John Street,
London EC1V 4PY

Printed and bound in the UK

This is a work of fiction. Names and characters are
the product of the author's imagination and any
resemblance to actual persons, living or dead, is
entirely coincidental.

Dedicated to The Brit Babes – a truly inspiring group of friends.
http://thebritbabes.blogspot.co.uk/

Prologue

'PLEASE, SIR. PLEASE! I won't let you down.'

David Proctor peered at the woman crouched before him. A haphazard pile of blonde curls was all he could see of her bowed head.

'I can learn. I can.' Her voice quivered with deep-seated yearning. 'I'll learn to be whoever you want me to be.'

The heated softness of her Scottish accent added a dimension to David's arousal he hadn't expected. No stranger to the world of submission and domination, he'd never met anyone so keen to be subservient to him before.

With his ego growing almost as much as his cock, which nudged against the inside of his suit trousers, David hunkered down beside the girl. Her bare buttocks bore the pleasing marks of his palm. The fading prints were a blotched pink now, but they'd blazed red only moments ago, when he'd pinned her across his lap, spanking her backside again and again in punishment for her repeated disobedience. Or rather, for her failure to obey, despite her repeated efforts to please him.

The cook's breasts, just over a handful in size, were dotted with freckles, and as he fondled them, David's mind seethed with images of all the things a willing slave could do for him.

Lifting her lowered head by the chin, David fixed his hazel eyes into her sapphire ones. 'But you refuse to climax when I tell you to.' His voice wasn't angry, but it was hard. David Proctor was, and would always be, an unyielding businessman. If there was nothing in any arrangement of long-term benefit for him, it wouldn't happen.

'I want to though, sir. I really want to, I ... Forgive me, but you make me hang on for so long before granting permission to come, and then I can't. I am so sorry, I ...'

'Sshhh.' David ran his fingers through the wisps of hair that had escaped her hooked-up ponytail. There was no denying that she intrigued him. With each stroke of her wavy locks, he pondered his situation.

The Retreat *did* need another submissive. And *soon,* if his business plans were to expand in the direction he intended. The man Fairtasia was sending to represent them was due any day now, and not long after that, their delegates would arrive.

'Please, sir?' The cook's pupils seemed impossibly wide as she held his eyes, and but for the occasional shiver of denied desire, her bare legs didn't move against the stone kitchen floor, proving just how good her stamina was already. 'Lady Tia could teach me.'

'Training ...' David spoke the thought slowly, as if to himself, mulling each letter over with his tongue, but the young woman leapt upon the word.

'Training! Yes, sir! Dr Ewen says Lady Tia is the best dominatrix there is.'

'She is indeed good, but ...' The Retreat's new owner reached his hands back to the girl's tits, and felt his cock stiffen further as her nipples pressed greedily against his skin 'I'm not sure Lady Tia's field of expertise will be sufficient. Spankings and beatings you can already take, and plainly enjoy.'

The girl dipped her face once more. She was obviously trying not to let her disappointment in her own shortcomings show. There was no doubt she was

2

submissive material, and yet not quite. Her deference to him, however, and his urgent requirement for an additional member of staff, made David's mind up for him.

'I think it's time I contacted a friend in England. I'm sure she'll send us the help we need.' As he manipulated the cook's chest with greater vigour, relishing the resulting gasp of pain-tinged pleasure that flew from her lips, David's round face gave a calculating smile.

His eyes had fallen upon the giant range in the centre of The Retreat's antique kitchen. Then his gaze travelled to the table next to it. A huge, old-fashioned pottery jar of ginger powder, and another of brown sugar, sat awaiting the sidetracked cook's attention.

For weeks, David had been contemplating how to impress the Fairtasia company delegation. He knew that the final securing of the contract he wanted from them so badly would depend on the outcome of the party The Retreat was hosting for them in a month's time.

In order for the head of Fairtasia to sign on the dotted line, and make their business arrangement official, the evening would have to be unforgettable. Now, as he looked about him, David knew *precisely* what theme that party was going to take. And how fitting it would be.

'Alisha.'

The cook jerked her head up hopefully at her employer's use of her first name.

'You may train to become The Retreat's new submissive. Lady Tia can begin your lessons as you suggest.' David unzipped the fly of his trousers. As he freed his dick, he had to suppress a laugh as the girl eyed it hungrily. 'You may also address me as David. I don't like "sir". I never have. Now suck me off.'

'Yes, David.'

'Good girl.' Extracting his mobile from his pocket, David tapped in a number as the cook's velvet mouth engulfed him.

The sucking of Alisha's lips and tongue working around his length was the only sound in the granite room as David waited for his call to be picked up.

'Ah, Fables Hotel? Could you put me through to Mrs Peters' office, please …? Not there …? Please tell her that Mr Proctor has a proposition for her; and that time is of the essence.'

Pocketing his mobile, David tangled his fingers in the cook's increasingly messed-up hair. Tilting his groin forward, admiring the way Alisha amended her position so she didn't gag, but took him deeper, David asked, 'Tell me, how much do you know about fairy tales …?'

Chapter One

THE CHIME OF the grandfather clock told Jess that it had been half an hour since the clipped edge to the manageress's voice had requested her immediate presence in the Victorian study.

Fully clothed, stretched over the study's large wooden desk, her hands out to the sides, her right cheek flat to the blotting paper-covered top, Fables' resident submissive was no nearer discovering what Mrs Peters had wanted when she'd asked Jess to join her.

No cords or cuffs had been used to keep Jess in place. Nor was her mouth gagged or her peppermint eyes hidden with one of the manageress's extensive collection of masks and blindfolds. Mrs Peters had told her submissive to remain precisely where she was, and Jess was far too sensible not to obey. She also knew it was to her advantage to make sure that not an inch of her moved until she was instructed to; because that way her orgasm-dependent body might get the attention it constantly required sooner rather than later.

Unlike her body, Jess's brain had proved not so easy to tame. As she lay there, her stomach muscles scrambling in a knot of erotic apprehension and expectation, her thoughts careered off on their own. A hundred possibilities about her immediate future flowed through her consciousness as Jess speculated about how her body might be used this time.

Miss Jess Sanders had worked at the five-storey Fables Hotel for six months now. Floors one to four of this popular establishment provided standard business and holiday accommodation. The fifth floor, however, catered exclusively for adults; adults who required very particular facilities alongside their room and meals.

Originally employed as the hotel's booking clerk, it had been a considerable shock to Jess when, after only a week in her new job, Mrs Laura Peters had made it very clear that she had every intention to train her to become a member of her specialised top floor staff. And Mrs Peters was very difficult to say no to.

As Jess lay stretched across the desk, resisting the temptation to brush away a strand of her red hair that had flopped from her fringe to fall into her eyes, she remembered how the hotel's overall manager, Mr Davis, had informed her about Fables' adult features. It had been stressed to her in no uncertain terms, that guests paid for the hotel's rooms and food only. It was *not* a prostitution or escort racket. Basically, it was like going on an expensive fantasy date.

Relaxing as best she could into the solid surface beneath her, using her reflective train of thought to deflect the mounting tremors dancing through her pussy, Jess considered what a good description of the service they provided that had been. The fifth floor was a place where extreme sexual fantasies came true. Somewhere anyone with the funds to pay for a room could live out their secret desires in safety. A hit of pride at being part of that service, of providing a means by which their guests' darkest lust-fuelled dreams could come true in perfect safety, sent Jess's thoughts off at another tangent. Whose dreams will I make come true today, she wondered, and how much will it hurt? An extra jolt of erotic anticipation hurtled directly to Jess's clit, causing her to halt her graphic musings; knowing how easily her imagination could lead to her downfall.

Aware that Mrs Peters sat in the wing-backed chair by the study door, silently watching her, Jess felt her nipples harden further, and forced herself back into the protective reflection of her recent past.

Jess's surprise when she realised Mrs Peters didn't have an administrative role, but a submissive one, in mind for her had taken weeks to sink in. Prior to arriving at Fables, her sex life had been almost non-existent, and she certainly hadn't experienced any submissive urges. It wouldn't have occurred to her that she could gain sexual gratification from the world of dominance, obedience, and physical and emotional submission. Somehow, though, Mrs Peters had seen through Jess's quiet, self-contained, shy persona. Spotting a buried supplicant potential laced with both intelligence and a level of empathy that was highly important when it came to serving their guests.

Swallowing without a sound, Jess lubricated her dry throat as she recalled how, in that very room, across the desk on which she currently lay with barely concealed impatience, she'd witnessed a fit and handsome young man beg for punishment from Miss Sarah, the hotel's dominatrix. Jess had never seen anything like it. The unexpected awakening that witnessing the show had engendered had filled her with a wealth of confusion.

That visit to the Victorian study had been the first step on the road to an intense training session, which had taken Jess on a voyage of self-discovery, and helped her build up a stamina and inner strength she'd never dreamt she could possess. It had led to months of entertaining clients within the hotel's specially designed fifth-floor rooms, which included a medical bay, schoolroom, dungeon, and the mysterious White Room.

Conscious that her memories, rather than holding back her arousal, were accelerating it, Jess hastily curtailed them. Closing her eyes for a second in an attempt to calm the increasing anxiety that the calculated silent delay was fostering, she knew in her heart there was no other job she could do now. Her body had been conditioned to crave non-stop tangible attention, and it would never forgive her if she gave up her daily diet of sexual punishment and gratification.

Anyway, Jess couldn't leave Miss Sarah.

And Miss Sarah would never leave Fables.

This contentment with her working life didn't mean Jess was relaxed in her work. A submissive never relaxed; a fact Jess had learnt the hard way only a few days after she'd been confirmed as a permanent employee on floor five. She winced at the memory as she lay there. Perhaps being in the study now was yet more punishment for the crime she'd unwittingly committed so early on in her hostess career? A professional slip she'd already paid for many times, and was never going to be allowed to forget. Jess shuddered against the table as the spectre of her mistake, and her boss's disdainful expression, crept up on her.

Under the watchful eye of Mrs Peters, Jess had spent an hour crawling on all fours, pretending to be the personal lapdog of a gentleman who'd wanted her to act like a bitch on heat. Shy, but obedient, Jess has played her part well, ending the session by carrying out the client's request for her to lick his cock until he came. She'd felt proud of herself as, with a blissed-out expression on his face, he'd come beneath her touch. Then she'd ruined it. The hour was up. The man had been dressing, when Jess stood up and addressed him as if she was his equal. The look on his and Mrs Peters' face would haunt her for ever.

Just thinking about her error made Jess's buttocks throb with recollection of the correction that had followed. It wasn't the spanking that had stung her, though. It was Mrs Peters' words. 'You appear to be under the impression you are the perfect submissive, Miss Sanders. Perhaps Miss Sarah has misled you in this. There is no such thing as a perfect submissive. The term is a contraction in itself. You would do well to remember that.'

A knock on the study door brought Jess back to the present. She tensed into statue stillness, the hard, unyielding surface beneath her forgotten for a moment as she strained to hear what was going on out of her line of sight.

The sound of three pairs of feet walking into the room revealed to Jess that she wasn't the only one Mrs Peters wanted to talk to.

With regal poise, her hands lodged on her hips over the dark green velvet dress she wore, the manageress moved behind the wooden desk upon which Jess was prostrated. Without having to be told, Mrs Peters' partner, business assistant, and artist, Sam Wheeler, took a seat on the red chaise longue to her left, making him the only person in Jess's direct eye line. The fact he didn't have his eyes lowered in deference to his woman informed Jess this was a staff meeting, not a training session. Any chastisement, therefore, was for her alone, and not the group at large. Jess frantically thought back over the past few days. Had she done anything else wrong? Or was this, as she had first suspected, Mrs Peters showing her her place?

From her limited viewpoint, Jess saw Lee Philips, the barman, receptionist, and occasional fifth floor assistant, pass before her and, as quietly as ever, prop himself up against the far wall.

That only left the final member of staff. The dominatrix, Miss Sarah. From the direction of her voice as she politely greeted her superior, Jess guessed she was sitting in the wing-backed chair her boss had so recently vacated.

Trying to deny the increase in her pulse rate, Jess remembered how afraid she'd been of Miss Sarah. The

9

dominatrix's tall, slim frame, the chestnut hair that framed her face and neck, her flawless porcelain skin, the unshakeable demeanour that belied she was capable of any emotion at all, were more than a little disturbing to someone as unworldly as Jess had been. Usually dressed in a corset, or some other garment that was so tight-fitting it gave the impression that, for Miss Sarah, breathing was an optional pastime, the dominatrix was an undeniably imposing figure.

The guests liked her because she radiated an air of authority. Without so much as raising an eyebrow, Miss Sarah's expression suggested she was someone you couldn't possibly disobey, thus taking away the guilt a guest might feel at wanting to have their backside whipped, or humbling themselves before another in the name of living out a fantasy. Their consciences could always fall back on the fact that Miss Sarah had *made* them do it. Miss Sarah had *ordered* them to. Which of course she had – but only because she knew they wanted her to. She could read a person's need to be controlled every bit as clearly as Mrs Peters seemed to be able to read her staff's thoughts before they'd even finished having them. Two skills that, even after six months of working with these women, unnerved Jess a great deal.

'Good afternoon. Thank you all for coming. I will keep this brief.' Mrs Peters' shrewd eyes appraised her newest recruit as she spoke. 'There is no reason to look so worried, Miss Sanders. Your beautiful behind is quite safe for the moment. You may sit upon the desk.'

Rising fast enough to be seen as obeying instantly, but not so fast as to make herself dizzy, Jess climbed onto the top of the antique desk as Mrs Peters had indicated. Sitting cross-legged in the very centre of its blotting paper-covered surface, so she could see her boss, but none of the other staff behind her, Jess experienced a sharp stab of disappointment that the spanking she'd assumed was coming had not taken place. At least, it hadn't yet.

'I have some news which requires the cooperation of you all.' Mrs Peters didn't move a muscle, but Jess knew she was simultaneously looking at every person in the room. 'Miss Sanders has, as ever, assumed her summoning here is because of a transgression which requires correction. In this instance, I am pleased to inform you that the complete opposite is true.'

Jess did her best to keep her facial expression blank, but her eyes almost betrayed her.

'I'm not sure if that's relief or disappointment in those forever dilated eyes of yours, Miss Sanders.'
Not daring to look round to see her colleagues' faces, Jess kept quiet. The dampening of her knickers, after being made to wait for something that wasn't going to happen, was increased by Mrs Peters' creeping a single, enquiring digit between her legs.

Saying nothing about her submissive's arousal, Mrs Peters gathered her thick, russet hair into a high ponytail, and strolled around the historically accurate room, the skirt of her long velvet dress rustling as she did so. 'I believe you have all, in one capacity or another, entertained one of our regular guests, Mr David Proctor.'

Jess's throat went from dry to dehydrated. All of the visitors to the fifth floor were demanding, especially of her, but David Proctor was the only one she seriously disliked. This dislike wasn't because his tastes were harsh, or the demands he made were more painful, or more humiliating, than those of the others. He was so ambitious, and single-minded, that she couldn't trust him to stick to the rules of safety. Proctor gave off an air that he knew more about what was going on at Fables than anyone else, including the staff. He could only be described as average in his appearance, but he was outstandingly influential, and the only man Jess had ever met who had no fear of Mrs Peters. Nor could Mrs Peters influence him like she could be other guests. David Proctor frightened Jess.

'David, as is clear from the amount of money he spends here, is a very wealthy businessman. And –' Mrs Peters paused, and for the briefest second Jess thought perhaps her boss didn't completely approve of what she was about to say, before her innate self-control took over '– he has decided to embark upon a new venture. An investment; an incentive if you like. Something extra to ensure his clients and business associates continue to work with him.'

Foreboding spread over Jess like a tidal wave. Her lower limbs were beginning to numb from staying in a cross-legged position, and she could feel prickles of nervous perspiration dot the back of her neck. Nothing that involved David Proctor could be good news.

A hush had fallen on the study. It had been quiet anyway. Not even Miss Sarah would have the nerve to stop Laura Peters in mid-announcement. However, the calibre of the communal listening had gone from being wary to tangibly tense. Jess could almost taste the apprehension filling the study. She wished it didn't arouse her quite so much.

Mrs Peters swept back to the desk. Her right palm stroked Jess's breasts through her thin cotton blouse. 'This investment involves the purchase of a business premises where fantasies can be indulged in without judgement, or the need for personal justification. In short, David is looking to recreate exactly what we do here at Fables.'

As her piercing jade eyes levelled on the tips of her fingers as they crossed Jess's shirt, Mrs Peters added, 'An idea which obviously appeals to you, Miss Sanders, if the peaked state of you nipples is anything to go by.'

Jess's cheeks flushed. Her generous chest, the feature which, beyond her natural deference, had first attracted her to Mrs Peters' attention, was nudging against the fabric of her bra and shirt with no regard for the consequences.

'Take your top off, girl.'

Even after six months working for the woman, Jess couldn't prevent her hands from shaking as Mrs Peters added, 'Then sit on your hands, Miss Sanders. It will make it less tempting for you to let your fingers stray without permission.'

Feeling only a glimmer of humiliation, rather than the full-on shame that would have engulfed her in the early days of her training, Jess complied. Cursing her overactive brain, which had already leapt ahead to the part in the proceedings where Mrs Peters ordered one of the men to fuck her, Jess wished she'd been instructed to take her panties off as well as her top. They were so wet that they were sticking to her crotch, making it increasingly difficult not to squirm as she sat in her yoga-type pose.

Having placed Jess into a more agreeably visual position, Laura Peters paid little heed to her as she went on, 'You will all appreciate, I hope, that we should be extremely flattered here at Fables. Not only is our work considered worthy of imitation, but David has asked for our express assistance in improving his new establishment.'

The temperature of the study was so high it had been bordering on stuffy, but goosepimples of cold spotted Jess's naked arms. Whatever her boss was about to say, she was sure she didn't want to hear it.

Not for the first time, she was grateful for all the exercise sessions Miss Sarah had forced her to endure. They had taught Jess a great amount of self-discipline, and as a result she'd developed the stamina and posture required to be motionless for long periods of time. Put through her paces three times a week, naked, often with a love ball or butt-plug in place, every single lesson had been like pure torture at first. Nowadays the sessions had taken on a more personal dimension. Miss Sarah claimed that ending their fitness routine a bout of mutual pleasure provided them with an excellent way of releasing the tensions of the day, and Jess found herself looking forward to them far more than she would dare admit – even to herself.

Jess wrenched her concentration back to what Mrs Peters was saying. 'The location of this new resort is a secret, but in order to ensure the calibre of his staff is as, and I am proud to quote Mr Proctor here, "as excellent, obedient, and inventive as those of the Fables Fifth Floor", he has requested that we loan him two members of staff to help train his fledging team.'

If the atmosphere had been tense before, it was positively bristling with static now. No one moved. Jess wasn't sure anyone was even breathing. One silent thought occupied the study. Please don't let one of them be me.

The minute's silence ended with a solo round of applause from Mrs Peters. 'Again you all prove to me that you are worthy of your places on the fifth floor. I can't imagine that any of you would want to leave, and yet not one of you so much as raised an eyebrow on the outside. Congratulations. I realise I rarely share my pride in your work, but on this occasion it seems fitting.' Far from feeling reassured, Jess was now really worried. Mrs Peters never said well done without there being a price to pay.

Beginning to pace again, Mrs Peters ran a proprietorial hand over the face of each member of her workforce, until she reached Jess. Flicking a finger across her sub's right nipple, she nodded in approval. Although her clear green eyes had flared, Jess's body didn't even twitch. Mrs Peters paused, surveying the whole room as she spoke. 'I trust that for the two-week period you'll be seconded into the care of Mr Proctor, you will both continue to do yourselves and Fables proud.'

Finally, when the tension that had smothered the room had become too much to take, Sam took a chance. 'So, which of us are to leave and, more to the point, who will fill their positions here while they are away? As you rightly say, our reputation for service is excellent, why would we risk it for Proctor?'

Although her eyes narrowed, Laura Peters didn't admonish Sam for speaking out of turn, a fact that made Jess's heart plummet further. If Mrs Peters had told him off, humbled him before everybody, then Jess could have safely assumed this was an elaborate exercise to see how they'd cope with such news. Now she was sure this wasn't something her boss had made up. This was actually happening, and two of them were about to be loaned out to a man she couldn't stand, and did not trust.

'The gap here will be filled by Lee taking on extra work.'

Jess heard Lee exhale as he sagged in relief against the William Morris wallpaper. Meanwhile, her own muscles knotted further and a wave of nausea swam up her throat. If Lee was staying that could only mean one thing …

Mrs Peters continued, 'And of course, I will take on more work myself.'

That means it has to be a combination of myself and either Miss Sarah or Sam … Jess felt sick. At Fables she was safe. Here, if she really did not want to do what a guest wished her to do, then she could get help, she could walk out, she could simply leave. But she didn't even know where this new place was. What if it was abroad, what if …?

Jess's wildly rampaging thoughts were interrupted by Mrs Peters. 'As I know you all to be intelligent individuals, you'll have worked out that it will be Miss Sanders and Miss Sarah who are to leave us for a while.'

Jess's hands slipped out from beneath her. Only self defence kept her lips from protesting.

'May I ask a question, madam?' Miss Sarah broke her previous silence.

'I'm afraid not.' Mrs Peters, who had unnerved Jess further by not telling her off for shifting the position of her arms without permission, said, 'I wish you and Miss Sanders to go and pack. You are being collected by David's associate in three hours' time. In one hour I wish you to be ready to leave, and standing in the White Room. There you will receive a suitable send-off. You are dismissed. I suggest you don't waste your hour on unnecessary conversation.'

Chapter Two

LAURA SAT AT the desk and looked at Sam. He was reclining upon the chaise longue, his long legs stretched out before him in a far more relaxed pose than he'd adopted during her announcement. 'You questioned me in front of the staff.'

He met her cut-glass gaze. Sam had known she wouldn't thank him for speaking out, but he couldn't shake the feeling there was more to her agreement to help Proctor than just being flattered by his kind words.

'I did.' Sam considered the consequences of continuing and carried on regardless. 'If you're about to ask me if I think you've made the right decision to lend him your key team members, then you may be disappointed by my answer.'

'Come here.' Laura reached out a hand.

Not fooled by what anybody else would have seen as a conciliatory gesture, the artist immediately rose and took her palm, pulling his lover to her feet as he did so. Not many women were as tall as he was, but then not many women were like Laura Peters in any way at all.

Standing less than an inch from her, he could feel the tug at his crotch as his eyes fell on the gorgeous bust currently trussed under velvet. Sam knew better than to either mention how much he wanted to touch her chest, or act on his physical reaction to it. That was not his decision to make.

When he had given up his graphic design business to work as a freelance artist and Laura's partner, the understanding had been very clear. She was in charge of everything except his art – including him. Sam Wheeler was her sounding board, her platform for ideas, the one she practised on and experimented with. He was the only one who got to see the occasional glimpse of Laura Peters the woman, not the mistress of the fifth floor. Therefore it disturbed him that, with a decision as big as this, Laura had said not one word.

Scraping a hand through his short, spiked hair, the manageress made sure her nails made their presence felt. 'I am well aware that you think I've made a bad call in agreeing to lend anyone to Proctor, let alone my two best workers, but you will have to trust that I have my reasons. I was only being polite when I asked how you think they took the news.'

Picking up Sam's hands, she placed them behind his back purposefully and undid his belt.

Refraining from commenting on what she was doing, Sam replied, 'If you were merely being polite, then you probably aren't interested in my opinion. However, as you have *politely* asked, I think Miss Sarah will cope well. She won't like it, but she will accept it. Miss Sanders, well …' His breath snagged in his throat as Laura folded back the top of his trousers and freed his erection from the confinement of his boxers. Wrapping it in her palm, she let the warmth of her body flow into the artist, so he had to work hard to keep talking. 'I think she is genuinely afraid, and probably believes she has displeased you in some way, even though you have said otherwise.'

Keeping her hand motionless, relishing the swell of his cock as it reacted to her inactivity, Laura held Sam's stare. 'You may well be correct. Now, tell me, is everything you require in the White Room ready?'

Accepting the change of subject, Sam said, 'Lee set my

equipment up for me earlier. I assume you have sent him to greet our guest?'

Privately impressed at the lack of expression in Sam's eyes, which belied exactly how badly she knew he wanted her to do more than hold his shaft, Laura inclined her head. 'Lee is to take David's representative to my office. I thought I should escort this visitor to the White Room myself.'

A tiny flicker in Sam's gaze told Laura that he thought this unusual as well. It wasn't like her to do something that she could order a minion to do for her. Storing away the fact he was querying her again for later, Laura let go of her lover's dick. 'Strip.'

Sam managed to hold in the groan that shot up his throat as she released him, but a faint, strangled grunt still escaped the edges of his clamped lips as he peeled off his clothes. He tried not to think about how good it would feel if his length was embraced within his companion's expert mouth, or deep within her pussy. He failed.

Stepping away from him, Laura gathered up her skirt in one hand, lifting it a little off the floor to make walking easier. 'I will see you in Room 54 in ten minutes.'

'What? But …' Like Jess before him, Laura had built Sam up and left him hanging.

'Don't even think about putting those clothes back on, Mr Wheeler. I think your role in the sending-off party will be achieved so much better if you're naked.'

'For fuck's sake, Laura, we've already discussed it and agreed what's going to happen. I was going to come along and observe, then …'

'I changed my mind.'

Jess knew she shouldn't be wasting time, but visions of her first meeting with David Proctor in the dungeon, many months ago now, were persistently clattering around her head. It had been the one and only time Mrs Peters had ordered Jess to dominate a client, and it had been a disaster.

David had required Jess to wear the incongruous combination of a business suit with a medieval-style leather chastity belt beneath, while she spanked him until he pleaded with her to stop. But as Jess had gingerly paddled his buttocks, everything about her new life had hit her in a rush of confused anger. She'd just begun to accept her role as a submissive, so being forced to swap sides had thrown her completely. Her brain had switched off, and David's instructions to halt the beating had fallen on deaf ears. She'd kept hitting him until his buttocks were raw, resentment for all she'd been put through in the previous weeks in the hotel exploding inside her, as it wrestled with the knowledge that she'd loved every single minute.

The cruel punishment Jess had received the second she'd come to her senses had proved to her that David may have acted like a submissive, but he was only willing to adopt that position on his terms. The whole thing had been an act; a favour to Mrs Peters to assist in Jess's bizarre training routine.

With feelings of uncertainty crowding her head, Jess couldn't shake the feeling that she was being cut adrift, and her world was about to be tilted on its axis once again.

Despite what her boss had said Jess was convinced she must have done something wrong to be sent away in the care of a man she hated.

Perhaps I was right in the first place, she thought, a vague glimmer of hope pushing its way through the chaos of her imagination. Maybe it was yet another lesson to ensure she didn't forget her place, and once she'd experienced a pretend send-off, she'd be told it was all a test, and she and Miss Sarah weren't going anywhere after all. It wouldn't have been the first time Mrs Peters had tricked her in that way.

Jess felt an almost childish need to be near the

reassuring presence of her colleague, and desperately hoped Miss Sarah would take charge, and tell her what to do. She had never knocked on Miss Sarah's door uninvited before. She'd been in the dominatrix's private suite on many occasions, but only by request or under orders.

Miss Sarah's voice, without a trace of a wobble, called out, 'Come in, Miss Sanders,' the moment Jess's knuckles had softly hit her bedroom door.

Jess crossed the threshold into her mistress's room. 'How did you know it was me, ma'am?'

'Who else would it be at a time like this?' Miss Sarah didn't look up at her visitor, but continued to sort neatly stacked underwear into the suitcase upon her double bed.

Jess watched as minute squares of silk and satin were positioned within the luggage. Miss Sarah really was packing. Her hope this was a joke evaporated. 'Did you know this was going to happen?'

The dominatrix spun on the soles of her Victorian boots, her dress rustling in a crunch of expensive material. 'You forget yourself, Miss Sanders.'

Immediately lowering her eyes, Jess experienced a frisson of excitement. Her body had been left hanging with unsatisfied want by Mrs Peters. Now, in the face of Miss Sarah's narrow, cat-like eyes, Jess became all too aware of her flesh's requirement for constant stimulation. 'I'm sorry, ma'am.'

'In this instance you are forgiven.' The dominatrix continued with her packing. 'I have no doubt you are feeling unsettled; however, I suggest you quickly go and gather together all the belongings you'll require for a few weeks away.'

'But?'

'Miss Sanders!' Miss Sarah snapped out her words with an air of finality that Jess knew better than to ignore. 'We have little time. I know no more than you do. And as we have no idea if we are going abroad or remaining inland, I suggest you add your passport to your supplies.'

Miss Sarah unhooked a row of corsets from her closet and, in a gentler tone, added, 'I honestly have no idea what's going on, Jess. I confess any scheme involving Fables' most demanding client, especially as he appears to be able to make Mrs Peters do something I suspect she doesn't completely want to do, makes me a trifle suspicious. However, we will find out in 45 minutes. Now, go and pack or Mrs Peters will send you away in the clothes you're wearing and nothing else.'

With a quick curtsey, Jess ran to her private bedroom. Devoid of the reassurance she'd hoped for, and mindful that Miss Sarah was probably right when she said Mrs Peters wouldn't hesitate to send her to her destination completely naked if necessary, she dragged her oversized holdall from under the bed.

The best plan she could think of to face this situation was to work without thinking, to adopt a level of reckless denial. Tidiness was going to have to go by the board. She could see no other way of getting even remotely ready in time.

Scooping up as many knickers, bras, stockings, and suspender belts as she could in a single armful, Jess dumped them in the bag along with her passport. These were followed by four tops, two skirts, some jeans, and a chunky jumper she kept purely for comfort wear during her rare days off.

As her toiletries bag was far too small to contain all her requirements for a fortnight away, Jess swept the entire contents of her bathroom shelf into a plastic carrier bag, and dumped it on top of her clothing. Pulling on her boots, a fitted cardigan, and a short-waisted leather jacket, Jess considered herself dressed for whatever journey she was about to go on. Stuffing her hairdryer, straighteners, and a pair of black kitten-heeled shoes into her bag, it occurred to Jess that if she was going to another hotel, she might well need her gym kit, and quite possibly a swimming costume, so she grabbed them as well.

Operating fast, her heart thumping, still not daring to consider where she was going, or who might be there beyond David Proctor, Jess glanced at her watch. Her haphazard packing style meant she had 15 minutes left.

Lingering in her bedroom doorway, scanning an eye around the small suite, Jess looked fondly at the neatly made bed that had been her refuge within the hotel. It was the only place where she could be Jess Sanders, the 25-year-old redhead with a pliant, curvy figure and shy but dry sense of humour, rather than Jess the submissive who did precisely what anyone and everyone told her to. The room was her bolthole, and she'd always been grateful for it. There had been times when Jess had wished she'd had company in her bed, but only fleetingly. It was vital to her sanity to have somewhere to enjoy some privacy. She began to speculate about where she was going. Would she have such a place for solitude there? Was she really going to be allowed to come back? She shook her head sharply. Thinking was definitely a bad idea.

Jess was about to close the door when she thought of something she might miss while she was away. Returning to her top drawer and rummaging a hand beneath her remaining shirts, Jess fished out a solid glass dildo and a pocket vibrator. If David Proctor is adopting similar policies to Mrs Peters, she thought, I expect I'm going to need these.

Resisting the urge to give her toys a flourish before she left, resolving to be every bit as pragmatic as Miss Sarah about the situation that had been thrust upon them, she carried her bag to the White Room.

*   *   *

The contents of Room 54 – the White Room – were never disclosed to the guests. It was used for those seasoned visitors who'd experienced the joys and horrors of life in

Rooms 50 to 53, and were after an element of surprise.

The first time she had visited this secret room, Jess had been presented with her final challenge prior to permanent employment with the fifth floor team. That experience, more than any other, had shown her once and for all that no other life would do for her now.

The second time she'd been in Room 54 there was no trace of the equipment she had used before. Every item in the room was changed at frequent intervals to keep things fresh for the guests and staff alike.

With her pulse thumping so fiercely in her veins she could feel it threading through the palm of her hand, Jess pushed open the door. In spite of being early, she was the still the last to arrive. Master Lee Philips was hovering impatiently inside the door. With a courteous nod, he snatched Jess's bag, picked up Miss Sarah's suitcase, and left with a speed that indicated how keen he was to get back again.

Jess blinked into the stark light of the room. No matter how many times she visited this space, the total whiteness of its floor, ceiling, and walls always made her eyes water. It was like walking into an unreal space, where time didn't really exist.

The second Jess's vision acclimatised, her eyes were drawn to Sam. Standing in the corner opposite the door, he was naked from head to toe. His cock looked as though it had been on the receiving end of Mrs Peters' deft touch, but hadn't been allowed any release. The sight of his condition brought Jess's craving for sex, which had been diluted by the shock of the afternoon's revelations, hurtling back to the surface. She began to regret having put on her tight-fitting travelling jumper and jacket, for her chest felt as if it was complying with Miss Sarah's theory that female breasts increased in size by at least 20 per cent whenever they were aroused.

Sam was standing next to his easel, upon which was a

large canvas. It displayed a charcoal drawing of a naked woman, her arms held out at her sides, her eyes closed, her mouth open in a howl that looked so real it could almost be heard.

Jess tore her eyes from the artwork. It was her.

Sam had sketched and painted Jess many times since his arrival at Fables, but this was an image she hadn't seen before. Unsure if she was disturbed or stimulated by the picture's presence, Jess was sure, however, that she was unsettled by the eyes of the unknown man who sat on one of three white wooden chairs placed side by side along the opposite wall of the room.

She'd built herself up to face David Proctor, and although she didn't like him, Jess had encountered him enough times to know that she could survive his games in front of all her colleagues. One glance at this new gentleman told her he was a very different proposition.

Tall and thickset, his dark skin shone against the stark plainness of the white wall, somehow enhancing its mouth-watering lustre. His cropped black hair framed his face precisely; his eyes, the colour of which was lost beneath incredibly long eyelashes, were narrowed as if he was suspicious of something. He was not smiling.

Next to this suited stranger, her back straight, her eyes fixed steadily ahead, sat Miss Sarah. She too had thought it sensible to dress for travel. Her Victorian garb had been exchanged for knee-high black boots, a short denim skirt, and a jumper similar to the one Jess wore herself.

The prickly heat of nervous arousal tripped down Jess's spine as the expectant group was disrupted by Lee's return. Slinking back into the room, the barman gave Mrs Peters a nod which could have been either apologetic or confirmatory, before he sat on the final white chair next to their guest.

The only other piece of furniture in the room was a large reclining armchair. Its presence spoke volumes.

Mrs Peters clapped her hands, and everyone froze. 'As you are aware, this is a goodbye celebration for Miss Sanders and Miss Sarah. A *temporary* goodbye.'

Noting the stress on the word "temporary", Jess surreptitiously angled her gaze towards their visitor. There was a faint hint of smugness to his gaze, but beyond that Jess couldn't read his features. It didn't help that she had already mentally undressed him, as she did with every client. It was a trick Jess had learnt early on in an attempt to anticipate, and thus perfectly serve, her guest's requirements. He is a big bloke, so he is probably, well, a big bloke. How will his dick taste? Maybe …?

'Miss Sanders!'

Jess's face blanched. How could she have drifted off at a time like this? Cursing the insatiable sexual appetite working at Fables had instilled in her, Jess murmured, 'Sorry, Mrs Peters.'

'Not a good first impression to give our guest, child.'

Jess swallowed but remained silent, her eyes and head dipped toward the tiled white floor.

'I have assured Mr Proctor's representative that you and Miss Sarah are the ultimate professionals. Able to instruct others in the art of domination and submission, and now, after that obvious lapse in concentration, you are going to have to work very hard to prove that to be true in your case.'

Feeling hotter than ever, Jess could feel her cheeks burn crimson. She didn't want to consider what expression she would have seen on Miss Sarah's face if she'd been brave enough to look at her.

'Anyway –' Mrs Peters' irritation at this early failure on the part of her submissive rang through her words '– I would like to introduce Kane to you.'

Miss Sarah rose from her seat and curtseyed before the large man who, at six foot four, was one of the few men who made both the dominatrix and the manageress look short.

Kane said nothing, but acknowledged Miss Sarah with a curt nod as she placed herself a pace behind Mrs Peters, stating quite clearly that she knew her place; and that place was at her manageress's side. The information Miss Sarah was imparting to the newcomer was clear. She was a trusted member of staff, and he would have to accept that.

'Kane has kindly agreed to collect you on Mr Proctor's behalf,' Laura addressed the two women carefully, 'but as I wish to give you a memorable send-off, our honoured guest will witness you take part in a training exercise first. This is a new scenario that has been requested by a group who've booked an adult party with us in five weeks' time. An event you will *both* be back in time for.'

Once again Jess heard the emphasis in Mrs Peters' voice, underlining that her girls would be safely returned to Fables, as if the matter was a cause for doubt. She wondered whose benefit it was for. Hers, Miss Sarah's, Kane's; maybe even Mrs Peters herself.

'Miss Sarah, if you will?' With a sweep of her arm, Mrs Peters transferred control of the proceedings over to her second in command.

Slipping off her coat, Miss Sarah walked towards Jess. 'Remove your coat and jumper, and undo your shirt. You will step out of your skirt. The remainder of your attire will stay in place.'

Excitement now vying for top billing with her nerves, Jess moved with as much dignity as she could manage. She was determined not to let either Mrs Peters or Miss Sarah down in front of David Proctor's henchman ever again.

Alongside the strain in her breasts, as they buffered against the inside of her black bra, Jess felt the seductive flap of her cotton shirt against her belly. Her boots echoed across the wooden floor. Walking to where Miss Sarah was pointing, about two metres to the left of the easel, Jess fought against the instinct to cross her arms over her chest so her hands had something to do.

As soon as Jess was in position, Miss Sarah spun towards Lee. 'Master Philips, remove your clothes and stand in front of the easel. Mr Wheeler, you will stand next to him.'

Conscious of the eyes of Mrs Peters and Kane upon her, and Sam's flagpole erection as he waited next to Lee, Jess re-examined the picture by her side. Her admiration of Sam's skill with charcoal and paper was well founded. Somehow he always managed to catch the intensity of her emotion as she came beneath whatever extremes of sensation she was being put through.

Miss Sarah's precise diction continued to ring out. 'During the party there will be eight people lined up before the easel. For now, as the time of departure for Miss Sanders and myself is imminent, we will proceed with only two players. I trust you are all familiar with the party game, pin the tail on the donkey?'

Jess felt a new layer of perspiration break out beneath her hair.

'However, rather than an image of a donkey, we have this stunning picture of our very own Miss Sanders.' Solely addressing the men, the dominatrix continued, 'You will be blindfolded, and given three chances to play the game. The aim is to pin a paper cock on the pussy; get a picture of a clamp on the nipple, and a third picture of a gag as near to the drawn mouth as possible.

'Whichever of you places your pictorial version of the sex toy nearest to the correct part on Miss Sanders' anatomy will be able to apply the real toy to the real Miss Sanders as your reward.' Miss Sarah pointed to a white wooden box that Mrs Peters had pulled from beneath her chair. It was brimming with nipple clamps, dildos, gags, and all manner of other adult toys.

As she finished talking Miss Sarah strode towards Jess

and, without a word, wrapped a padded black silk mask over her eyes before yanking down her sodden panties. 'You will kneel, Miss Sanders, with your legs open wide. I do not wish there to be even a semblance of pressure near that gorgeous pussy of yours. Place your hands behind your back.'

Jess obeyed, wishing she'd been allowed to take her boots off, as their backs rubbed uncomfortably against her folded thighs. Her head teemed with visions of what might happen next, as the sound of Miss Sarah's footsteps echoed across the floor as she approached the practise contestants.

Trying to work out who was going first, Jess picked up a shuffling sound. She suspected it was the light tread of a blindfolded Lee as he was steered to the easel with three pictures in his hands. A mild murmur of amusement from the audience seconds later left Jess speculating how close he'd got to the fake erogenous zones he was aiming for.

Another minute passed, and Jess heard the heavier footfall of Sam approaching the easel. Jess fleetingly considered if he minded his creation being ruined by having drawing pins stuck into it, but she was brought back to the more pressing issue of who would fuck her in front of Kane as Miss Sarah said, 'Interesting aims, gentlemen. You may remove your blindfolds.'

Not sure if the dominatrix was amused or being sarcastic, Jess wished she could see. Trying not to shuffle her knees, which were becoming increasingly uncomfortable as she sat open legged, she clenched her teeth. Her tits were already anticipating the bite of the silver clamps that were coming her way, and she resolved not to allow herself to react to the hurt they'd cause in the face of their taciturn visitor.

Mrs Peters' unmistakable stride, accompanied by another set of feet, which had to be those of Kane, approached the easel. 'Perhaps, as this is such a close contest, you would do us the honour of declaring the winner, Kane.'

'I would be delighted.' This was the first time Jess had heard the guest speak, and it was with a sense of surprise that she heard the rasping gravel of a Scottish accent.

There was a pause, as if Kane was considering his response, and Jess supposed that Sam and Lee must have been very near the mark with some, if not all, of the targets. Not that it should have surprised Jess; they knew her anatomy very well indeed.

'It is clear the cock belonging to this gentleman here is the winner by some way, while his comrade's tit clamp was marginally nearer. As to the mouth, that really is too close to call. If I may be so bold, Mrs Peters, I suggest both gentlemen tend to the rather luscious body over there that is, quite evidently, gagging for it. And I will apply the gagging device myself. Yes?'

'Certainly.'

All Jess's attempts at mental relaxation faltered as the idea of Kane's chocolate-coloured shaft sliding between her lips took hold. Her earlier speculation as to his size and taste returned with a vengeance as she was hoisted to her feet by Miss Sarah, her legs knocked further apart to maintain the lack of self-imposed friction.

As her mistress's hands made short work of Jess's remaining clothes, she couldn't shake the feeling that his had all worked out rather conveniently for Kane. Had they even played the game with blindfolds? Had the outcome been predetermined?

Jess didn't have time to let paranoia take hold.

'Come with me.' Miss Sarah grabbed hold of Jess's right tit, using it to steer her across the room.

Stumbling blindly, her already hypersensitive flesh reacting to the touch of her mistress, Jess found herself being half lifted and half shoved onto the reclining chair in the middle of the room. Lying back, her hands trapped beneath her, she couldn't suppress a shriek as the whole chair abruptly swung flat with a jolting thud.

Like an inappropriately attired ringmaster leading a circus, Miss Sarah commanded Sam to don a condom and get into position. There was barely any hesitation before Jess felt his weight sit astride her legs. His length disappeared inside her slick opening with an accompanying groan from his throat that was so heartfelt Jess was convinced Laura would punish him for it later.

The submissive didn't have the chance to consider Sam's fate. Miss Sarah was speaking again. 'Master Philips, the clamps if you please.'

Miss Sarah ran a soft hand over Jess's forehead, sending extra zips of desire on a beeline for the "v" between the younger woman's legs. 'I'm sure I don't have to tell you, Miss Sanders, that, as with all sessions on the fifth floor, you are not to climax until permission is given.'

Wishing Kane had gagged her *before* the clamps were added, Jess saw the light before her shrouded eyes dim slightly as the shadow of Lee fell over her. Seconds later, her whole frame flushed from heated pink to scarlet as the initial burn of clawed sensation smarted her nipples and galloped with lightning speed through every nerve of her being.

Once Lee had finished snapping the metal pinches into place, he straddled Jess's body, sitting only an inch or two in front of Sam, who was already finding it difficult not to move, his cock twitching urgently within her.

Inside Jess's head the countdown had begun. How long? How long before she could let go and free her simmering orgasm? Jess clamped her jaw together as she waited for her tits to stop blazing; for the lemon juice sting to blend into the angry, more manageable, throb of blunt pain that would follow.

Experience told her she needed another 30 seconds without her tits being touched so she could gather enough resolve to ensure she'd last as long as she'd be expected to. The moment she'd had the thought Jess regretted it, for, with predictable timing, she heard Miss Sarah say, 'You may move, gentlemen.'

The dominatrix had hardly finished the sentence when Lee's fingertips started to caress the nipples that stuck through the clamps. He kissed the surrounding globes, while Sam pumped steadily within her. Red lights and orange lights burst like fireworks behind Jess's closed and blindfolded eyes. It was a warning sign. She was too close already.

She would not let Mrs Peters down. Only sheer willpower, and the fact Jess was digging her teeth so violently into the sides of her mouth that any second now she'd draw blood, was stopping her from making a noise and climaxing under the two men already in place. Hurry up, Kane, she begged silently. Hurry up!

'If you would be so kind, Kane.' Miss Sarah spoke politely, but Jess noticed she was using the same firm tone she used for their most troublesome clients. 'As you can see, we have a range of gags available. Or perhaps you'd like to use the one nature has equipped you with.'

Mr Proctor's henchman didn't reply, but Jess could hear the rummage of equipment as his hand sorted through the supplies.

Her focus was fading, and she was sure Kane was deliberately delaying his verdict. Lee's digits were working faster on her tits, causing silent tears to run in streams along the contours of Jess's face as his dick rubbed against her stomach. Meanwhile, Sam had increased his pace.

At last Jess became aware of an unfamiliar salty aroma. It was the scent of fresh cock. Kane had obviously decided to plug her lips himself. A decision she had no doubt he'd made long before the charade of looking through the gags.

Kane stood with his feet on either side of the lowered

chair, his tip playing around Jess's lips for a distractingly long time, before he plunged himself into her throat.

His shaft was even wider than she had imagined. Jess choked against his girth for a split second before relaxing her throat. Accepting his rapid pumping, she breathed through her nose as, with an unexpected lack of finesse, Kane fucked her face.

With her hands cramping beneath her, her body a mere thing with which others could play, Jess sensed her resolve begin to crumble. She knew there would be no permission forthcoming from Mrs Peters for her to climax. It would be a case of hanging on as long as she possibly could, and hoping she'd done enough to impress.

It was with surprise and considerable relief, therefore, that just as Jess was about to scream her frustration around the dick gag, Mrs Peters proclaimed in a loud, imperious voice, 'Miss Sanders, you may come.'

Jess let go of the bundle of lust that had filled her from her toes to her chest in one burst. Her body jerked so vigorously against the reclined chair she wasn't sure how she didn't buck the men off.

Her jarring movements and frantic, muffled moans triggered Lee's climax, his come dashing Jess's flesh in time to Sam filling her channel with the shuddering of his own, held-back orgasm. Then, as Jess's mouth gasped puffs of air out of its sides, Kane's load hit the back of her throat, forcing her to fight back the need to cough.

Kane stepped back. His hooded eyes watched her closely as, to prevent herself from choking on his seed, Jess let his cream run down her chin.

For a second, her world spun as the heady success of taking three men at once filled her with perverse pride. She'd done what Mrs Peters had required. She had not cried out as she'd come and she had endured the humiliation of Kane's spunk covering her face, rather than embarrassing herself and her superiors by having a coughing fit. Surely that would make her life a little easier in the time between getting dressed and leaving Fables?

Kane, however, was not so easily impressed.

Climbing off Jess's face; Kane spoke to Mrs Peters in a fashion that not even Sam would have risked. 'Your submissive is of a woefully poor standard. She can't even swallow! Mr Proctor will expect better than that. Dress her quickly.'

There was no audible reply from anyone in the room.

Jess felt light-headed as a collection of hands pulled her upright. Her wrists were freed, and her clothing replaced before she'd had the chance to lick some moisture back into her lips, or wipe away the juice that stuck to her thighs, or the come on her face.

Then, with the blindfold still in place, Jess found herself being thrown into a fireman's lift over Kane's shoulder. She shrieked as blood rushed to her head, aware that she was not the only one protesting, but Miss Sarah's words, as she hurried after Jess, were being paid as little heed as her own complaints.

As the stale atmosphere supplied by the hotel's air-conditioning system was replaced by fresh air, the banging of several doors against Jess's flailing arms and legs told her that they were leaving Fables by the back door.

The last thing Jess heard, before she found herself thrown into the back of a car, was the commanding voice of Mrs Peters.

'Dignity, Miss Sanders. Remember your dignity. Miss Sarah, look after her. I'll see you *both* in two weeks. Do Fables and yourself proud.'

As Miss Sarah's less resistant but equally offended body was deposited next to Jess, the car began to move …

Chapter Three

PREENING AT HER reflection in the mirror, Lady Tia tugged the body-hugging black dress into place around her abundant figure, so that the plunging neckline showed off her copious bosom.

Picking invisible flecks of lint from the clinging fabric, The Retreat's resident dominatrix swished her hips from side to side, critically assessing the hang of her thick, black hair. Then, drawing on a pair of elbow-length, black silk fingerless gloves, Lady Tia examined the gleaming gloss of her black nail varnish, and double-checked the layer of bright red lipstick that coated her pouting brown lips.

Finally satisfied with her appearance, she turned with all the purpose of a medieval galleon about to do battle.

She did not like the news her superior had imparted to her that morning. Not one bit.

Dr Elena Ewen smiled quietly at the screen of her laptop. It had taken a lot of work to make this happen. She hadn't been able to believe how easy it had been to find David Proctor after all these years. Although she'd been the one who'd set in motion a course of action that had let David believe he'd found her, and that he was the one who'd come up with the idea that such an establishment would help secure some new top-flight contracts. Now all she had to do was keep him in check, and get on with running The

Retreat.

As a child, Elena Ewen had always been the best at everything. Always the cleverest, the prettiest, the most popular, and, most important of all, the one the boys wanted to get to know as well as possible, and the girls had been more than a little curious about. Even during her teenage years, Elena had been smart enough to know that what she actually did, and what people thought she did, could be two different things. She hadn't wanted a reputation for the wrong things – even if that reputation was sometimes well deserved,

It had been at university that the course of the rest of her life had been determined. That was when she'd met a woman who would tilt her already jarred perspective of life over the edge of generally accepted normality into a world where control equalled power, and power equalled control. It was only a short step from there to see that the ultimate tool in the quest for power and control was sex.

The knock at the door was brief, only functioning as an attempt at politeness, before Lady Tia wafted into Elena's study in a haze of musky perfume. As she clicked on her screensaver, the Scotswoman peered at her assistant over the rim of her glasses. 'Good evening, Lady Tia. Thank you for coming so promptly.'

'I am not happy about this situation.'

Dr Ewen's smile stayed in place, but not so much as a hint of it hit her slate grey eyes as she gave a brittle response. 'To the point, as ever.'

'I see no reason to be any other way, especially as I suspect this will have a greater impact on our work here than you imagine.'

Totally unintimidated by the immaculate presence towering over her desk, Elena replied with complete assurance, 'I expect there to be an impact on our work here. I expect it to improve. To lift us from the small, albeit successful business we have established here serving select holidaymakers to a thriving concern with a constant flow of business trade. Customers Mr Proctor has deemed "special guests". Ladies and gentleman of some means who, for reasons he may or may not choose to share with us, he has decided to reward with our services rather than financially. This is an opportunity for a new clientele I propose to exploit fully.

'We are to be a treat. A memorable experience that will ensure his clients wish to work with him again. Never –' Dr Ewen paused for emphasis '– has our work here been so important. Mr Proctor's influence in the world of business in general, and in PR specifically, is considerable. This alliance can only do us good. We will, as I have explained to you *twice* before, benefit from these changes. Your position here is not under threat. Nor will it be. That is not why David is having the women brought here.'

Bristling at the implication that she might feel threatened in some way by the two bits of girls being shipped in from the south, Lady Tia curbed the barbed remark that was forming on her tongue. Elena Ewen may have been half her size, but she was the mistress here at The Retreat, and only a fool would forget that her petite, aristocratic frame was capable of keeping even the strongest dom in his or her place.

Adopting a more civil tone than the one she felt like using, Lady Tia said, 'I can assure you that I do not feel threatened. However I do resent the fact that this man has, in only a space of six weeks, purchased this place from under us, dismissed our female submissive, and –' Lady Tia spat out her final words, her displeasure getting the better of her common sense '– thinks we require training, when he knows full well you and I have far more years of experience than Laura Peters could ever dream of.'

Rather than reacting with a return of the venom being aimed at her, Elena stood and moved to the plush sofa that ran along the side of her office. Picking up her laptop, she gestured for her companion to approach her as she sat and lifted the screen. 'I trust you are not wearing underwear?'

Recognising the question for what it was, an instruction and not a query, Lady Tia inched up the skirt of her dress, revealing her muscular chocolate legs, and a shaved pussy that seemed to have the ability to pout as broadly as its owner's mouth.

Inclining her head a fraction in approval, Elena patted the cushion on the sofa next to her. 'I would like you to keep your skirt high and sit here.'

As she obeyed, Lady Tia's eyes were still set in disapproval, but the more defined rise and fall of her breasts was clearly detectable to her manageress's expert eye.

Dr Ewen pointed toward the laptop's screen. 'You see this woman?'

Lady Tia studied the scene as the computer was balanced on her boss's lap. A young, shapely woman was fastened to a white rope hammock, and her ample tits were squeezed through the gaps in the weave. The slight pot of her tummy was squashed against the rope, and her reddened face was a vision of climax-preventing concentration.

'Let me introduce you to Miss Jess Sanders. You will be meeting her in approximately one hour. She's been working at Fables for six months. This is a recording of her final training session before being accepted on to the staff permanently. If you continue to watch you will see that she is not alone.'

As the camera angle panned outwards, Lady Tia saw that a man had been laid beneath her, and a battle of wills was obviously in progress to see which of them would break and plead for release first. 'Do you know the circumstances behind this session, doctor?'

'No. I do know, however, that the gentleman you can see is Mrs Peters' partner; both in a business and a personal sense.'

'She has a lover of her own?' The dominatrix's immaculately plucked eyebrows rose in disapproval. 'I hadn't considered her weak enough to have a full-time companion, let alone emotional connections.'

Elena nodded. Her eyes didn't leave the screen, but her left hand moved to Lady Tia's thigh. 'Laura Peters writes her own rules.'

Forbidding herself from focusing on the cold hand against her skin, Lady Tia twisted her head sharply. 'You didn't tell me you knew her?'

Refraining from answering, Elena walked her fingers very slowly towards her companion's mound, resting them below the heart-shaped flesh, before clicking the computer on to another screen. 'This is Miss Sarah. Reports on her are good. One hundred per cent good, in fact. The consummate professional. Whereas Miss Sanders is relatively new to this lifestyle and continues to makes mistakes. But then, what use is a submissive that doesn't make mistakes? I've always thought the whole point is that we can punish them for their errors.'

The dominatrix watched the screen with hawk-like eyes as Miss Sarah, her slim body perfect in Victorian clothes, chastised a man bending over a desk. So that was the competition. Lady Tia didn't care what Dr Ewen said; there was only room for one dominatrix at The Retreat, and that was her. She wasn't stupid enough to share her thoughts, however. It was time to think tactically, especially as she suspected her own resolve was about to be tested.

'I reluctantly have to confess I'm impressed.' Lady Tia continued to scrutinise the image before her, not allowing her gaze to switch even for a second towards the palm so near her core. 'Miss Sarah has excellent technique and poise. Her expression is serene yet indomitable. I would hazard a guess that it is very difficult to read her reactions.'

Dr Ewen, whose own expression was frequently impossible to assess, was not fooled for a moment by the compliment Lady Tia was laying on the woman she was already sure she considered a rival. Nor was she misled by Tia's lack of reaction to the fingertips which she was now edging very quietly up and down her thick thigh. 'David has informed me that Mrs Peters suspects these two women of having formed an intimate alliance beyond the requirements of work.'

This time Lady Tia did react, her voice keen. 'Suspects, but isn't sure?'

'Let's just say that neither of them has been foolish enough, or unprofessional enough, to give their association a name. But the very fact these women care for each other could be useful to us. Something that, should we need to, we can use to our advantage.'

The smile on Lady Tia's face was sardonic as her mahogany eyes blazed with the hint of malevolent plans. If there was nothing she could do to prevent David Proctor from inflicting these "experts" upon them, maybe there were ways to turn the situation to her advantage.

Snapping the laptop shut, Elena abandoned her companion's body and rose to her feet. The legs of her satin trousers brushed together as she sat at her desk, steepling her fingers in front of her. 'It occurs to me, Lady Tia, that while our guests are here you may well be called upon to prove yourself capable of withholding the very brand of discipline you dish out. I think we would be wise to have a refresher course, prior to their arrival.'

Managing to refrain from vocalising once again her disapproval at what was happening; Lady Tia wisely inclined her head. Her body had anticipated pleasure from the moment Elena had instructed her to raise her dress. 'As you see fit, doctor.'

'You are a skilled woman, Lady Tia, particularly when

it comes to the administration of the whip.' Elena let her eyes roam from the dominatrix's bare toes to the top of her bushy head of hair. 'You'll have seen from the video, however, that Miss Sarah is also skilled, particularly in the arena of spanking. Do you know where she was taught?'

'Not with me, doctor. I have not seen nor heard of her before today.'

'And I'm sure you would have if she'd been on the London club circuit like yourself. Interesting …'

Lady Tia said nothing else. Her pussy pulsed with craving as she regarded Dr Ewen, wondering, not for the first time, just how old her employer was. Her grey hair, and the intimidating slant at which she kept her glasses, suggested an age much greater than her flawless skin would suggest.

'You will remove your dress and undergarments.'

Lady Tia obliged, her stance portraying her as a woman every bit in control of herself.

'Hands and knees, please.'

As soon as Lady Tia was in place, her breasts hanging like twin pendulums, Elena walked around her second in command, enjoying seeing the woman prostrate before her. She briefly considered touching the cocoa-coloured butt, smoothing it beneath her palms before she brought it to a shine with a paddle she'd extracted from her desk drawer, but time was too short for such self-indulgence.

Swinging her arm back and upwards, Elena landed the first strike. The thwack it made against the brown skin spoke of satisfaction and anguish. Yet Lady Tia did not move. Her arms and legs remained planted firmly where they were as her boss hit again, starting to develop a rhythm.

A dozen strikes passed in quick succession as Lady Tia began to breathe deeply; her fingers grasping at the carpet, her ears alight with the sound of the weapon repeatedly cutting through the air.

41

Dr Ewen's voice barely registered her exertion as she worked. 'You may rest assured, Lady Tia, that I am counting the hits as I work ...' *Smack!* 'A figure I will remember and then, at a later date, compare with the number of blows your frailer counterpart will be able to sustain.'

'Yes, madam.' Riding out the blows, Lady Tia kept her voice calm, yet there was no denying the sheen of sweat on her forehead as three more blows landed on her rump. Each strike crashed against alternate cheeks, neither increasing nor decreasing in ferocity, but remaining at a constant level of painful.

Elena continued to talk, as if she was doing nothing more interesting than sorting her paperwork, 'Of course, I am not a fool ...' *Smack!* 'I do not trust Proctor, and he would be foolish to trust me ...' *Smack!* 'I know where my loyalties lie, and unlike the skinny girl from the south –' *Smack!* '– you will receive a reward if you can take more blows than I think you can.' *Smack!*

'May I ask, madam, how many blows do you think I can manage?'

'Lady Tia, you know better than to ask.' *Smack!* 'However, these are not normal circumstances, and the thought, perhaps, that I will shortly be sucking on those chestnut nipples, and, should I see fit, lavishing some attention upon your always wet pussy –' *Smack!* '– should be an incentive to keep you going for a while longer.'

'Yes, madam.'

'You should see your backside. The colour is what I can only describe as apple red; although admittedly an apple that has been dropped and bruised. What fine marks these will be to show off to our guests.'

Lady Tia bit back a reply. She hated having marks upon her flesh as much as she loved administering them to other people. Marks suggested weakness, and weakness was for submissives and guests, not for her. Yet, even as she recoiled from the assumptions Miss Sarah and Miss Sanders might make when they saw her battered arse, Lady Tia's imagination had placed Dr Ewen's matchstick body against her own, getting beautifully lost in voluptuous flesh.

At the 25th stroke, Lady Tia gave her first moan. Her teeth had been clenched together so hard, they were beginning to make irritating grinding noises.

Watching the pattern she was forming with a practised eye, Elena judged it was almost time to stop, whether Lady Tia begged her to or not. Pussy juice gleamed on her victim's legs, and the aroma of sex hung in the air. While Elena had needed to exert her authority over her dominatrix, she didn't want to damage her beyond bruising either.

Throwing back her arm in the same arch she'd repeated for the last 29 hits, The Retreat's mistress was about to congratulate her assistant, when Lady Tia blurted out, 'No more!'

A self-satisfied smile crossed Elena's face. 'You may roll over, Lady Tia. Place your hands beneath your backside so you can feel how roasted it is.'

Normally, Dr Ewen would have ended the session there, ignoring the fact that there would be a pressing in the pit of her dominatrix's stomach, evidence of her desperation for the deliverance of an orgasm. Today, however, she required Lady Tia to be sharp and collected when their guests arrived, which meant allowing her the climax she privately yearned for.

Tucking stray hairs from her greying ponytail behind her ears, Elena knelt between her domme's legs and leant forward. Attaching her mouth to Lady Tia's right nipple, sucking with a finesse that she knew would bring her second in command to a swift and rewarding orgasm, Dr Ewen gave the succulent pussy before her two sharp slaps.

With almost surgical precision, her boss slid a finger

inside Lady Tia's channel. The dominatrix held in the urge to cry out as, trembling with the shock of her conclusion, she rolled against the rough carpet.

Once her task was complete, Elena returned to her feet, wiping her fingers on a tissue, her voice business-like. 'As you dress, I'd like you to give me your opinion of Alisha.'

'Alisha? The cook?' Lady Tia's eyebrows rose for a second time, as she replaced her clothes, her racing pulse slowing with every addition to her attire. 'May I ask why?'

'What do you know about her?'

'Only that she is a dab hand at peeling potatoes, is far more intelligent than she pretends to be, and is extremely good at having her arse spanked when we require extra help. Beyond that, I know nothing of her at all.'

Tapping her fingertips together as she articulated her thoughts, Elena said, 'If Proctor's plans go as he wishes, we could have a steady turnover of guests here within two months. This will require us to have more than the three of us on the regular staff. Alisha is an attractive young woman. I'd be interested in your opinion.'

Lady Tia considered carefully before asking, 'You see her as a possible submissive?'

'You will not have missed the way she appraises both the male and female guests when they come here. If I'm correct, I suspect Alisha would happily follow a command to be hog-tied, and paddled by a stranger with the same ardour she displays for us. Such a staff member could be very useful.'

'And this idea has come from Proctor, I assume. He's besotted with the girl despite her inconvenient shortcoming?'

'No, this idea has come from my common sense, Lady Tia,' Dr Ewen snapped. 'The shortcoming you mention need not be an issue for your concern. Now, if you would be so good as to go and prepare for our southern guests, I will join you in the lobby as soon as they arrive.'

As soon as Lady Tia had gone, Elena sat back at her desk. She knew Proctor wanted Alisha trained, but she wasn't sure of his motives – not yet, anyway.

Chapter Four

JESS MAY HAVE been blindfolded, but she knew she'd been bundled onto a plane. The claustrophobic nature of the atmosphere, combined with the distinctive smell of expensive leather, and the hum of air conditioning, made her location unmistakeable.

The pair of strong hands that had gripped her shoulders manoeuvred Jess into a chair that was far too comfortable to be on a charter flight. It had all the luxurious hallmarks of a first class compartment or a private plane.

Of course it's a private plane, Jess told herself. As if I could be taken on to a standard flight like this!

No one had spoken in the car. During the journey from Fables to whichever airport they'd been driven to, every erotic scenario possible, from the mild to the brain-bogglingly outlandish, had passed through Jess's head.

As a seatbelt was buckled across her lap, and the engines roared into life, Jess felt more disorientated and dizzy by the second. Her ears popped as the plane soared skywards, heading for its required altitude.

Her muscles clenching to new heights of tension, Jess became aware of movement, and an unfamiliar female voice saying, with a gentle Scottish purr, 'You may disengage your seatbelts now, gentlemen.'

'I must say, I'm very grateful to Mrs Peters for sending me two such ripe specimens.' Jess jumped in her seat. She hadn't expected to hear David Proctor's voice echoing around the interior of the plane, the unfamiliar acoustics making her unsure if his stocky body was looming over her or if he was merely sitting nearby.

The voice that replied was more sceptical. 'Having seen them in action, David, I am yet to see what has so enthralled you about these women.'

Kane was still here. Damn! Jess, her hands linked together in her lap, wished she could block out the conversation between the two men, but knew that if she didn't hear what was said, her imagination would fill in the blanks anyway, and probably invent a scenario even worse than the reality of the situation.

Proctor's sigh as he replied to Kane's caustic comment felt somehow suffocating, as if it was filling Jess up from the inside out. 'Well, ladies, I can't pretend I'm not disappointed. I had such high hopes. Kane is an excellent judge of sexual prowess, and I felt sure you'd impress him in the White Room. Yet, from what he tells me, you, Miss Sarah, did nothing but stand feebly by and watch, while Miss Sanders lay motionless as she was given the time of her life by three obliging gentlemen, my compatriot included.'

Miss Sarah's sharp tut of response was deliberately audible.

'You wish to speak, Miss Sarah?' David's voice was sugar sweet, and if Jess hadn't met him before, she could *almost* have believed it was a genuine invitation. The staff of Fables, however, knew better, and the dominatrix remained silent. Besides, her tut had been eloquent enough to make her feelings clear without elaboration.

'So she is wise enough to hold her tongue on occasion?' Kane's curt accent oozed sarcasm.

Although she couldn't see him, Jess was sure Proctor would be glaring from herself to Miss Sarah and back again as he spoke. His words dripped mock-sorrow. 'If I'd considered for even one moment that you'd fail to impress my respected associate, then I would never have asked Mrs Peters for you.'

Proctor paused long enough for Jess to feel queasy again. 'You have precisely 75 minutes to convince me I haven't made a terrible mistake in borrowing you. If you fail to impress, then I will leave you at our destination, and you'll have to make your own way home in disgrace. I can't begin to think what the other members of Fables will think if you scuttle back with your tail between your legs.'

Lying bastard. Despite her anxiety, Jess seethed silently. She knew David was talking crap. He would never abandon her and Miss Sarah in the middle of nowhere. Mrs Peters' revenge would be extreme, to say the least. She was convinced he was in full "bullshit show-off" mode in the presence of Kane.

Trying to remain rational, Jess allowed herself space to think. Why was he trying so hard to impress Kane if he was simply a colleague? She was damn sure David knew Kane was playing down his White Room experience. Anyway, no man could keep his dick as stiff as Kane's had been if they didn't like what they'd been seeing. Plus, it had been his choice not to use a gag, and in the back of her head Jess could hear the cacophony of appreciative sighs and groans that had issued from Kane's throat while she'd held his shaft in her velvet grasp.

Deep in thought, Jess was surprised by the sudden removal of her blindfold, and found herself looking into the smiling face of a uniformed air stewardess.

Predictably slim, yet curvy in all the right places, the hostess had a tan that was plainly out of a bottle, and which clashed alarmingly with her jet black hair and overdose of make-up.

Jess who, beneath all her erotic musings, had harboured unrealistic hopes that she might be allowed to sleep on the flight, saw how unlikely that now was. The stewardess, her light blue, fitted blouse showing off her braless tits beneath, her skirt short enough to reveal the tops of her stockings, hovered by David, as if awaiting instructions.

It had been a while since Jess had seen Mr Proctor, and she was struck afresh by the falseness of his expression. Everything about him had always seemed implausible, as if his whole demeanour was being used to perpetuate the idea that he was a nice guy, and not the ruthless businessman Jess knew him to be. Average in height and build, it was as if the very ordinariness of David's short, greying hair with its overlong fringe, and the unremarkable shade of his green eyes in his circular face, had to be compensated for with constant reminders of his wealth. A wealth which he flaunted with every garment he wore and every item he owned.

Rather than dismissing the stewardess, he gestured towards her, 'Ladies, let me introduce you to Alisha.'

Jess looked at the girl more closely. She had "footballer's wife" written all over her, but perhaps it wasn't just her tan that was false?

'Alisha is a member of staff at your new place of employment.' David gave her a smile that may well have been genuine, but still managed to make Jess feel uneasy. 'She's been intrigued by what I've told her about my visits to your team in Oxfordshire. So naturally, when Alisha asked if she could witness your expertise for herself I was only too delighted to agree. As you have yet to impress my colleague here –' David gestured to Kane '– now seems the perfect time to show him and Alisha what you are really capable of.'

While smarm poured from Proctor's tongue, Jess battled not to exchange knowing glances with Miss Sarah. Instead she focused on the figure now perching on the chair next to her boss. She couldn't have been more than 22, making her at least half David's age, and three years younger than Jess herself. Alisha was giving off an air of confidence that didn't sit quite right with the frequent flick of her eyes from David to his guests, and back again.

Was her confidence fake too? Had David simply ordered her to act like that for him? Jess began to feel as if she was watching some sort of bizarre theatrical performance.

Glancing at Kane, who sat on the chair across the small aisle from David, Jess couldn't mistake the look of contempt on his face. He was observing Alisha with even more open suspicion than he'd spared on either Jess or Miss Sarah. So, he wasn't convinced by this woman either …

Jess's train of thought was interrupted by Proctor. 'Miss Sanders, stand, and raise the overhead locker above your seat.'

Rising to her feet and clicking the locker hatch open, Jess took a step back so the plastic door could swing upwards. She had expected to find either ropes, paddles, and handcuffs; or life jackets, whistles, and the other items of safety equipment that should be stored on an aircraft. She had not expected to see three neatly stacked piles of clothing.

This time Jess did glance sideways at Miss Sarah, who cast a warning flash of her eyes straight back at her as Proctor addressed them. 'The red outfit is for Alisha. I think that colour will suit *her* best, and of course, she is a *much* smaller size than either of you two.'

Jess winced inside; David really couldn't be so stupid as to think that teenage flattery would work on his female companion. She might have looked like a college cheerleader, but Jess was becoming more certain by the second there was more to Alisha than met the eye.

'The blue dress is for Miss Sarah; the brown for Miss Sanders. Garments which reflect your respective statuses. Change quickly.'

Passing out the bundles of clothing and examining her own outfit, which had a distinct Cinderella feel to it, Jess stripped, until only her underwear remained. She was about to pull the low-busted, tattered-edged dress over her head when David stopped her. 'No, Miss Sanders; take off your underwear as well. I think you'll find the costume more flattering worn with nothing beneath.'

Miss Sarah, who'd also stripped to her underwear, stopped in the act of picking up her allocated dress, which, with its tight-fitting top and flouncy skirt, could either have been Cinderella at the "going to the ball" stage of the story, or possibly Sleeping Beauty, Rapunzel, or any other random fairy tale princess in fact. She wordlessly undressed to the flesh, before edging the cheap polyester material over her head.

Alisha, meanwhile, had disappeared into the bathroom cubicle to change, only returning once her pure satin Red Riding Hood outfit, complete with cloak, miniskirt, and black basque were in place. As fantasy clothing for adults went, these three outfits would probably feature high on any fetishist's wish list.

'You'll note that in the interests of aircraft safety, I have dispensed with the high-heeled shoes that would normally add that extra element of interest to your garments, except for yours, of course, Miss Sanders. Cinderella always had bare feet in her servant days. Most fitting for an experienced submissive such as yourself, I'm sure you'll agree.'

Remembering his instruction on their very first meeting back at Fables, Jess used his Christian name in reply. 'Yes, David.'

Alisha, who held a Red Riding Hood-style wicker basket, curtseyed towards her employer, proffering it in his direction. As he swished back the chequered tablecloth that had been laid across its top, the broad smile that crossed Proctor's face plunged Jess's heart to her feet.

The brown bodice of her dress squeezed Jess's chest up and out, so that her cleavage was displayed to its best advantage. Her nipples were only just hidden by the keenness of its elasticated top, which was so tight she could already feel its pattern imprinting on her skin. The skirt, on the other hand, which was cut into strips of wispy netting, barely covered her backside. If Cinderella really had worn an outfit like this when she was cleaning, then with every stretch and bend to dust or sweep she would have shown off her arse to perfection.

Miss Sarah, positively regal in her ankle-length, puff-skirted dress, also had her breasts compressed to the point of popping out from its faux satin material. The thunderous expression on her face, however, was far from the serene visage normally associated with fairy tale princesses.

'Alisha, I think you could learn a great deal from these women.' David took the basket from her hands, and extracted a strip of red ribbon. 'Use this to secure Miss Sanders' wrists. She will put them together for you without argument.'

Mindful of Mrs Peters' final instruction – *Do Fables and yourself proud* – Jess obediently placed her palms together in front of her waist, and watched Alisha wrap the wide ribbon around her wrists with rather more expertise than expected. Not her first time at doing this, then …

'Miss Sarah, to me, please.'

The dominatrix, every inch of her displaying a haughty indifference to the men watching, did as she was bidden.

Rummaging in the basket, purely to effect Jess thought, David produced what he'd been searching for, and held it up like a trophy. 'Miss Sarah, I'd like you to teach Alisha how to use this to bring your submissive to the point of ecstasy, but slowly. Make it last. Make her wait.'

Jess, her blood pumping with the speed of a delayed train trying to make up time, felt her throat close on itself as her superior lifted a heavily frosted cupcake from

Proctor's palm. Of course, what else would Red Riding Hood have in her basket?

'Kane, I know they didn't impress you before, but this will be good.'

Jess didn't know whether to be flattered or bemused by Proctor's faith in her. No one had ever tried to stimulate her with confectionery before, and she really wished her brain hadn't already filled itself with visions of Miss Sarah rubbing the icing star that was stuck in the top of the cake over her breasts in a steady, rotating motion.

Obviously wanting to get this charade over with as soon as possible, Miss Sarah took charge. 'Alisha, if you'd step this way, I will talk you through what I do, as I do it.'

In a tone that brooked no argument from anyone, Miss Sarah went on. 'Turn around, Miss Sanders. Lift your tethered hands, and hold onto the back of the chair before you.'

Jess had been so sure that it would be her chest that would be the focus of the cake's attention that the order to turn sent a flare of disappointment rippling through her breasts as they were pressed against the back of the leather chair.

'Alisha, I require your assistance as well as your *complete* attention for this lesson. As you can see, Miss Sanders' skirt is cut into many lengths, so just lifting it up in one piece is not an option. Use one of your hands to hold all the strips of netting out of the way.'

As Alisha's fingers gently gathered up all the stray pieces of skirt, Jess felt the heady frisson of an unfamiliar hand holding the fabric in the small of her back, and four sets of eyes levelling themselves on her posterior.

'Thank you, Alisha. Now, observe.' Miss Sarah contained her smile as Jess's backside quivered a fraction at the first touch of the stiff, sharp-edged, icing star. Trailing it in a misshapen figure of eight from one buttock to the other, using the anus as the cross-over point, Miss

53

Sarah noted how each pass forced Jess to focus harder on not fidgeting her feet.

'If you look closely, Alisha, you will see different points on the arse produce different reactions from our submissive, as does the amount of pressure applied, and the manner in which we hold the cake.'

Miss Sarah swivelled the cake around in her fingers, so she was now holding its top and pushing the sponge base against Jess's butt. 'I suspect, however, that I'm not telling you anything you don't already know.'

Not giving Alisha the chance to reply herself, David interjected sharply, his brusque tone betraying his own arousal. 'This is *all* very new to Alisha, if you would continue.'

Filing his overreaction away to be considered later, Miss Sarah kept her attention on the younger woman. 'Now that I have flipped the cake around, if I press it while keeping it moving, the crumbs will leave a trail across her flesh. Get the amount of pressure correct, and the cake won't be destroyed.

'You will also notice, if you get in close, that despite being extremely horny, Miss Sanders isn't moving or making a sound. She has, after all, been *very* well trained. She is diverting her feelings away from the climax she craves by the clenching of her toes, and the digging of her fingernails into the chair against which she is leaning. Do you see?'

'Yes, Miss Sarah.' Alisha spoke respectfully, but Miss Sarah remained unconvinced by her willingness to learn about the art of domination. Something about the way her chest was filling her bodice as she stood nearer to Jess, her hands fidgety in their keenness to touch, made her think that this young woman was better suited to a very different role in David's new establishment.

Jess closed her eyes. She could feel Alisha's rapid breathing on her thighs, and it was taking a little more effort than she would have liked to admit not to twist around so that the stewardess was faced with an eyeful of pussy.

'Would you like to take over with the cake?'

Alisha looked up at the mistress, her oddly bright blue eyes giving out mixed signals of excitement and trepidation. 'Yes, Miss Sarah.'

Giving her the cake, whose icing was beginning to crack into hairline fractures, as if a skier had been racing over and across a snow-capped mountain, Miss Sarah leant forward and whispered into Alisha's ear, so that only she could hear. 'And of course, if the subject of your administrations has no idea what you are going to do next, then their imagination can do as much work on your behalf as you do yourself. You may touch Miss Sanders any way you wish. Until I say otherwise, you are in charge.'

'Miss Sarah, I think we should all hear what ...' David stepped forward, a protest about to burst forth from his open mouth, but Miss Sarah put up her hand, stemming his objections before they'd started.

'You asked me to educate the girl. Let me do so. Miss Alisha, proceed.'

An uncertain glance from Alisha, who had clearly realised she was no longer working from whatever script Proctor had given her, and wasn't sure who to obey, told Miss Sarah that her suspicions about the girl were correct. As the dominatrix wondered what David's real agenda with Alisha was, she added, 'If you don't know where to start, consider what you would like to feel if you were Miss Sanders.'

After a moment's hesitation, Alisha knelt and, easing the icing star out of the cake, placed one of its points directly over Jess's anus.

The strange sensation caused her concentration to waver, and an unpermitted groan slipped from Jess's lips. She braced herself for a slap of correction. A slap that didn't come as Red Riding Hood gently cartwheeled the star, point by point, up her crack until it reached the top of her butt, then ran it down again.

With her nipples rubbing against the thin, cheap material of her outfit, Jess edged her bum out a little to afford better access. As Alisha continued to roll the icing shape up and down, Jess fought to contain the frustration building in her throat at the delicious hesitancy of the touch. Was the girl really nervous and inexperienced, or knowledgeable enough to know that going slowly would ensure Jess's body inflamed faster with each teasing touch?

Sighs of contentment from the audience made Jess stiffen. So consumed had she been in the sensations provided by such an unlikely tool of provocation that she'd forgotten about David Proctor and his grumpy sidekick. Steeling herself, Jess had almost managed to gather herself together when a thin tongue started to lap up the sticky trail across her butt.

Jess's groan morphed to a protracted whimper. She could feel the dawn of her climax bunching in the pit of her stomach. Only the thought of Miss Sarah's annoyance if she came before she was bidden kept the submissive from pleading out loud for this unusual stimulation to either stop, or to go on for ever.

'Turn around, please.'

The sound of Alisha, and *not* Miss Sarah, issuing the instruction was unexpected, and as Jess twisted at the girl's request, her heart hammered in her ears. She had guessed what was about to follow, and she wished she hadn't worked it out. Wished it wasn't so predictable; but wished, more than all of that, that Alisha would hurry up and just do it.

'Miss Sarah, would you hold her skirt up for me, please?'

The dominatrix's eyes narrowed; she had been so sure

she'd assessed this girl correctly. Now, as Alisha continued to issue instructions to her submissive, she was less certain. It was a feeling Miss Sarah didn't like.

'Lift your hands, Miss Sanders. You may steady yourself by placing them on top of my hood.' As she spoke, Alisha pulled the red hood over her head, hiding her expression from all three onlookers, as she crouched before the submissive and, just as Jess had hoped for, eased the icing star up inside her channel.

A protracted breath whistled from Jess's lips as the shape widened her in places; but not everywhere, and not enough. This was a situation quickly remedied by the application of a pair of red-lipsticked lips, hungry and searching. Not searching for Jess's engorged and neglected nub, but for the star, which Alisha's tongue fiddled around within its cushioned hiding place with prolonged, cruel strokes.

After what felt a gorgeously tormented lifetime to Jess, Alisha hooked the now shrunken star out with her tongue, and consumed it with two crunches. Then, moving back, her eyes shining, pussy juice smeared across her cheeks, she unceremoniously slammed the entire cupcake against Jess's clit. The submissive came with an intensity she would never have thought possible from a small, round, iced, vanilla-flavoured sponge.

No one had spoken after Jess had come. No one had told her off for coming without permission. No one had congratulated Alisha on her technique. No one had commented when Miss Sarah had changed back into her own clothes, and Jess, with her limbs shaking from post-climactic shock, had followed suit.

Kane had held his tongue when David escorted Alisha to the bathroom, his cock so rigid beneath his suit trousers that Jess was amazed it hadn't broken through the zip fly unaided.

Jess wasn't sure how much time had passed between leaving her Cinderella drabs behind and the jet descending onto the runaway, but it couldn't have been many minutes before the "fasten seatbelts" sign had flashed on and both she and Miss Sarah had been blindfolded once more.

Having been bundled with slightly less speed than before from the plane into another waiting car, they were driven for at least half an hour before a now familiar pair of giant hands came to Jess's face, and undid the blindfold for a second time.

Kane, his face remaining an expressionless blank, silently watched as Jess's vision adjusted to the light.

The first thing she noticed, apart from Kane, was that it was now dark. The second was that Miss Sarah was sitting at the opposite side of the limo's back seat, also blinking and holding a blindfold.

As soon as Kane moved to the front of the vehicle, the words "are you all right, ma'am?" formed on the tip of Jess's tongue. A hand signal from Miss Sarah stopped her uttering them. Jess understood. They might have been alone in the back of the car, which was closed off from the front with a screen, but that didn't mean Kane wasn't listening to them.

Hungry, tired, and more nervous than she'd ever been in the presence of Mrs Peters, Jess looked out of the window. Trees and hills bordered the roads. She didn't think they'd been in the air long enough to be abroad, and yet this neither looked like, nor felt like, England.

As if understanding Jess's unspoken query, Miss Sarah said, 'I think, although I may be mistaken, that this is Scotland.'

'Have you been here before, ma'am?'

'I've visited a few places here, but it's a bigger country than people often think. I've not explored it as much as I'd have liked.'

Scotland? Miss Sarah could be wrong, of course. Even

as she had the thought, Jess dismissed it. She'd never known Miss Sarah be wrong. She was over 600 miles from home. A chill ran though the submissive. Anything could happen, and hardly anyone would know where to look for her.

Miss Sarah saw the trepidation on Jess's face, which she guessed went far beyond wondering if she'd survive the sexual excesses asked of her. After a quick scan of the back of the car to make sure that they weren't being filmed, she placed a reassuring hand on Jess's knee.

It was a tiny gesture, but it went a long way to steady Jess's rising nerves as the car began to move again, swerving from the streetlamp-lit main road, into a dark, narrow driveway lined on either side by rows of dense woodland. Now Jess was sure Miss Sarah was right; the nature of the pine trees casting their shadows across the road had Scotland written all over them.

As the vehicle turned again, the women found themselves faced with a small, stone castle framed against the gloom of distant mountains. But was it a real castle, or a pretend one? It had a tall, slim turret and so many towers that it instantly made Jess think of Walt Disney films.

Jess found herself reaching for Miss Sarah's hand, and was mildly surprised when the mistress took it. One look at her face showed her it had also occurred to Miss Sarah that, no matter how beautiful the floodlit vision of Scottish heritage before them was, its picturesque nature would be a stark contrast to the experiences they'd face within its thick, granite walls.

'Is that a proper castle?' Even as Jess whispered her enquiry, she realised it was a ridiculous thing to ask in the circumstances, but it was at least non-controversial.

Miss Sarah answered her quickly. 'Yes. When it's sunny, it will even appear pink because of the make-up of the granite. Disney copied the design of Scottish castles for his fairy tale films.'

Was it a coincidence or deliberate that they'd been obliged to wear fairy tale fancy dress, and now were at a fairy tale castle? Jess's ponderings were cut short by the unlocking of the car's doors.

'Out.' Kane, proving once again he was a man of few words, looked faintly amused as he watched the women clamber out of the limousine with as much dignity as they could muster. 'You will stay here.' He smirked. 'Not that there is anywhere to flee to if you decided to do a runner.'

Holding her tongue until Kane was no more than a shadow as he approached the castle door, Jess spoke in hushed tones. 'May I ask a question, ma'am?'

'You may, although I cannot promise an answer.'

'If I understood Mrs Peters correctly, we're here to teach the new staff. I can't do that! I'm a submissive. I do what I'm told by other people. I don't tell people what to do. Look what happened when I had to order Proctor about in the dungeon. It was a disaster.' An involuntary shiver ran the length of Jess's spine as she recalled her first meeting with David. She'd managed to shut it out for months and now, as she stood on the grand gravel driveway, it seemed to be the only memory her head had space for.

Miss Sarah's snort of fake laughter made Jess flinch. 'I suspected you'd misunderstood. I am certain it will be me training the submissive, not you. I suspect you'll be the practice subject for the mistress or master of this establishment, and perhaps a model for me to demonstrate on, as you were on the plane.'

'My God! I ...' Jess couldn't finish her sentence, uncertain whether this situation was better or worse than the one she'd been imagining.

Miss Sarah carried on, her tone less derisive; her eyes firmly on the castle door, anticipating the return of Kane, or at least someone to fetch them from the cool of the night into whatever temporary future awaited them. 'But of course, I could also be wrong. So far, nothing we have encountered has made much sense, but I'm sure it soon will.

'Perhaps our opinions about our new colleague's progress will be asked for, perhaps not. My advice to you, Miss Sanders, is to say nothing that doesn't need saying, to trust no one but me, and expect whatever David Proctor has planned to start the very second we set foot inside that castle.'

Chapter Five

JESS WASN'T SURE exactly what she'd expected to happen once they'd been escorted into the castle. What she *had* been sure of, however, was that Miss Sarah was right. The moment they crossed the threshold into David Proctor's territory, they'd be subjected to some kind of sexual action that would make their in-flight entertainment look mild.

The submissive had spent the final part of the journey mentally preparing herself for an instant stripping, beating, and group fuck by every member of the staff she was there to meet. She'd contemplated being fastened to some sort of table or chair, so that her naked frame could be examined and teased to the point when her endurance broke; and being the target for every sort of sex toy ever invented. What Jess had not expected was nothing.

When she and Miss Sarah had finally been ordered to approach the castle, they'd stuck close together, walking slowly. As they'd stepped before the main door, someone from within had let out a whistle, and a male-shaped shadow had appeared from the gloom of the night. Steering Jess by the neck, the stranger had taken her inside, while Kane emerged from the door and shoved Miss Sarah in a totally different direction.

Ushered through the large entrance hall, with barely enough time to take in more than the solid, whitewashed walls, and the profusion of bold tartan chairs and sofas, Jess had been vaguely conscious of a group of people standing to one side. They mutely observed her being swiftly manoeuvred past them.

Still held by the back of the neck, she was frogmarched along a narrow corridor by a slim young man Jess hadn't been able to see clearly in the dark. Whoever he was, he had kept purposely behind her as they strode through the castle, and she hadn't dared ask him anything as she saw that a spiral staircase of bare stone lay ahead of them.

Two minutes later, they'd reached an open wooden door. With no corridors to either the left or right, there was no other way to go but through, and Jess had suddenly been reminded of Rapunzel, who'd been imprisoned in a room at the top of a tower with nowhere to run.

The guide held her by the shoulders. His unspoken instruction that she should not try to look at him was made clear by the intensity of his grip. With an unexpected burst of speed, the man then took a step down, at the same time urging Jess firmly forward. No sooner had she stepped into the room than the door was snapped shut behind her, and Jess had found herself alone in a circular space which had curtains drawn all the way around it.

Five minutes later, she was still taking slow, deep breaths as she tried to soothe herself. Whatever was happening would be for a reason, and if she knew David Proctor like she thought she did, Jess was sure that somewhere in the room there was probably a camera observing her every move, gauging how she was reacting to this enforced situation.

Standing still, she cast her eyes around the room. If life at Fables had taught her anything, it was that the more detail she took in about her surroundings, and the more attention she paid to every word spoken to her, the more she'd learn, and the better her chances of survival and erotic contentment would be.

'So, I'm inside the turret, then.' In the centre of the room, a spindle-backed wooden chair sat next to a matching table. 'All that's missing here is a spinning wheel. Forget Rapunzel, this is Sleeping Beauty!' Jess muttered to herself as she walked around the rug-covered stone floor, skirting the very edges of the room as if she was a tiger patrolling the surrounds of its cage. She ran her hands across the floor to ceiling dark purple velvet curtains. Unsure if she wanted to see or not, she drew them back.

The majority of the room's walls were constructed of large blocks of bare granite, but as Jess threw open the third curtain, she stepped back in surprise. A wooden door, about four feet high, and two feet across, had been built into the curve of the stone. 'OK, so maybe this isn't Sleeping Beauty after all. Maybe it's Snow White.'

With her heart thumping, Jess placed her hand on the brass doorknob, and bent to see what was through the doorway. 'Oh thank God!'

It was a washroom. A modern shower cubicle, sink, and toilet were plumbed into the exquisitely tiled carpeted semicircle. Making use of the facilities, Jess wondered if this was to be her room; where she was to spend all her time when she wasn't doing whatever it was that Proctor expected her to do.

Returning to the larger room, Jess continued to throw back the curtains, wondering if any other cubbyholes were secretly attached to this turret. No more doors appeared but, drawing back the last pair of drapes, Jess jumped as she came face to face with her own bedraggled reflection.

A huge, round mirror stared at her. 'So maybe this is Snow White! Complete with the scary mirror on the wall and the dwarf-sized door. Which means, I only have the Wicked Queen left to meet.'

As soon as she'd spoken the words she slammed her hand to her mouth, wishing she hadn't said them out loud. Until that point she'd considered herself to be doing well. She'd shown whoever was watching her via the camera she was convinced was installed in the turret somewhere that she was capable of acting calmly, and was brave enough to explore, not merely sitting and cowering on the chair awaiting her fate. Now she'd blown it. I might as well have lain down on the floor and wanked without permission, Jess thought crossly. Instantly, she wished she hadn't had that thought either, for some solo comfort from her fingers over her ever-damp clit would been have more than welcome.

Beginning to shiver, realising that the curtains hadn't been there to hide things, but to keep the heat in the room, Jess put the heavy velvet drapes back in place, starting with the one over the mirror. She'd never liked looking at herself in mirrors, and the sheer size of this one, along with the brilliance of its shine, unnerved her as it reflected back her dishevelled red hair and tired eyes. 'Not exactly the fairest of them all!' she quipped.

Sitting at the little desk, Jess reasoned that this couldn't be her bedroom, as there was no bed. That meant that, despite the fact it was almost one o'clock in the morning, she was being kept there for a reason other than to get some sleep. The idea of a wicked queen came back to her mind. No one had mentioned a mistress equivalent to Mrs Peters. Until now Jess had assumed that David would run this place, but now, as fatigue took a firmer hold, Jess saw how unlikely that was. Hot shot businessmen don't run places like this; they get other people to run them for them while they sit back and get off on the results. Surely though, she thought, allowing her eyes to close for a few seconds, if I can survive Mrs Peters' regime, then whoever runs this place will be no problem. She snapped her eyes back open. Or could they be worse?

Not wanting to speculate on the woman she had already labelled the Wicked Queen, who might not exist beyond her overactive imagination anyway, Jess looked at the table. Her eyes fell on the only items it held: a brand new

65

notebook and a pencil. Was she supposed to write something down? If so, what? Holding her hands in her lap, wishing she'd known she was going to have to dress for the cool Scottish climate, not to mention the draughty nature of castles, Jess's thoughts drifted towards Miss Sarah. Where was she? What was happening to her?

'It is a pleasure to meet you, Miss Sarah.'

Her back as straight as ever, her chest thrust out, and her shoulders back, Miss Sarah returned the greeting, 'And you, ma'am. Forgive me, but there was little time at departure, and Mrs Peters did not inform me of your preferred form of address.'

Dr Ewen looked into the face of the woman before her. The video footage had not done her justice. Not only was Miss Sarah striking, she was also beautiful. She didn't need to see Lady Tia's face to know that she already hated the newcomer.

Removing her glasses for a second, giving Miss Sarah a better look at her shrewd, silver eyes before the spectacles were slid back into place, Dr Ewen said, 'If Proctor has one failing, it is that once he has made a decision, he likes it acted upon instantly. He doesn't always give thought to details such as time.'

Her expression wooden as she mentally weighed up the woman who was to be her boss for the next fortnight, Miss Sarah was also conscious of the powerhouse of a woman who stood behind her. Her face might have remained neutral, but that didn't stop hate leaking into the atmosphere from her every pore. Dr Ewen might have been in charge, but Miss Sarah had no doubt at all it was the woman behind her who was going to cause her the most inconvenience. Probably at every available opportunity. After all, Miss Sarah thought as her new companions mutely observed her, if this was the other way around, and she had come to Fables, I would make her life

66

hell.

Allowing only a moment of silence, Elena Ewen introduced Miss Sarah to her current surroundings, 'This establishment is called The Retreat. We have existed for almost a year, and have a steady trade. We provide a haven, an escape from the pressures of technology, and require all mobile phones, laptops, and other distractions of modern life to be left behind once you enter the castle grounds. Here our guests can relax and be precisely who they want to be. I trust you and Miss Sanders have no such gadgetry?'

'No, ma'am. Mrs Peters does not allow them either.'

'Excellent.' Dr Ewen sat a little straighter as she went on. 'When Mr Proctor came across us a few months ago, well, let's just say that things changed quickly. We are currently in the process of improving and expanding our staff to suit the requests of his particular brand of client.'

Miss Sarah inclined her head a fraction of an inch to prove she was both listening and understood as the manageress went on.

'I am known to visitors as The Retreat mistress, but you may address me as Dr Ewen, and you will treat me with the same respect as you would give to Mrs Peters.'

'Of course, Dr Ewen. Thank you.'

The atmosphere softened from brittle to formal as Dr Ewen proffered a hand towards the other woman in the room. 'May I introduce you to Lady Tia, my right hand, and The Retreat's resident dominatrix.'

'I'm honoured.' Intending to avoid every chance for resentment, Miss Sarah curtseyed, showing Lady Tia that she accepted her seniority, even if it was only because she'd got here first.

Lady Tia, however, had already decided that she wasn't going to let Miss Sarah off the hook so quickly. With her hands glued to her hips, she made her feelings about Proctor's plans very plain with one word. 'Indeed.'

Pointedly walking around Miss Sarah, Lady Tia addressed Dr Ewen. 'It would be wise for us to see what we are dealing with here. I find it difficult to believe that someone so young has had as much as experience as you or I in the ways of domination.'

As she spoke, Lady Tia stopped behind Miss Sarah and passed her hands around the petite waist, cupping each of the newcomer's breasts in her palms. 'About a handful. A promising start, I suppose. Although –' she glanced pointedly at her own hefty cleavage '– it is not of the standard our customers are used to.'

Viewing Miss Sarah as an asset rather than a person, following the lead of her assistant, Dr Ewen nodded. 'How about her hips? They look sturdy, but are they sturdy enough?'

Lady Tia seized one of Miss Sarah's hips in each hand, and squeezed her bones through her flesh, causing her to exhale rather louder than she would have liked.

'I would say they were fine for our purposes, but to be sure I am going to have to strip her. May I, doctor?'

'You may.' Elena Ewen tilted her head to one side as if considering all options. 'To begin with, however, I think you should only remove her upper layer of garments. David reported to me that this specimen looks astounding in corsetry.'

Dr Ewen made the statement as much to gauge her second in command's reaction to the fact that someone else might be considered to look better in basques and stockings than she did, as to actually see Miss Sarah in her finery. There was no question that Miss Sarah had a more conventionally acceptable figure than Lady Tia did, and her poise was superb. Elena smiled inwardly; this was going to be fun. Lady Tia had needed taking down a peg or two for some time. Perhaps this was the means by which that would happen.

Miss Sarah knew the scrapes of the sharp, black

fingernails that assaulted her skin were not accidental, and privately awarded her opposite number a point. She would have done the same; grazing the skin a little, seeing how much indignity her equal could put up with. As her blouse hit the floor, and she stood in a black G-string, an exquisite boned black bra, her stockings and boots, Miss Sarah judged the time was right to meet her new employer's steady stare.

The tiniest hint of amusement flashed in Elena's eyes. The girl was good at this game. Lady Tia was excellent with the guests, and she could dominate in her sleep, but Miss Sarah evidently understood the politics as well, and took the game to a psychological level as well as a physical one. She was already sorry she was going to have to let Miss Sarah go back to England when her work here was done.

'No corset today then? A shame.'

'Forgive me, doctor, but I was not informed where we were travelling to, or how long our journey would be. Corsetry, as you will appreciate, is not suitable for extreme heat or extended uncomfortable journeys.'

This time Elena allowed the smile to show. 'And of course, we now have the sight of you in your basque to look forward to. I would be much obliged, Miss Sarah, if you would wear your most popular corsetry tomorrow.'

'Of course, Dr Ewen.'

Lady Tia continued to run her hands over Miss Sarah, manipulating her flesh. Interchanging her touch from light to firm, feathery strokes to pinching, she was determined to make her react in some way; to at least make her nipples peak, or juice run from her pussy. So far, she had been disappointed, for although Miss Sarah's nipples were plainly pert beneath her silk underwear, no other physical reaction was evident. Not once had her face coloured or her speech faltered; nor had her feet shuffled or her hands clasped in an involuntary movement.

A wave of unaccustomed discomfort slipped through Lady Tia's substantial frame. She had the unpalatable feeling that if she didn't exert her position of power soon, then this statuesque interloper would take it from her simply by doing nothing.

'Your self-control is excellent.' Lady Tia spoke from behind Miss Sarah, hoping she'd react and bend to face her, and thus give her an excuse to punish her for moving without permission. But Miss Sarah stood exactly where she was, refraining from answer.

'And I can see why the Fables guests visit you on a regular basis,' Lady Tia continued. 'Mrs Peters was kind enough to send us a recording of you applying the cane to a gentleman in the study at the hotel. Your weapon control was very precise.'

Knowing Lady Tia wasn't really complimenting her, Miss Sarah continued to avoid comment, while watching Dr Ewen with unblinking interest.

Running her fingers through Miss Sarah's loose russet hair, teasing out the tangles that had formed during her impromptu journey, Lady Tia continued, 'As Dr Ewen stated, I am the dominatrix in charge here. Although we all, myself included, answer to Dr Ewen –' she paused, and doffed her head respectfully to her boss, mindful of not pushing her luck too far '– the remaining staff, be they employed in our small office, in housekeeping, or the kitchen, report directly to me. This means that while you are within The Retreat, you and your toy will consider me your first port of call before bothering Dr Ewen with any enquiries or requests.'

Miss Sarah silently noted Jess's relegation to a mere toy. It was vital she listened intently while being informed of her place in the scheme of things here. A position that was clearly much lower in the order of things than Lady Tia, who, with more skill than Miss Sarah would have liked to admit, was tipping her semi-naked body enchantingly into arousal.

In any other circumstance, Miss Sarah would have practised her well-honed art of distraction to fend off such inconvenient feelings of stimulation until she was off duty, but she did that by phasing out of her client's conversations, and thinking of the mundane tasks she would have to do once they'd gone. Here and now, phasing out was too dangerous an option; she had to stay alert and on top of every word, be it spoken or merely implied.

Keeping her hands moving in steady strokes, Lady Tia crouched on her haunches, and brought her face close to Miss Sarah's pearl buttocks. Then, taking a fleshy arse cheek in each hand, she eased them apart, examining the neat backside in intimate detail.

Miss Sarah made a split-second decision. If Lady Tia continued in her minute examination, she would discover that her body would very much like a finger to probe between her butt cheeks, or a tongue to lap along her spine, just like anyone else would. Perhaps an initial defeat to this woman would be a good idea? Politic, perhaps?

Having made her diplomatic decision, Miss Sarah, feeling the intense pressure of Lady Tia's digits massaging her buttocks, sighed sharply.

'So, you are not as ironclad in your self-control as we were led to believe!' Lady Tia was immediately triumphant.

Dr Ewen, however, remained silent, sitting on the top of her desk to observe the performance. She was convinced that, for one of them at least, this was an optional performance, albeit one she would enjoy.

Lady Tia, with her eyes flashing devilment, said, 'With your permission, doctor, I would like to see our honoured guest as nature intended?'

Elena, ever the voyeur, nodded curtly, continuing to envy Laura Peters for her good fortune in finding this woman. If her dominatrix was up to this standard, then how good would her submissive be? Observing carefully, she found herself fascinated as Miss Sarah was fully undressed, and decided to change how Lady Tia intended the session to go.

'As we suspected; only average breasts.' Lady Tia inspected Miss Sarah with a continuing firm grip, stating "waxed pussy", as if she was about to compile an inventory. Miss Sarah shuffled her feet as a finger was slipped within her channel to check its width. 'Wet, and yet with a level of control that prevents her internal juice from straying and giving her state of stimulation away. Unusual and potentially useful.'

Crossing her arms, Dr Ewen ordered, 'I would like you to lie upon the carpet, Miss Sarah.'

Obeying instantly, taking a brief satisfaction from the flash of annoyance that crossed Lady Tia's face as her plans were interrupted, Miss Sarah placed her back upon the plush carpet.

'Put your arms out to each side, and bend your knees while widening your legs.'

Dr Ewen turned to Lady Tia. 'There are many tests I intend to carry out so we can ascertain what Miss Sarah can teach us, and perhaps what we can teach her. For now, however, it is very late.'

The Retreat mistress raised her chin imperiously as she stared at Miss Sarah. 'In normal circumstances, I would require you to withhold your pleasure. Tonight I require to see how fast you can come. I wish to see you let go. And I should warn you, I am excellent at knowing a fake orgasm when I see one, so don't even think about cheating.'

For the first time since leaving Fables, Miss Sarah felt wrong-footed. Until now, although she didn't like the situation, it had been almost textbook when it came to what she had expected to happen. Letting herself go, however, was a skill she hadn't perfected in the same way as *not* letting herself go. Dr Ewen was evidently as clever as Miss Sarah thought.

Confident once again, acting as if her boss wasn't there, Lady Tia stood astride Miss Sarah's waist, her luscious bulk towering over her. 'You are obviously an intelligent woman, and I have no doubt that you are extremely good at what you do at Fables. This, however, is *not* Fables.'

Taking off one of the long silk gloves she wore, Lady Tia leant forward and, dangling the fabric down, teased it over Miss Sarah's nipples. Watching the woman's sapphire eyes closely, she worked quickly, knowing that she was being assessed as much as Miss Sarah was. If Dr Ewen wanted the other woman to come off quickly, then she would oblige; but it would be quickly with at least a modicum of style.

Conditioned for so long to hold in her reactions, Miss Sarah was quiet for a moment, her breathing steady, as the delicious wipe of the silk buffered her tips with a technique that she could only admire. It sent a rush of adrenalin to her pussy.

Crouching back on her haunches, Lady Tia fixed her eyes on the glistening mound before her, and trailed the glove from Miss Sarah's chest to between the open legs. The dominatrix smiled quietly as the pussy visibly twitched in response.

With closed eyes, Miss Sarah allowed her head to fill with images she would never normally permit. She could see Jess, her tits heavy and succulent, as she lapped at her nipples. She pictured being in the dungeon at Fables with a whip in hand, punishing row after row of hot, fit men. She saw a slave eating from her navel, and …

Sensing that Miss Sarah was simmering on the edge of climax, Lady Tia stopped moving the teasing cloth and, with expertly calculated timing, smacked a palm onto her cunt.

The shout that escaped Miss Sarah's lips was as much a shock to her as to her companions as, with an unexpected single kiss to her pussy lips, Lady Tia sent her into a body-wracking orgasm that made her lose her rock-solid concentration, and bring her own hands to her breasts to caress the nipples that, after receiving minimal attention, felt terribly neglected.

It was Lady Tia's laughter that snapped Miss Sarah out of her climactic condition. A mocking snigger that infused her with a resolve to make sure the bigger woman was left in doubt of her own skills at the earliest possible opportunity.

Blanking Lady Tia, Miss Sarah asked Dr Ewen, 'May I rise?'

'You may.' Elena said nothing of her liking for the show she'd witnessed. 'And replace your underwear, Miss Sarah. You have one more job to complete before you can have some well-earned sleep. '

Lady Tia, looking marginally smugger than Elena would have liked, opened a drawer in a nearby cupboard, and produced a yellow cloth tape measure. 'If you have quite composed yourself, Miss Sarah, we will go and see your toy.'

Chapter Six

JESS LOOKED AT her watch again. She'd been alone for an hour. Each passing minute had brought a new level of anxiety with it. Convinced that this period of solitude was planned precisely to unnerve her, it annoyed Jess that it was working so well.

Beginning to wish her unknown escort had tied her to the chair so she at least had the comfort of knowing she had no choice but to stay there, Jess tried not to think about the fact that she hadn't even attempted to open the door. If it was locked, she was a prisoner; if it wasn't, she'd be able to walk out. Jess felt she was better off in ignorance. Anyway, if she left, where would she go? Geographically, she had no idea where she was beyond that she was in Scotland in the middle of the night.

Jess was shocked at how disquieting she found this possible freedom of choice. She'd become so used to confinement. It had never occurred to her how free and in control she felt when she had neither freedom nor control.

The growing sound of boots against stone steps made Jess sit up straighter, and she found she was holding her breath as the door opened. Exhaling with relief as Miss Sarah came in, Jess was about to speak, but her words died on her lips. Miss Sarah was being followed by another woman.

Jess's eyes widened with desire-driven uncertainty at the sight of the stranger. Her dark skin glowed with health, her round, stately body was all billowing curvaceousness; tempting, yet somehow dauntingly untouchable. Instantly, she became the focus of the room.

'Miss Jess Sanders, may I introduce one of our hosts, and our temporary immediate superior, Lady Tia.' Doffing her head in deference to the other woman, Miss Sarah's gaze met Jess's for the briefest of moments. The gesture told her how important it was that she should do exactly what was asked of her, and that she should do it well, for the woman with them itched to punish someone, and that someone was very likely to be her.

'I am pleased to meet you, Miss Sanders.'

Lowering her face to the floor, she replied meekly, 'I am honoured, ma'am.'

Lady Tia reached for the bottom of her clinging dress, and pulled it over her head in one swift, coordinated move. 'I feel to some extent that I know you already.'

Doing her best not to gape at the voluptuous, basqued body that had been revealed to her, Jess remained quiet.

'As I've informed Miss Sarah, Mrs Peters was kind enough to send my employer a few recordings of your work for us to study. Your hammock experience was particularly impressive. It isn't often I come across a submissive who can think so clearly at the height of their chastisement. I commend you.'

Unsure if she should reply, Jess's eyes flicked towards Miss Sarah. A blink of her eyelids confirmed it was OK for Jess to speak. 'Thank you, my lady.'

'Now –' Lady Tia paced the circumference of the circular room '– prior to me showing you your sleeping quarters, I have been instructed to get you measured up for some party outfits.' She brandished the tape measure she held before Jess. 'Please stand, Miss Sanders.'

Approaching the curtain that hid the mirror, Lady Tia yanked it across, noting Jess's lack of reaction. 'I see that you've already explored the room. Most sensible, although

I'm not sure it was permitted. I will find out from my superior in due course.'

A cold chill tripped up Jess's spine. So, this was the Wicked Queen.

'Miss Sarah, if you could stand here.' Lady Tia kicked the rug away and pointed to a spot on the cold stone floor directly before the mirror. 'Remove your boots, and all items of clothing. Only when you are naked can we be sure to get the measurements 100 per cent accurate.'

Awarding her rival yet another point for making her stand naked on a cold floor, thus ensuring that her enforced motionlessness was as unpleasant as possible for a body that was already tired from the rigours of the day, Miss Sarah did as she was bidden.

Holding out the tape measure to Jess, Lady Tia stood to Miss Sarah's right.

Taking the proffered seamstress's tool, Jess was struck by the contrast between the dominatrices. Their flesh, alabaster next to dark, younger next to more mature, toned next to pillow soft, sent unexpected shots of lust through Jess's system as she struggled to focus on what was being asked of her.

'As you measure your companion's limbs, waist, chest, and neck, you will record the results on the pad provided. Begin.'

Unrolling the tape measure, Jess's unease grew. Where to start? She had never been into needlework, and now she came to think about it, she wasn't sure if she'd ever used a tape measure before.

'I'm waiting, Miss Sanders.'

Lady Tia wasn't actually tapping her foot, but Jess could feel impatience radiating from her. The sequin-encrusted basque that harnessed her breasts was rising and falling fast, making Jess suspect that Lady Tia was already getting off on the fact that she'd soon be punishing Jess, whether she made a mistake or not.

Deciding she'd do her best to please Miss Sarah, as pleasing Lady Tia had clearly been a lost cause before she'd even walked into the room, with a shaking hand, Jess took the pad and wrote a list of the measurements she thought would be required.

Politely asking her colleague if she could raise her right arm, Jess placed the end of the tape measure under Miss Sarah's armpit. She ran the measure along its length, and wrote down the number, before repeating the procedure on her other side.

Mumbling, 'Excuse me, ma'am,' Jess moved to Miss Sarah's waist and lifted her arms out of the way so she could circle the tape around her hips. Hoping she was measuring in the correct place, Jess recorded the resulting number quickly, before kneeling. Her proximity to her mistress's pussy, the gentle aroma of a recent climax assailing her nostrils as she placed the end of the measure against Miss Sarah's inside leg, forced Jess to concentrate harder on reading numbers, and not on how easy it would be to lap her tongue over the swollen clit. Her hands began to shake more visibly.

'And now her torso.' Every word from Lady Tia was undercut with dissatisfaction, but Jess wasn't sure if this was because she was doing a good job and therefore couldn't be told off, or if she was messing it up. 'I trust you know how to do that?'

'Forgive me, Miss Tia, but I do not.'

'*Miss* Tia?'

Jess's cheeks coloured as soon as she realised her mistake, the thunderous and yet victorious anger on the older woman's face unmistakeable.

'I'm so sorry, my lady,' Jess blustered, her hands dropping to her sides, not daring to glance at Miss Sarah's exquisite reflection in the mirror. 'Please accept my apology. It was pure habit, Lady Tia.'

'Habit is no excuse.' Lady Tia, who'd so far been

disappointed at how well Jess had undertaken the task, felt a surge of triumph swell within her. 'I think Mrs Peters has let you have it easy. I was educated in a very different way to your manageress, and it's my rules you will follow here. Not hers.'

Miss Sarah, who'd been watching events via the mirror, spoke with protracted care. 'Lady Tia, Miss Sanders is, as you will soon discover, an excellent submissive. We all know that you've been looking for an excuse to test her from the moment Dr Ewen told you of her presence under your roof. I suspect, although she is far too sensible to admit it, that, far from being an accident, Miss Sanders deliberately misnamed you so the lesson you intend to give can begin. It is very late, and for some of us, it has been an extremely long day.'

Jess wasn't sure who was the more surprised by Miss Sarah's speech, herself or Lady Tia. Never, in all the time she'd known her, even on those occasions when she suspected they'd become closer than perhaps they should, had Miss Sarah ever publicly stuck up for her.

Her fake anger stolen from her, Lady Tia found the genuine article rumble in her throat. 'How dare you talk to me like that in front of your toy?'

Jess froze. The tape measure in her fingers was suddenly slippery with perspiration.

Lady Tia attempted to stare her into submission, but Miss Sarah infuriated her further by keeping her voice at an agreeably pleasant pitch. 'I was merely suggesting that you proceed with the plan you have for Miss Sanders. I for one would appreciate seeing you in action. As Dr Ewen made clear, I have an opportunity to learn from you.'

'Remove your toy's clothes. All of them.' Lady Tia spat out each word, not willing to indicate that Miss Sarah had been correct in her assumption, however obvious it had been from the outset.

Without another sound, Miss Sarah, grateful to leave

the icy stone floor for a moment, stripped Jess with a speed born of practice.

'A ripe body.' Lady Tia nodded in approval. 'It is nice to see that not all of England has been conned into thinking a fat-free body is the most attractive.' She traced the tip of a single fingernail across Jess's abdomen, making her skin ripple with longing. 'How these young girls think they are going to hold their lover's attention with nothing more to offer than a toned stomach and pubescent tits is beyond me.'

Glad she didn't have to reply, and thinking of all the women she'd seen in the course of her work who matched that description, but were far from dull, Jess waited, a lump of apprehension forming in her throat as Lady Tia tugged the tape measure away from her limp fingers.

Watching as Lady Tia wrapped the thin fabric around her wrist, leaving approximately six inches hanging free, Jess noticed that the end of the tape was tipped with a narrow strip of steel to prevent it from fraying. She gulped; she did not want to think about what damage that strip might do in practised hands. Trying to control her breathing, Jess found her usual inner willpower was getting away from her in the face of the disgruntled dominatrix.

'Miss Sarah, you may leave.'

'Thank you, my lady, but I will stay. After all, I have no idea where I'm supposed to go. Plus, how can I learn from you if I am not here to see you at work?'

This brief, brittle battle of words bought silence for a second before Lady Tia responded, 'Very well. If you insist on remaining, Miss Sarah, then we might as well make use of you. In fact –' a sadistic gleam flashed in her eyes '– the recording of this session could become an excellent training tool for my own submissive. That is, after all, why you are supposedly here.'

'*Supposedly* here?' Miss Sarah's face remained

expressionless, but her voice was beginning to betray her as she faltered out the words.

'Did we not agree that Mr Proctor had another motive? I can't help wondering if he is in collusion with Mrs Peters to replace you. All evidence so far shows quite clearly that neither of you are as good as you think you are.'

Jess chewed the insides of her cheeks to prevent herself from protesting on Miss Sarah's behalf. She knew that she herself had a long way to go before she could be considered a worthy sub, but Miss Sarah was the best.

She didn't want to think about the possibility that Lady Tia could be right, and all this was an elaborate way of Mrs Peters getting rid of them, but Jess was unable to prevent her earlier fears racing back to the surface. That couldn't be true – could it? Mrs Peters had said quite clearly, as they'd been bundled out of the hotel, that both she and Miss Sarah would be coming back. But then, she had said a lot of things …

Miss Sarah calmly parried her opposite number. 'I am sorry we have disappointed you so far. It is early days, however. I can assure you that Mrs Peters is expecting us in Oxford, and we shall, once our work here is complete, be happy to go home to Fables. We are not here to usurp you. We have no need to do that, nor do we wish to.'

Lady Tia laid her smooth palms on Miss Sarah's shoulders and pushed her so that her bare back was pressed against the impressive mirror with a slap of skin against glass. 'You have said that before, miss. You protest too much.'

'I can't imagine you fear anything, my lady.'

It was a clever answer, and for a moment Jess felt the atmosphere thaw from ice age to merely arctic as the two dommes regarded each other. The actual air temperature, however, was dipping. The stone walls that had been cheated of their velvet curtains were sucking the remaining heat from the small, circular space. A shivering she couldn't control crept over Jess, and she wished Lady Tia would hurry up and get on with the inevitable whipping.

Still, Miss Sarah wasn't shivering. An outbreak of goosepimples across her flesh showed how good at self-control she'd become, as her back stuck to the cold glass behind her, and her naked feet coped with the chill of the flagstone floor.

Picking up the wooden desk chair, Lady Tia placed it in front of Miss Sarah, with just enough space for her to move between the chair and the mirror. Then, pointing from Jess to the chair, Lady Tia inclined her head as she saw the submissive sit as Mrs Peters had taught her. Back straight, legs wide, and butt forward so that her pussy was accessible for whatever her companion saw fit. Jess's hands lay lightly on her knees, and her eyes dipped to a place on the floor that fell just short of Miss Sarah's turquoise-painted toenails.

Unable to criticise, Lady Tia continued with her amended plan. Standing to the right of Miss Sarah, with her back to Jess, she took the end of the tape measure and began to rub it over Miss Sarah's porcelain skin.

'While your mistress was meeting my boss, Miss Sanders, I was lucky enough to discover how quickly her nipples respond to the sweep of silk. I've never seen anyone come so quickly.'

Jess frowned. She couldn't imagine Miss Sarah coming willingly in front of this woman.

'Your look of concern is touching.' Lady Tia lowered her hand a little and Jess, unable to stop herself, lifted her eyes to the mirror. A tiny cloud of concentration was clear in the reflection of Miss Sarah's blazing green eyes as the tape measure's tip was circled around the circumference of her breasts at a steady snail's pace.

Addressing Miss Sarah, but looking at Jess, Lady Tia continued, her voice as sleek as melted chocolate. 'It was of great interest to Dr Ewen and myself to learn from

David Proctor that you and your toy have formed an alliance that borders on the personal. Such lack of professionalism was unexpected. Dr Ewen in particular was surprised that Mrs Peters allowed such behaviour, although as we have learnt that she herself enjoys a permanent fraternisation with a gentleman who was previously a guest, maybe she is willing to overlook a weakness she has become prey to.'

Lowering her gaze once more, Jess felt her blood freeze in her veins. They'd told no one. They hadn't even told each other. How had Proctor found out? He must have just been fishing; digging dirt for the sake of it, while accidentally hitting on a half-truth. The submissive didn't dare tilt her eyes upwards again.

Although tell-tale spots of pink highlighted her cheeks, Miss Sarah spoke with her usual clarity as the end of the tape measure continued to zero in on her flesh. 'Mr Proctor has provided you with false information. I imagine he thinks such "knowledge" will provide you with some sort of leverage over us. As of course it would, if it were true. However, it is not. You should ask yourself, Lady Tia; why did he feel the need to give you such dud ammunition? Does he think you need to believe such lies to increase your own strength of will?'

As the level of tension, sexual and malevolent, rebounded around the turret room, Jess was reminded of two tigresses pacing it out, sizing each other up, before their fight for the territory truly began.

Her colossal chest giving the impression that it was going to burst free from its harness all on its own, Lady Tia abruptly swung around, and slapped Jess across both breasts.

The shock of the unexpected smack sent a whistled howl from Jess's lips, causing her to shuffle on her seat. She dug her fingernails into the flesh of her thighs to prevent herself from moving further.

Without stopping to admonish Jess again, Lady Tia took the cold metal end of the tape measure, and pressed it against Miss Sarah's right nipple. Jess stared in horror as, with that one simple move, Miss Sarah was reduced from controlled dominatrix to a woman panting sharply through pursed lips, having difficulty remaining static against the mirror.

White now, rather than merely pale, Miss Sarah spluttered as Lady Tia swapped sides, torturing the left nipple in the same way. Her hands, which had been hanging at her sides, now gripped the edges of the mirror's frame, her toes curled into clenched balls.

'The question is –' Lady Tia didn't release any pressure as she brought the clawed fingertips of her free hand down sharply against Jess's chest, leaving a graze which stung like a paper cut '– which of you am I going to satisfy, and which will I forbid to climax?'

Letting go of Miss Sarah's breasts, she smiled at the inflamed crimson tips. 'As I seem to have found your weak spot very quickly, I'm trying to decide if it should be Miss Sanders or you I should torture with a withheld orgasm? Although I suppose that would be unfair, really, as you've already had one climax from me tonight, whereas your toy's body couldn't be more blatantly desperate for a fuck if it tried.'

Jess had been referred to as a toy by many people and on many occasions, but there was something about the way Lady Tia said it that frightened her. After all, when toys were worn out or finished with, they got thrown away …

Unrolling the tape measure, Lady Tia hung it around her rival's neck. Taking hold of both ends, she crossed the fabric strip so it formed a yellow X between Miss Sarah's tits. Jerking the tape taut, she ordered Miss Sarah to lean forward, before tucking the free ends behind her, so it was trapped between her bare back and the mirror.

'I bet you can imagine how good this is going to feel, Miss Sanders.' Lady Tia taunted Jess as she lapped her own agile tongue around the edges of the tape cross, where the fabric touched Miss Sarah's abused and sensitive skin.

Jess could imagine all too well. Never had she felt so jealous of an object. She wanted to be wrapped around her mistress's torso, wanted it to be her tongue that attended to the burning chest, to kiss better the sore patches that were already beginning to bruise around her nipples.

Grasping her own legs harder, Jess felt the trickle of juice escaping her pussy. The woman she'd forever think of as the Wicked Queen had barely touched her, yet it was as if she was experiencing every touch to Miss Sarah's flesh upon her own.

Only when Lady Tia's mouth had journeyed over each edge of the cross did she stand back, and allow herself to wallow in the sight of Miss Sarah, who was clinging onto her composure, but only just.

The Retreat's dominatrix grinned; the breathing of the submissive behind her was even more laboured than that of her mistress, even though nothing had happened to her … yet.

With a rough tug, Lady Tia grabbed the centre of the tape measure cross, and snatched it from Miss Sarah's flesh. The burn of the fabric as it was ripped away from her back caused Miss Sarah to emit a sharp yell, and her knuckles whitened further as she held the mirror harder.

Lady Tia's eyes bored into Miss Sarah's, daring her to blink, as she rolled the tape measure into a tight coil. 'Miss Sanders, stand up. Turn around. Lean over the chair so that your butt is presented to me. Spread your legs.'

Bracing herself for the beating she'd expected from the moment she'd been bustled out of Fables, Jess knew Mrs Peters would not have been pleased with her performance so far, and she was determined to do better. She'd survived so many erotically charged spankings over the last six months she was sure that, if she kept control of herself, this was one area where she could impress the bigger woman.

It was with considerable surprise, therefore, that Jess felt Lady Tia's thick fingers swiftly come to her pussy. Spreading her labia with one hand, she stuffed the coiled measure inside Jess with the other, letting about six centimetres of its length hang from her body like a misplaced tail.

Gasping at the blissful intrusion, Jess fought to stem the climax which wanted to race through her stomach and down her throat at the same time.

Ignoring her struggle, Lady Tia barked, 'Stand up, Miss Sanders, and go to your partner.'

As Jess shuffled her feet slowly across the stone floor, Lady Tia issued another order. 'Miss Sarah, step away from the mirror and come here.'

As Miss Sarah obeyed, Lady Tia smiled at the mirror. 'What a nice smeared outline you have left.'

Jess stared at the mirror; it had indeed temporarily captured the outline of her superior.

'You can even see where your buttocks have been, and your liquid has escaped and made a mess against the glass.

'On your knees, Miss Sanders. I have no doubt you enjoy licking your mistress. Now you can, or at least, the remains of her reflection.'

The measure was beginning to feel increasingly awkward within her. The strip hanging free tickled her thighs, and sent shocks of longing to her pussy as Jess shuffled closer to the mirror. Lowering herself to her hands and knees, very conscious that the tape could fall out at any moment, Jess ran her tongue over the sweat marks left by Miss Sarah. With every creamy lick, her mistress's liquid tasting as though it had been sprinkled with dust, Jess's muscles cramped with tension as she tried to guess what Lady Tia was doing behind her back.

Jess didn't have to guess for long. Two hands came to her rump, smoothing and probing every section of her buttocks, before initiating a crescendo of slaps against her rounded arse. With her face pressed against the heated glass, Jess closed her eyes so she didn't have to witness the grotesqueness of her squashed reflection.

As the slaps she'd dreaded and longed for built in power, Jess felt a hand move with catlike speed. A strangled scream shot like a bullet from her throat, as Lady Tia yanked the tape measure from her sodden channel. The top of Jess's head was sent banging into the mirror as a climax ricocheted through every part of her, and her exhausted body flopped helplessly to the ground.

Chapter Seven

JESS WASN'T SURE how they got from the turret to the room that was to be their sleeping quarters. She felt as though they'd been walking along corridors for hours before Lady Tia had unlocked a wooden door and, without a word, shooed her unwanted guests inside.

Having been led through the castle naked, and shivering with the particular brand of cold that only comes from damp stone, Jess was too far along the road of exhaustion to care that she and Miss Sarah had been allocated only one bedroom between them.

Sitting on the edge of the king-sized bed, Jess tried to take in her surroundings, but beyond registering that the room was of a standard square shape and size, and that the walls were covered from floor to ceiling with book-filled shelves, she was too tired.

'Miss Sanders.' Miss Sarah pointed to the foot of the bed. 'That is your bed. This one belongs to me.'

Jess's brow creased in confusion. She couldn't see another bed. Dragging herself reluctantly to her feet, she shuffled to the end of the iron framed bedstead, and saw a tiny camp bed. Low to the ground, its mattress was thin, its covers insubstantial and cheap. It was so small it had been completely hidden from view by its companion furniture. With resignation, recognising that this was probably another test from the mind of Lady Tia, Jess climbed beneath the covers as Miss Sarah switched off the light.

Wishing she had some sort of nightwear, Jess wondered where her luggage was as she attempted to get comfortable on the feeble mattress. Rather than increasing her comfort, every movement she made led to the discovery of another insufficiently padded spring. Her channel still smarted from when the tape measure had been ripped from her body, and the sensation of it uncoiling as it was removed, the metal tab at its end knocking against her sensitive skin, replayed itself on continuous loop in her head. Jess found herself becoming aroused all over again as she wriggled within the confines of the slim bed.

Her muscles felt tense. Her mind refused to settle as it bounced with unanswered issues concerning The Retreat, and images of Miss Sarah's body suctioned against the Wicked Queen's mirror, and the girl in the Red Riding Hood costume who'd fucked her with a cupcake.

Longing for sleep to overtake her, she lay listening to Miss Sarah's restless movements. Surely the dominatrix couldn't be uncomfortable or cold. Jess was just considering how sore her superior's nipples must be feeling, and if she was secretly longing for Jess to kiss them better, when Miss Sarah got out of bed, switched on the light, and began to hunt around the room.

Blinking her tired eyes, Jess watched in silence as Miss Sarah climbed on a stool, naked, and stretched a hand up to the top of each bookshelf in turn. Her slender fingers tilted back one volume at a time as she searched in every nook and cranny.

After a while of observing Miss Sarah's creamy buttocks, Jess knew that if she didn't say something soon to distract herself from the desire to get up and kneel before the other woman's gorgeous body, then her mattress was going to become wet with her wasted juices as well as lumpy. 'Please, Miss Sarah, what are you hunting for? May I help?'

Twisting sharply, a finger to her lips, Miss Sarah

shushed a chastened Jess and continued her search through the next row of books.

Ten minutes later, as Jess was about to risk raising her voice again, Miss Sarah stepped lightly down from the stool. She nodded to Jess, her face satisfied, the bloom of bruises across her breasts visible as she brandished a copy of Dickens' *A Tale of Two Cities*. 'Rather fitting, don't you think, Miss Sanders?'

Without explaining what she meant, Miss Sarah retrieved a pair of stockings from her discarded travelling clothes, climbed back onto the stool, and spoke into the space where the book had been.

'Forgive me Dr Ewen, Lady Tia, Mr Proctor; I fully understand the need for cameras and recording equipment in the main rooms and corridors, but not in this one. We are allowed one place of sanctuary at Fables, and my first suggestion as an advisor to you for the improved running of The Retreat is that you grant your own staff this same courtesy. One place of privacy.'

Snapping out the tiny microphone and camera she'd found secreted there, Miss Sarah blinded and muffled them by stuffing her stockings over them, before placing the Victorian classic back over her discovery.

'Is that where we are Miss Sarah, The Retreat?'

Without answering, her hands lodged on her hips, Miss Sarah faced Jess. Kicking the stool to the side of the room, she said, 'For tonight at least, we have privacy. Tomorrow we may both pay the price. It will all depend on Dr Ewen.'

'Our temporary manager?'

'Manageress. It seems our hosts have not shared any information with you yet. I assumed the young man who escorted you into the castle would have filled you in on your location and the set-up here.'

'Not a word, Miss Sarah.'

'Are you warm, Miss Sanders?'

'No, ma'am.'

'But you are tired. As am I.' Miss Sarah regarded the former booking clerk. 'Yet I suspect that, like me, you feel it's unlikely you'll sleep. We are too keyed up by events. A dose of normality would do us good.'

A frisson of expectation filtered through Jess's veins. Forcing herself to deny the smile that wanted to hit her lips, she wasn't able to stop it reaching her eyes as she replied, 'I'm sure you're correct, ma'am.'

Picking up the top cover of her bed, Miss Sarah wrapped it around her naked shoulders, shrouding her body in quilting as she stood with her back against the nearest bookshelf. 'We have a large space here, Miss Sanders; I think we would do well to make use of it.

'For some time now I have been meaning to devise a shortened version of your exercise routine, so that we can fit it into even the most hectic of schedules. As it has been three days since you last had a structured exercise session, now seems the ideal moment to develop such a routine. As a reward for each completed movement I will, to the best of my ability, answer any questions you may have about our current location. A location that is, to answer your earlier question, known as The Retreat.'

Jess said nothing, already foreseeing erotic elation, her mind conveniently forgetting how exhausted she was.

'Get up, Miss Sanders.'

Wriggling free of her insubstantial bedding, Jess already felt warmer at the prospect of what was to come than she had been curled up in the camp bed.

'Face the bookshelves.'

Jess did as she was bidden, wondering what exercise she could possibly perform so close to the built-in unit. As she inspected the oak bookshelf at close quarters, she saw how worn it was; how time had taken its hard edges and polished them to a marbled patina. It had obviously been securely in place for hundreds of years.

Miss Sarah took her submissive's arms, stretching them

out along the shelves. Allowing herself to be positioned so her chest was angled closer to the shelving, Jess found her eyeline focusing directly on book after book of fairy tales. From the works of the Brothers Grimm to Hans Anderson, and various other interpretations in between, they were all bound in a manner which, even to Jess's untutored eye, spoke of their antique value.

As Miss Sarah's hands placed Jess's ankles closer together, she couldn't help thinking back to the turret room and its fairy tale connotations. This castle might look like something straight out of Disney, but Jess knew exactly how a few of the original fairy tales had gone. They were not stories she would tell any child without expecting nightmares to follow immediately afterwards.

Her silent counting of the number of fairy tale links she'd made since Kane had bundled her into the plane was cut short by the insistence of Miss Sarah's palm against the flat of her back. She was pushing Jess in a way that ensured her torso was tilted back a fraction, so her large, almond nipples were buffered against the edge of the wooden shelf.

'On my mark, you will bend your knees so that your breasts travel from the shelf on which they currently rest to the one beneath, and back again. Each flex will only be considered successful if your nipples touch both shelves. You may keep hold of the shelves to aid your movements. You will continue to pump your legs until I tell you to stop. As you work, Miss Sanders, you have permission to ask me four questions. Only four. What it is you wish to know the most?'

Four questions. Already picturing how enflamed her chest was about to become, and hoping Miss Sarah would kiss it better afterwards, Jess tried to marshal her thoughts. She already knew this place was called The Retreat, and she was in Scotland, that Miss Sarah's equivalent was called Lady Tia, and she'd learnt from listening to their verbal sparring match in the turret room that this place was run not just by David Proctor, but also by a woman called Dr Ewen.'

'Begin.'

Bending her knees, Jess lowered herself, so that her breasts flopped from one shelf, scraping against the books' spines below, until they hit the next row of oak. Sticking her backside out a fraction to ease the discomfort on her tits, Jess clasped the horizontal shelf supports to either side of her harder. Rising up again, knowing it wouldn't be long before her nipples felt as bruised as Miss Sarah's after her encounter with the vengeful Lady Tia, she let out a blast of shocked air. Miss Sarah's hand had smacked her butt.

'I didn't tell you to stick your arse out. I wish it to remain tucked in.'

'Sorry, ma'am.'

'Are you?' Miss Sarah spoke sharply, 'I think that you wanted me to spank you. Tell me the truth, Miss Sanders. Did you wish for me to hit your rear?'

Jess, who for once hadn't actually considered that her backside could be spanked at the same time, but knowing that Miss Sarah would never believe a denial said, 'I did, Miss Sarah, sorry, Miss Sarah.'

'Keep it in.'

'Yes, Miss Sarah.'

Jess had only completed three knee bends, but her breasts were already reaching the stage where being scraped against the wood was more of an irritation than a turn-on. Grateful the shelves were so polished with age that she didn't have to worry about splinters, Jess kept her legs moving, the muscles in her thighs tightening, her limbs beginning to shake rather faster than they normally would have done, revealing how worn out she was.

Knowing she wouldn't be allowed to stop until she'd asked her questions, Jess took a deep breath, and asked the first query that came to her lips. 'Who was the young man who took me to the tower room?'

Miss Sarah, her hand poised and ready to slap Jess's butt should it stick out further than permitted, replied quickly, 'I have no idea. No male has been mentioned to me beyond Kane and David.'

Jess felt herself slowing. Her fingers grew sticky against the shelf as her gaze repeatedly shifted from the row of fairy tales to a line of Jane Austen novels on the shelf beneath. Unsure if she was allowed to make any noise beyond her asking four queries, Jess suppressed the whimper of discomfort that built within her as her tits continued to be agitated between the two lines of wood.

'What is the submissive here like?' Jess's voice was getting more unsteady as her arms joined in the ache with her legs.

'I have yet to make her acquaintance. I know there is one, though, so if you were worrying about Proctor having been even more economical with the truth than usual, and you've been brought up here to be their sub, rather than help train the staff here, then you can let go of that fear.'

Miss Sarah indulged in a brief grin as Jess let out an audible sigh. 'Thank you, ma'am. It had occurred to me that he may have been trying to trap me.'

Closing her eyes as she kept moving, Jess could feel the tell-tale signs that her body was crossing over from the annoyance of repetitive abrasion to the point where her flesh would miss the friction provided by the wood should she be ordered to stop. Her nipples were rose red, her chest was tender, and bubbles of nervous energy danced in her veins.

Whispering through her controlled breathing, Jess asked her third question. 'I'm a little frightened. Doesn't anything scare you, ma'am?'

Normally Miss Sarah wouldn't have countenanced even hearing, let alone answering such a matter, but these were not normal circumstances, and something in her made her want to be honest with this girl. To return some of the trust Miss Sanders continually showed her. 'Of this situation, no. I am not afraid. It will be a challenge, and then it will be over. Does anything frighten me? Only one thing, Miss Sanders. Fire. I hate fire. A fact I trust you'll keep to yourself.'

'Of course, Miss Sarah.' Jess had hardly finished speaking when her knees buckled and she slouched forward. The entirety of her bust slammed against the line of fairy tale books, before tumbling off again in her haste to correct her position, as Miss Sarah's expertly aimed palm smacked against her backside.

'That's two of my answers you've responded to, and I did not give you permission to reply to me!'

'No, Miss Sarah, sorry, Miss Sarah.'

'Such slips are dangerous, Miss Sanders! How are you going to do yourself, Mrs Peters, and myself justice if you can't even complete this mini exercise set to my satisfaction?'

Sweat dotted Jess's skin as she carried on pumping her knees. Suddenly she was very aware of how late it was, and of how much had happened since she'd left her own bed in Oxford that morning. Her arms began to spasm, and as she bullied her body into keeping moving, Miss Sarah slipped a single digit between her legs.

As the finger swept over Jess's slippery clit, her body was tripped into a head-fuddling climax which tipped her against the books. Miss Sarah's voice rose over her groans of tired ecstasy. 'You have one last question.'

Panting out her words, not yet steady enough on her feet to face her mistress, Jess asked, 'How are we going to impress Lady Tia and her staff when she already hates us?'

Sighing, placing an unexpectedly light palm on Jess's right hand, Miss Sarah gently led her to the double bed, and pulled back the bedding. 'We are tired. Come and sleep. Tomorrow I intend to discover exactly what Mr David Proctor is up to.

'Despite our differences, there is one thing we all appear to agree on, whether we are from The Retreat or Fables; Proctor is not a man to be trusted.'

As she lay next to her submissive, passing a hand around Jess's shattered but peaceful body, Miss Sarah spoke her final words of the day. 'My best advice to you while you are under this roof, Miss Sanders, is to be the best submissive you can possibly be, and stay alert. Stay very alert!'

Chapter Eight

THE NOTE THAT had been slipped under their bedroom door was short and to the point.

You will report to the hallway at exactly 10 a.m. for breakfast. Miss Sanders will not wear underwear.

Jess stretched her aching limbs as she read the message and checked the time on the ornate carriage clock positioned on the nearest bookshelf. It was already 9.30. Bleary from lack of sleep, she turned to see Miss Sarah walking from the adjoining shower room.

Dabbing the last droplets of water from her naked body, her eyes fell to the piece of paper. 'You have our instructions, Miss Sanders?'

'We are expected in the entrance hall in half an hour.'

Allowing her towel to fall to the floor, Miss Sarah gestured to the door. 'I suspect our luggage is outside. Please fetch it.'

Dragging the two bags into the room, Jess watched as Miss Sarah opened her case. Her brow furrowed. 'Interesting.'

Apprehension at what the day might hold sent a rush of nervous bubbles through Jess as she saw the expression on her mistress's face. 'Miss Sarah?'

'I believe my belongings have been searched.' She began to fasten her peppermint green corset around her chest. The hint towards affection Miss Sarah had displayed the evening before had completely gone as she asked,

97

'Miss Sanders, do you remember what I told you last night?'

'I am to listen to everything, only speak when I'm spoken to, and trust no one but you.'

'Good girl.'

At exactly five to ten Alisha placed a tray of toast and coffee on a table in the centre of the hallway. Her hands shook a little, making the teacups rattle, as she thought back to the previous day.

The visiting dominatrix had intrigued her. After only a few minutes in Miss Sarah's presence, Alisha couldn't imagine anyone saying no to her without expecting serious consequences. The newcomer was a world away from the more clichéd image of a domme that Lady Tia presented, and while she was certainly respectful of Lady Tia, she was already in awe of Miss Sarah.

Placing three empty cups and saucers on the table, Alisha continued with her line of thought. She knew that although Miss Sarah fascinated her, it was the guest submissive who had captivated her the most. She'd heard that Miss Sanders was good, and David had extolled her virtues to the point at which Alisha had found herself becoming jealous of a woman she'd never met.

Alisha knew that Dr Ewen and David harboured hopes that she could be like Jess, although they hadn't said as much in so many words. She'd been told all about how Jess had been spotted when she worked as a booking clerk. David had gone on and on about how Miss Sanders' potential had been so obvious that the only one who hadn't seen it was Jess herself. Alisha wasn't like that. She wanted to be – but she wasn't.

The memory of the flight from London made Alisha's palms perspire, and she wiped them quickly over her crisp white apron. She still wasn't sure how she'd managed to keep so calm on the plane. If David hadn't been so precise with his instructions, the cook was sure she'd have lost her nerve. She almost had when, on her knees before Jess, she'd inhaled her beautiful personal aroma. But although Alisha loved to be chastised, in the face of the inscrutable Kane she hadn't dared put a foot wrong.

Since her late teens, Alisha had fantasised about being bound and pressed into submission by men and women alike. She would masturbate night after night, picturing them spanking her arse, her breasts, and her cunt, until she could take no more, and was reduced to a begging mass of climactic flesh. In reality, the problem was that even though this wish had been granted for her since Mr Proctor had swept in and taken over, Alisha couldn't quite let herself go – not properly. Consequently she rarely climaxed, despite her overwhelming desire to do so, and was left in a frustrated state of semi-satisfaction most of the time.

She could be on her knees before David, desperate for her to fuck him after being teased and tormented and slapped in an eye-wateringly delicious manner for ages, yet something inside her prevented her from orgasming. She didn't know if it was because David always made her wait so long that when she was finally given permission to come, she couldn't let herself go, or if her pride was getting in the way; or if there were other issues she just hadn't worked out yet. All Alisha knew for sure was that she wanted to obey David, and that she wished he'd hurry up and allow the training he'd promised her to begin.

As each day went by, Alisha expected David or Dr Ewen to dismiss her, or tell her they'd changed their minds, and she would only be required to work in the kitchens, as per her original job description. Each day, however, they found her a fresh task. Sometimes she was a practice target for a new whip or paddle, so that Lady Tia and Dr Ewen could see what sort of marks the tools made. Sometimes she was tied to a chair and forced to watch The

Retreat's established submissive take fuck after fuck, without even a finger being laid upon her.

Every new session added to Alisha's confusion as The Retreat staff treated her like a thing rather than a person. An item that was stuck between a submissive and a handy extra female pair of hands, tits, arse, and a constantly slippery pussy for the amusement of each other as they prepared for the new "superior class" of guests David promised would be flooding through the castle doors very soon.

When Alisha had been informed the Fables team were coming to help complete staff training prior to The Retreat's reopening, she'd assumed they were coming to help train her. The experience on the jet, however, where following David's instructions had led to her being more dominatrix's accomplice than submissive, had only served to confuse her further.

With the Fairtasia delegation party in only two weeks' time – a gathering that Alisha assumed would be of a bacchanal style – she still didn't understand what her role in the proceedings was going to be. Although, knowing David's obsession at the moment, she thought, it'll probably be more Grimm fairy tale than Greek orgy, although God knows why he likes those twisted stories so much.

The sound of approaching footsteps made Alisha turn her head, and glance through her fringe towards the doorway. Air caught in her throat as she took in Miss Sarah's tastefully sequined pale green corset, suspenders, knickers, and bottle green velvet boots. Again, within the safe confines of her head, the comparison to Lady Tia was instant and impossible to ignore. The woman from Fables screamed style. Lady Tia simply screamed orders.

If Miss Sarah was surprised to see the pseudo-stewardess before her, with her curly blonde hair free from the black wig and her emerald eyes devoid of the blue contact lenses that Proctor had insisted she wear on the flight, then she hid it well.

Alisha bowed a fraction as she greeted the guests, 'Miss Sarah, Miss Sanders, I hope you slept well.'

'Thank you.' Miss Sarah neither confirmed nor denied their lack of adequate rest, but stood beside the profusion of predictably tartan armchairs and sofas with a collected ease that Alisha knew she could fake, but was sure she could never actually feel.

'If you'd like to make yourselves comfortable and take breakfast, Dr Ewen will be along presently.' Alisha curtseyed and left, wishing she could stay and observe what would happen next.

Pouring herself and Jess a cup of strong coffee, Miss Sarah spoke without looking up. 'I can hear the question marks crashing around in your head from here.'

'Sorry, Miss Sarah.' Jess wasn't quite sure why she was apologising, but thought it was the safest option.

'You are wondering if the girl who has greeted us with breakfast was the one who fucked you with a cupcake yesterday. Consequently, although you've only been awake for a short time, the thought has already got you moist. In other words, Miss Sanders, you are the pliant slut Mrs Peters has conditioned you to be.'

Unsure if this was a compliment or a complaint, Jess's face coloured a violent pink as the swelling of her bra-free chest beneath her white shirt blatantly confirmed what Miss Sarah had said to be the truth.

'Yes. It was her.'

'May I ask a question, ma'am?'

'If you must.' The dominatrix motioned towards the toast. 'You should eat. I suspect you'll need a lot of energy today.'

'What is she? I don't see Alisha – if that really is her name – as a dominatrix; but she doesn't feel like a submissive either.' Jess hesitated before, sensible of her place, adding, 'Of course, I could be wrong.'

Smearing a spread of marmalade on top of her toasted bread, safe in the knowledge that the conserve wouldn't dare fall off and stain her clothing, Miss Sarah aimed a half smile towards her submissive. 'Your perception never ceases to impress me, Miss Sanders. The blonde hair and green eyes suits her. The jet black-haired, blue-eyed doll thing made her look a little too "reality TV", don't you think?'

Opening her mouth to confess she hadn't noticed it was a wig at the time, Jess found herself abruptly shushed. Someone else was coming.

Jess automatically stood as Miss Sarah rose to her feet, inclining her head in recognition of the woman striding confidently nearer on silent, gliding feet.

'Miss Sanders, I presume?'

'Yes, madam,' Jess murmured, refraining from any additional comment as she saw Dr Ewen for the first time.

Miss Sarah pointed to the third cup on the table. 'Good morning, doctor. May I pour you a drink?'

'You may, thank you, Miss Sarah.'

Jess didn't know where she was supposed to look, if she should remain standing, or sit back down. On the brink of uncertainty, she felt on edge, and paradoxically very turned on. Whatever was going to happen to her next was in the command of the thin, imposing woman whose stare lasered through her minimal clothing like some sort of sonic ray.

The Retreat manageress quickly brought Jess's moment of doubt to an end. 'Miss Sanders, go to the boathouse by the loch. You may eat your toast on the way. Our resident submissive is expecting to meet you there. You'll find it by walking out of the front door, and heading left. Walk along the walls of the castle for about 200 yards, until you see the water. Then follow the thin gravel path. The boathouse is another 100 yards from there. You can't miss it.'

As the main door to the castle shut behind Jess, Dr Ewen turned a flint gaze, not unlike that of Mrs Peters, toward Miss Sarah. There was a suggestion of unspoken amusement and respect evident in her tone as she sat, her teacup held in the poise of a typical English lady of the manor. 'I can see that reports of your decisive actions and cool common sense were not exaggerated.'

'Thank you, doctor.' Miss Sarah put her own cup into its saucer without so much as a chink, and angled her chin upwards a fraction while she waited for her companion to elaborate.

'After some consideration, and a discussion with David Proctor, I've decided to adhere to your request and not replace the microphone you broke.'

'I am grateful. I am sure you understand that in order to give you our best work we need a little time off duty.'

'However –' Elena stood, acting as if the domme hadn't spoken '– if you or Miss Sanders prove to be rather less than we've hoped for, then it will be put back without your knowledge.'

Getting to her feet as well, Miss Sarah allowed her eyes to roam around the hall, taking in the three doors and the two corridors that ran off it.

'David tells me that Laura Peters is still able to give the impression she can read minds. I trust you realise, Miss Sarah, that this isn't the case, and that she is just extremely good at reading people.'

Instead of answering, Miss Sarah said, 'I hadn't realised that you knew Mrs Peters.'

'The fact I'm stating, Miss Sarah, is that her ability to second-guess people is a skill Mrs Peters was taught, and she learnt it from the same person I did. I suppose I'm telling you this so you understand that, like your manageress, I am no soft touch. Consider this a warning.'

'Point taken, doctor.'

'I understand there are five specifically designed rooms for the guests to use at Fables. Here we have a different set-up.' Elena gestured to the first closed door to their right-hand side. 'The Retreat used to offer breaks for two or three guests at a time. We'd provide an advanced form of adult entertainment, as you yourselves do at Fables. Now Proctor has taken us over – with my agreement, I should add – The Retreat has two primary functions. That is to say, once it reopens it will have a practical application outside of sexual entertainment.

'The second part of our service will be to act as a seasonal conference and meeting centre. That is already largely set up and will start running during the autumn and winter months. So, this is the lay of the land.' Elena pointed ahead. 'That room leads to my office, the next to the conference hall.' She swung her arm to the left. 'That door is the entrance to a lounge for any guests who wish to opt out of our offered activities for a while.'

'Such a space is a good idea, Dr Ewen.'

Taking a step towards the corridor immediately in front of her, Elena carried on her monologue. 'This way leads to the stairs for the main suite of seven bedrooms, five for guests, one for myself, and one for David when he is in residence. The other corridor is much longer, and winds around the rest of the castle; it has doors leading off to the dining room, kitchen, and storage rooms, and at the very end sits the steep staircase to the turret room Lady Tia showed you last night. If you wish to go outside to the boathouse and loch, then you can leave via the front door, or through the kitchen.'

Miss Sarah nodded in approval. 'I can see that this is a perfect location, and that much of your equipment is pretty much built in, with the stone pillars holding up the ceilings so perfect for bondage and submission sessions. Not to mention that this is a stunning location for those visiting

Scotland for the first time, but where in Scotland are we?'

Walking down the corridor that led to the kitchen, Dr Ewen beckoned for Miss Sarah to follow her. 'The layout is indeed excellent for our requirements. I am not, however, at liberty to share our exact location with you. If you'd follow me, I will finish measuring you for your party clothing. Miss Sanders was unable to complete the job properly last night. I will also require you to give me Miss Sanders' measurements. I suspect you know them by heart.'

The freshness of the morning breeze felt like balm against Jess's skin, tickling her commando pussy with a pleasantly tender caress. It had been a long time since Jess had been exposed to real fresh air, and it went some way to calming her anxiety as her feet crunched over the gravel path at the side of the castle in the direction Dr Ewen had indicated.

Appreciating the blueness of the sky, and how it framed the purple mountains behind, Jess saw how the pine forest they'd driven through the night before gave way to a rough hinterland of heather and erratic boulders as the earth flattened toward the loch, before roughening up again on its opposite side.

The loch water, stirring gently in the spring breeze, gave the impression that it was holding its breath; as if it was waiting for something to happen. Given the storytelling aura this place seemed to radiate, Jess half expected the Lady of the Lake's arm to break forth from the centre of the water and hold Excalibur aloft.

Knowing she was letting her mind wander to put off thinking about what might happen in the boathouse, Jess experienced a resurgence of the trickle of dread-lined arousal that had tingled at her crotch in the hallway.

Almost on the edge of the loch itself, the log-built boathouse was much larger than she'd expected. Enclosed on three sides, but open at the front, it had been designed to provide easy access for the collection of boats stored within.

A couple of metres from the building, Jess halted. Gathering herself, she remembered Mrs Peters' final words, repeating them like a mantra in her head. *Do Fables and yourself proud. Do Fables and yourself proud* ... She wiped her sticky palms on the back of her short denim skirt, and crept with small, hesitant steps into the boathouse.

Exactly in the centre of the open-sided log cabin, backed by tiers of rowing boats and skiffs and lying on an old upturned wooden fishing boat, was a young man.

A thick width of black leather tethered him in place. Face up, his hands were stretched up over his head, and his erection, which must have received recent attention to be in such a state, stuck up like a mast.

Jess was stunned. She had been sure The Retreat's submissive was Alisha. It had never occurred to her that it might be a man.

Despite her instant desire to take his flagpole shaft in her lips, Jess kept her mouth shut. She understood that she was being tested as much as he was. Probably more so.

Unable to drag her attention away from all six foot of his nakedness, Jess examined every inch of him; his closely cropped sandy hair, his lust-glazed, pleading blue eyes, and his work-honed musculature, which suggested that he was used to manual labour. From the tan on his face, neck, arms, and lower legs, Jess guessed that this work was outdoors. She was also sure this was the man who'd escorted her so anonymously from the limousine to the turret only the day before.

Convinced that she was not allowed to talk to this man, as her instructions had only been to come here and find him, Jess decided to take the safer option of doing nothing. Unfolding a chair from a stack by the wall, she sat next to him, trying to decide how old he was. Late 20s, she suspected.

Jess had been in the presence of many men and women who'd come to Fables to experience what life was like at the wrong end of a whip, and the air of excited expectation combined with erotic fear from these newcomers was distinct. This man, although clearly apprehensive about what was to come, had evidently accepted his position. There was no vibe of personal confusion wafting from his bound body. This submissive was not in need of either her or Miss Sarah's instruction.

As Jess sat staring at him, her thoughts as to why she was there at all were dislodged by the mounting need to sit astride the cock. She was sure it was pointing at her – taunting her with its quiet necessity to screw her. Determination to show whoever was watching them – and she was sure someone would be – that her self-discipline was a lot stronger than they'd bargained for stopped her doing just that.

As she continued to examine the handsome specimen before her, Jess sat with her hands under her thighs to stop herself from being tempted to reach over and trace the contours of his physique.

Minutes passed, and the space between the two submissives became tangible, until, finally, the fair-haired man broke the tension and twisted his head towards Jess. His lips parted as if to plead for her touch, but she gave an urgent shake of her head, and he returned to his position, staring up at the roof of the shed without saying whatever he'd intended to.

'Very good, Miss Sanders.' David's appearance at the entrance to the boat shed made Jess jump. He was waving a smartphone in his hand, which he'd clearly been using as a webcam to view her arrival. 'Master Richards, you could learn a lot from this young lady.'

Immediately on her guard, always uneasy if David paid her a compliment, Jess waited with bated breath. Whatever

Proctor had planned was about to begin.

'Miss Jess Sanders, may I introduce you to Master Jason Richards? I would like you to undo his waist restraint and assist him to his feet. You will not touch any more of him than you have to.'

Taking care to avoid all contact with his skin, Jess worked the leather strap undone, and eased Jason upwards, so that he sat with his legs spread astride the upturned vessel.

'Excellent.' David repositioned Jess's chair so that it was at a right angle to Jason. 'Sit down again, Miss Sanders, and observe. At no point are you to look away.'

'Yes, Mr Proctor.'

'I told you when we were at Fables to call me David.'

'Sorry, David. Thank you.'

Jason, his eyes blurred with the need to spurt his load, looked incredibly uncomfortable with his shaft stuck bolt upright against his stomach.

'Master Richards is relatively new to this life, Miss Sanders. He is usually to be found maintaining the estate's woodland, but I suspected he had an aptitude for this life from my first visit some months ago, and although he has a lot to learn, I have high hopes for the honing of his ability.' As he spoke, David undid the zip fly of his suit trousers, and sprang his erect dick from his boxers.

Wondering if her instincts had been wrong, and maybe Jason was a newcomer to this life after all, but just a fast learner, Jess said nothing as she heard the unmistakable sound of David's hand fisting his own cock. Refraining from giving into temptation and looking at Proctor, she maintained eye contact with Jason, willing him to do well for both their sakes.

'Master Richards, now it is your chance to watch. Your hands will remain tied in your lap, but at no point will they touch your erection. Miss Sanders, stand, turn, and touch your toes. I know that will not represent a problem for you after all the exercise sessions Miss Sarah has put you through.'

Embarrassingly aware that no lubrication of any sort would be required in addition to her flowing juices should Mr Proctor wish to thrust straight into her, Jess bent double in front of him, her skirt riding up over her bare butt, her hands around her booted ankles.

'Master Richards, you will notice I have no need to finger this girl up, for as every good submissive knows, you should always be ready to receive your master or mistress. In your case this will mean an ability to harden up at will.'

Jess was considering how the hell any bloke could do that if faced with something that turned him off and not on, when the tear of a condom packet opening brought her back to more immediate concerns.

The possessive hold of David's hands on her hips sent her mind reeling. This was so out of character. She hadn't been tied, spanked, or criticised. What was he up to?

'Jason, you will not move, or speak, or come.'

Jess didn't have to see Jason's face to know that it would be a study in frustrated concentration. And if he really was as fresh to this life as David maintained, then she was fairly sure she knew what Jason would be thinking as well. He'd be wondering why he didn't tell Proctor to piss off, why he didn't stand up and walk away ... and on top of those thoughts, drowning out all common sense, he'd be experiencing the ache in his groin, the craving at the very pit of his belly, the overwhelming curiosity to see how far he could go before he'd taken as much as he could take.

Yet it didn't feel like Jason was new to this. Miss Sarah's advice rang out in the back of Jess's head. *Trust no one but me.*

'I know exactly how badly you'd like to impale this young woman, Master Richards,' David happily chattered to the hapless spectator, 'but I suspect if that option was permanently withheld then you'd settle for a suck of my dick, or perhaps you would rather it was me who was bent over, so you could shunt my arse?'

The sound of Jason gulping filled the space, which was quiet but for the distant ripple of the breeze across the surface of the loch. Even though David's words were aimed at the pupil, they were having an additional effect on Jess's state of arousal, and her braless tits, squashed against her own legs, were agitating for the caress of a hand or mouth.

As the teasing tip of David's penis journeyed over and around the entrance to Jess's channel, neither entering nor touching her clit, she felt the blood that had rushed to her head make her dizzy, and she was very grateful that he was holding her hips so firmly.

'You see, Jess, Jason hasn't completely accepted his position. I know you went through similar feelings in your early days. He is also reluctant to admit that the idea of piercing my butt is as appealing to him as fucking you.'

The more David spoke about Jason's submissive shortcomings, the more Jess felt he was protesting too much.

'You should see his dick, Miss Sanders. It is so wired I could count every vein.'

Jess was almost relieved David had said that. Giving her information designed to goad her as much as Jason was far more in character for the man, whose cock was now buffering against her butt.

'And Master Richards –' Proctor was gloating now '– Miss Sanders here is positively fluid.' He let go of one of her hips and scooped up her pussy cream with his finger. 'Here you go.' David stuck the finger out to the semi-tethered young man. 'Taste her.'

Although all Jess could actually see were her legs, and those of Proctor behind her, his designer trousers bunched around his ankles, in her head she could clearly picture Jason's lips parting keenly.

She knew how she tasted. She'd lapped up her own juices from a variety of dicks, tits, mouths, and pussies enough times to know that her flavour erred towards a mixed fruit cocktail with a hint of honey. The thought of this stranger gobbling her juice before he'd so much as touched her, when she knew he badly wanted to, made Jess proud of him. She hoped Master Richards was as determined not to fail. Jess was certain that if he did, it would be her fault.

'I see you enjoyed that snack, Master Richards.' David eased his hands down Jess's thighs, and a whistle of loss escaped from her clamped teeth as his dick moved away from her opening.

From her bent-over position Jess could see David's cock as he bent his knees. His shaft was thicker than she remembered. Its tip shone, illustrating how much his own stamina was being tested alongside that of his employees.

Jess closed her eyes; she had to forget Jason now. Forget that he was naked and hot and desperate to get inside her. Every ounce of her focus was required to make sure that the male breath she could feel against her pussy didn't trigger her orgasm.

David's face was so close to her core, it felt as though he was puffing hot butter over her. Each word he uttered increased the flow of pre-climax that was wafting through her frame. 'I think it only fair that I should remind myself of Miss Sanders' taste as well. I would like you to observe Jason. See how statute-like Miss Sanders can remain, even while I'm licking out her insides.'

Clever bastard. Now Jess really couldn't move, for she had no doubt the punishment for contradicting, and therefore humiliating, David would be even more severe than if she slipped up and accidentally came without permission.

The tongue action lacked any real skill, and Jess felt she'd be tipped onto the ground as its relentless poking pushed into and around her channel. The muscle occasionally glided over her nub, creating a rainbow of coloured dots that dazzled her eyes beneath her closed lids, but Jess had no idea if that was deliberate cruelty, or accidental.

Jess could hear faint whimpers coming from her right, and suddenly, rather than willing Jason to succeed, she was willing him to fail – fail before she did.

As David ate from Jess, he unexpectedly smacked his palm flat against her butt. The gasp of shock that shot from her made her flush with shame. She should have been prepared for the slap, but her thoughts had been elsewhere.

On the second spank, however, her reaction was composed, and the tension she'd felt bristle in David eased off. 'I'm sure you can imagine how pert Miss Sanders' nipples are right now, Jason. And do you see how pleasing her arse looks now it has been slapped? I would like you to pay particular attention, and observe this next move without blinking.'

Jess was repositioned with speed. Her head spun as she was pressed onto her hands and knees. Her shirt buttons were ripped at, rather than undone, so Jess's tits hung down while David thrust into her like a dog taking his on-heat bitch.

The pitch of his voice as David moved within her told Jess how florid his face would be. She'd seen him on the point of coming often enough to know exactly how much he would resemble a bright red balloon. 'She is so good and tight, Master Richards. Can you see how her breasts hang just below the flap of her open shirt? I wonder how badly you want to crawl beneath her and tongue them.'

His hands dug into Jess's waist as he continued to manoeuvre back and forth, riding her like a rocking horse, her tits kissing the air, her bobbed hair flopping over her face. A voice in the back of Jess's head began repeating her new mantra. *Do Fables and yourself proud. Do Fables and yourself proud ....*

'Shall we ask Jess, Master Richards? Shall we see if she would like your teeth on her chest?'

As he opened his mouth, unsure if Proctor's query was rhetorical, or if he should answer, Jess realised that, for Jason, words were not the issue. An animal-like growl came out of his throat before any syllables had the chance to form, and she was conscious of a spatter of come spotting her backside, and smearing against the wooden floor next to her. Not a finger had been placed on him, and yet Jason had come.

David's voice rang out like thunder as his own pumping stopped its regulated pace and his balls banged hard against Jess's backside. Taking out his annoyance at Jason's disobedience on her body, he pummelled Jess as if she was little more than a sturdy blow-up doll.

As his own climax came, David reached beneath Jess with both hands, and sharply tugged at each nipple, making her yelp with welcome pain as her own orgasm shuddered through her, making her arms quake at the elbows.

'Stand up, Miss Sanders,' David cracked out his words, the friendly charade forgotten. 'I didn't give you permission to come either.' He shook his head theatrically. 'This is most disappointing.'

Pulling up his trousers, David brushed at his suit, removing some rogue flecks of dust. Undoing the strap that bound Jason's hands, he barked, 'Dress.'

Tilting his head toward Jess, David ordered, 'Go to your room, Miss Sanders, replace your blouse, and then report to the kitchen. You will help prepare lunch.' Then he strode from the boathouse, in the opposite direction to The Retreat.

Watching Proctor disappear, Jess wondered what the

hell Miss Sarah would make of her morning report. The last half-hour had all the hallmarks of a regular guest entertainment session, not a training exercise for a new submissive. Despite the fact that Jason had come, his stamina had still been incredible. He can't be the one we've been brought here to teach, she thought. It has to be Alisha. Doesn't it?

Chapter Nine

'LAURA HAS IMPECCABLE taste.' Dr Ewen looked Miss Sarah up and down. 'And David was quite correct, you do look stunning in that outfit. Thank you for remembering to wear it today.'

'I am flattered you like it.' Her basque no longer properly in place, but pulled down so that her pearly breasts sat above its boned top, Miss Sarah sat as instructed on the edge of a large, scrubbed wood table and looked around the huge kitchen.

'Lady Tia will like it too, I am sure.' The Retreat mistress picked a metal ladle from a nearby utensil pot and caressed the back of its bowl over each of Miss Sarah's nipples in turn, watching her reactions like a hawk.

'Thank you, doctor.' Miss Sarah held her posture as together as possible despite the darts of desire that travelled with lazy stealth through her punished breasts. She found her mind wandering more than she'd normally permit it to. She wished to ask why they'd been brought up to The Retreat to train a dominatrix who plainly required no training, and just who the submissive that Jess had been sent to see was. She held her tongue, however, wise enough not to underestimate the woman before her. Politeness did not mean the doctor wouldn't spare the rod if she deemed it necessary.

'Am I correct in assuming that you are rarely on the receiving end of attention such as this?' Elena kept up the light, circular movements, noting with interest the bruises on each tit that were too new to have come from anyone other than Lady Tia.'

'You are, doctor.'

'Does Mrs Peters never test you? Make sure you remain sharp for your guests?'

'She does. We're all tested at least once a month – without warning.'

'I'm very pleased to hear it.' Elena exchanged her methodical rotation of the kitchen utensil for a light tapping of the ladle's bowl against each nipple in alternating actions. There was no doubt it hurt, but if Dr Ewen hadn't been watching for the microsecond's flash of hurt that had betrayed Miss Sarah, she'd have missed it.

After a few minutes Dr Ewen clattered the ladle onto the table, walked to the nearest drawer, and took out some dessert spoons. Then she lined the new cutlery in a regimented row next to the ladle.

Miss Sarah mentally recoiled, and she had to force herself not to jump to conclusions. She knew she was supposed to be worried by what she saw. It was a classic technique she had used on clients a hundred times before. It did not mean the spoons would be used for anything other than making her insides churn with an apprehension it was more important than ever that she kept to herself.

'Please don't concern yourself with the silverware, Miss Sarah. It is there for Alisha to use in a cookery project.' Elena flicked her eyes to her wristwatch. 'Lady Tia will be here in three minutes' time.'

Not giving her temporary boss the pleasure of seeing the unease stirring inside, Miss Sarah regarded the woman before her, holding her unblinking stare with her own.

Picking the ladle back up, Elena continued to her polish her companion's tips. 'Might as well have some fun while we wait.'

Miss Sarah didn't reply, the muscles in her neck

invisibly tensing. She was silently counting off every second of the time until Lady Tia was due to sweep into the room.

'I suppose you could call this session a punishment for your actions last night, although as I said in the hall, your audacity did impress me. Or you could think of this as a further demonstration of your talents. Or, perhaps, you could be about to do what you were brought here for, and teach Lady Tia how to refine her not inconsiderable skills.'

Filing away the fact that Dr Ewen believed her dominatrix needed some lessons to be contemplated at a more appropriate time, Miss Sarah was relieved to hear the sound of the oak door to the kitchen swinging open.

'Ah, Lady Tia, prompt as always.' Dr Ewen nodded at her assistant with outward satisfaction, but suddenly her temporary employer's expression didn't ring true to Miss Sarah. In fact, less and less of the place rang true, but she couldn't figure out why. Knowing she needed to think through her disquiet in peace later, she kept her body perfectly still and bent her neck so she could see Lady Tia.

The dominatrix was also corseted, but in a silver material that was so shiny even the face of a vampire couldn't have escaped its reflection. Her shoes, high-heeled and strappy, were decorated with little squares of mirror, and the effect against her chocolate skin was stunning. Unlike Miss Sarah, she wasn't wearing any knickers, and the round of her ample rump had sparkles of light from her corset dancing across it.

Unlike on their first meeting, Miss Sarah could now admire the curve of Lady Tia's neck, as her hair was piled upon the top of her head in a puffball of a bun. Huge chandelier earrings hung at each side of her head. The entire impression was that Cinderella had gone to the ball without remembering to put on her dress. Jess was right; this place had warped fairy tale written all over it ....

'I confess, Miss Sarah, I've acted a little unfairly, for I

117

have already informed Lady Tia what you will both face this morning, but I suspect you would have guessed as much anyway. I suspect you are used to Mrs Peters changing the rules as she goes along.'

Miss Sarah lifted the corners of her mouth into a convincing smile. 'I would expect no less. Lady Tia is, after all, your second in command.'

'I knew you would understand.' The shrewd slate eyes moved over the seated dominatrix for a split second. 'Lady Tia, if you would care to sit next to Miss Sarah, my assistant for this session will be here any moment, and then we can begin. We need to be out of the way before Alisha arrives to start preparing lunch.'

The sharp, questioning twist of Lady Tia's head toward her boss told Miss Sarah that although she knew what was to come, her rival dominatrix hadn't known as much as she'd thought she had. Miss Sarah's estimation of Dr Ewen grew further.

The door opened again, and Kane came in. A flash of emotion, possibly annoyance, possibly something far more complicated crossed Lady Tia's face. As tall as Lady Tia, physically Kane was every bit her equal, and for a moment Miss Sarah wondered if perhaps they had once been partners. She returned all her attention to Dr Ewen, who spoke again.

'Good morning, Kane, thank you for joining us. If you could prepare things as arranged?'

Pausing long enough to take a good look at Miss Sarah's exposed breasts, Kane began to layer thick towels across the top of the huge, free-standing range in the middle of the room.

Miss Sarah's heart rate doubled at the sight. They knew! How? There was only one thing that she was truly afraid of, and that was fire, and unless she was becoming paranoid, the heat in the kitchen was largely emanating from the range Kane was dressing. Miss Sanders was the only one she'd ever told of her fear, and there was no way she'd have betrayed her.

Their bedroom must have had more than one bug hidden it. Miss Sarah's feet felt as if they'd become glued to the floor while her brain addressed her limited options. If she ran away she'd have not only lost face here, but with Mrs Peters as well; but if she stayed …

She felt sick and angry, the way a submissive was supposed to feel, not a dominatrix. Fixing her thoughts on how she'd explain her failure to Laura if she fled, Miss Sarah forced herself to observe Lady Tia. If she was frightened of the heat, then she wasn't showing it.

Working either side of the pipe chimney that rose proud at the back centre of the cooker, Kane continued to pad up the thick, fluffy towels. Then he tested the top of each pile with the palm of his hands as if to make sure some, but not too much, heat was radiating through the fabric. A thumbs up towards Dr Ewen, and the smartly suited man placed two low wooden stools next to the back of the range, one either side of the chimney. Dr Ewen smiled at him like a malevolent nightmare.

'This will be a competition and an illustration of your skill. I think you'd agree that in order to be the best dominatrix you can possibly be you need to understand how to take it as well as how to dish it out. Your own body has to be as aware as that of your subjects of how we react under different pressures, environments, and levels of pain and pleasure.'

Returning to the pot from which she had retrieved the silver ladle, Dr Ewen took two long-handled wooden spoons. 'A little predictable, perhaps, but sometimes it's nice to have a change from whips and paddles, don't you think?'

Neither woman replied as Dr Ewen passed Kane one of the spoons. 'So, as Lady Tia knows, the object of this exercise is to see which of you can stand the most blows to

119

your behind without moving, pleading for us to stop, or climaxing. A simple enough task – too simple, in fact. So I have decided to apply an incentive ... something that will make you want to get this over with as quickly as possible, just as much as you want to be the one who lasts the longest. An interesting juxtaposition I think you'll find.'

Pointing to the range, Dr Ewen put out a hand to Miss Sarah, who took it and climbed down from the table, while Kane led Lady Tia to the range.

'Miss Sarah, remove your knickers, please, then I wish you both to stand upon the stools and lie across the towels; they will protect you from the possibility of burning on the range's top. Your backsides should be at the very back of the range, so that your pussies are free from its edge. Chests should be pressed against the top of the towels. Arms and heads will hang over the front of the cooker.

'The range is currently on at a low heat and, as you can see, the towels hang right over its front, so your face, hair, and arms will be protected.'

As she obeyed, Miss Sarah regretted that she hadn't put her hair up, for it hung like a curtain over her face, obscuring her inverted view of the room. Warmth oozed into her, but it was a pleasant heat, and despite Miss Sarah's phobia associated with the fact there was a fire in the metal box beneath her, she had to acknowledge that it was no worse than being strapped into the medieval-style rack in the dungeon back at Fables.

Kane walked around the range, making sure the women were safe, before pulling away the stools to leave their feet dangling in mid-air. This meant that all their weight was now on their chests, a fact which instantly gave Lady Tia an advantage, as her top half was much heavier than her companion's.

The polishing of the back of a wooden spoon head on her backside told Miss Sarah that the action was about to start. The gathering of breath she'd intended to be silent as she mentally prepared for a beating came out with a ragged and uncharacteristic groan she hadn't intended to vocalise.

Busying her spoon in circles around Lady Tia's backside, Dr Ewen said, 'I should tell you, Miss Sarah, that before he took up his current employment, Kane was a fireman. He is therefore able to ensure that this scenario is safe. I would not do this if he was not here.'

Not sure if this news reassured her or not, Miss Sarah didn't have time to ask what exactly Kane's new employment was, for he was running the tip of the spoon handle up and down the crack of her buttocks. With her arms dangling, she wasn't sure how to hold them so they didn't accidentally get burnt on the lower part of the range, which the towel didn't quite reach. Glancing through her curtain of hair, she looked towards Lady Tia. The bigger woman had clasped her hands together, and lifted them to rest on the back of her neck. Wondering if Lady Tia had been in this position before, Miss Sarah copied the gesture, making sure she swept as much of her hair as she could out of her eyes at the same time.

'Ready, Kane?'

There was no reply from the Scotsman, but Elena continued to talk, making Miss Sarah assume that he'd agreed. 'Lady Tia, you are well aware of how many hits you have to take before I'll be even remotely impressed. Miss Sarah, your task is to show me how many you can take. Of course, as a matter of personal honour, I've no doubt that you will wish to endure more than your companion.'

The prickling heat beneath Miss Sarah was forcing her to centre her mind as Kane continued to trail the handle along her butt crack. She had already assumed that a spanking was imminent, and wished they'd just get on with it.

'Knowing that you are experts in your field, and in the interests of not being here all day, I have set a time limit, which I have chosen not to share with you. On the count of three we will proceed.' Miss Sarah heard Kane step closer. 'One, two –' the spoon was raised from her arse '– three.'

Smack! The first hit connected with the centre of Miss Sarah's right arse cheek, sending a bloom of heat through her skin that was rivalled by the slowly increasing warmth against her flattened boobs.

Slap! The second stroke met her symmetrically on the opposite cheek, and by the time the burly Kane had tenderised her flesh nine times, the boned top of her corset was digging up and into the underside of her breasts. As Miss Sarah gasped through each swipe of wood, she tried not to think about the advantage Lady Tia had in being allowed to keep her tits covered by her basque. Not only would her corset not be cutting into her, but it would also be affording the other woman an extra layer of protection between her body and the heat beneath.

Kane swung his spoon with a fervour that sent ripples of stinging fire shooting from Miss Sarah's abused backside, into her crotch, and up through her swollen tits.

It must be my imagination, she thought. The range can't be getting hotter. As Miss Sarah began to feel she was in a heat sandwich, Kane started to treat each of her butt cheeks as if it was a clock face upon which he was striking off the hours.

Sweat gathered at the back of Miss Sarah's neck and across her chest, sticking her basque to her flesh. There was no doubt; the range was getting hotter.

Don't panic, she told herself. They want you to panic. Don't. Miss Sarah couldn't stop herself from wriggling her chest back. The movement eased the intensity of the temperature from the towel bedding a little, but had the effect of sticking out her butt more, so that Kane's enthusiastic arm had an even easier target area than before. She'd lost count of how many strikes had transformed her peach backside into the crimson mass she knew it would be. Even winning the challenge didn't matter. All she wanted was to get off the range as quickly as she possibly could.

They knew. They must have overheard her telling Miss Sanders. Miss Sarah cursed her carelessness for a second time. There must have been two receivers hidden in her bedroom; how else would they know to tailor this challenge so she'd have to face her only major nightmare?

The room, which until now had resounded only to the thwack of each hit of wood against flesh, filled with the echo of Dr Ewen's discontent. 'Miss Sarah. You moved. Don't think I missed that little infraction. Lady Tia has not flexed so much as a finger, and although you have easily coped with 25 hits each, that puts her ahead. As punishment, Kane will increase the heat.'

It took every scrap of her discipline not to cry out and jump down as the sound of the flames below being fanned with an influx of air filled her ears. The towels were no longer simply hot, but had taken on the sticky heat of a sauna. Only self-respect kept Miss Sarah where she was.

The continuing spanks to her arse felt like nothing now. Numbness had taken over, and her nerves only tingled with lust, not pain, as, in a contradiction of sensations, Miss Sarah's frightened body desperately wanted the spoon to move, to twist and curve, and land with all the precision its wielder could yield onto her oily clit.

'Thirty-five apiece!' Elena shouted the result so loud that her words rebounded off the granite walls. 'Sixty seconds to go. Lady Tia is ahead.'

Even as the mistress spoke, the back of the spoon landed upon the opening of Lady Tia's anus, and the low-pitched squeal that fell from her lips to the floor could not have been called reasonable noise.

'I spoke too soon. The situation is now equal – and we are at 40 hits.'

Feeling as if she was being slammed against the wall of

a blast furnace, thinking that surely their protagonist's arms must be getting tired, and that Dr Ewen was a lot stronger than she looked, Miss Sarah gritted her teeth. Her palms were clammy; her brain catapulted between visions of getting third-degree burns, and her body blissfully climaxing against an oven in a scream of terrified delight.

The air was heavy with the aroma of sex, sweat, and scorched fabric. Miss Sarah glanced across at Lady Tia, relieved to see she was not the only one suffering from the rise of steam from the towels. Her competitor's face was ruddy with heat, the necessity for an orgasm etched across her face.

'Ten, nine, eight …' With each number of the longed-for countdown, Miss Sarah felt her resolve slipping. 'Seven, six, five …' Just one hit to her cunt would be one too many, and as her arse was targeted with renewed vigour, her will to hang on grew as well. If she could survive this, she could survive anything The Retreat could throw at her. She was no submissive, and this was her chance to prove it. 'Four, three, two, one … *Stop*.'

There was a clatter of wood against stone as Kane and Elena's weapons hit the floor. 'It seems that we need to initiate phase two. Congratulations, ladies, I didn't think either of you would take 55 hits in such circumstances. I am impressed. But you will stay exactly where you are until one of you fails.'

Unsure how much longer she could fight her fear, Miss Sarah heard the door to the kitchen scrape open, and Dr Ewen call, 'Ah, Alisha, Miss Sanders. How fortunate you should arrive now. I have a job for you.'

Chapter Ten

'MISS SANDERS! I asked you to come over here.'

Jess felt a shiver trip down her spine as the reality of what was taking place before her sank in. There really were two women bent over a range which was pumping out enough energy to heat the entire kitchen.

Catching up with Alisha, who'd already reached Dr Ewen's side, Jess obediently waited to hear what she was expected to do, trying not to let her gaze stray to Miss Sarah as she did so.

'I assume Mr Proctor sent you here to assist Alisha prepare lunch for the staff, Miss Sanders?'

'Yes, Dr Ewen.' Jess, who'd rushed to the kitchen after changing in her room, had encountered Alisha on the other side of the kitchen door, and hadn't had the chance to say so much as good morning to her yet.

'Excellent.' Elena gestured to the prone women before her. 'As you can see, the range has been nicely fired up and is all ready for you to cook on.' She turned to Alisha. 'What are you going to make?'

'Traditional Scottish drop-scones, doctor, to be served with a selection of cheeses, chutneys, and preserve.'

'Delicious. Well, don't let me keep you both. Go and prepare your batter, and I will make sure you have space to cook them.'

Dismissed, Jess followed Alisha to the other side of the kitchen, wondering how she was supposed to cook anything remotely edible when her wits were entirely with Miss Sarah. She didn't know how to make drop-scones, or even what drop-scones were.

The low level of noise behind them was eerie as two sets of lungs failed to suppress heavy breaths, edged with a surfeit of anxiety, which filled the kitchen like a ghostly presence.

Knowing she was going to have to ask what to do, Jess whispered to Alisha, 'How do we make them? Do they take long to prepare?'

Replying as covertly as she could, Alisha replied, 'They're dead easy and quick to do. We have to cook them on the range's stove, though.'

Alisha was getting an iron griddle pan and a huge mixing bowl out of the nearest cupboard, when Dr Ewen broke the uneasy quiet. 'I think perhaps two batches of mixture might be a good idea.'

The next ten minutes dissolved in seconds. Doing exactly as Alisha instructed, Jess fetched milk and eggs from the larder, spooned out flour, and stirred and stirred until her arms ached, and every millilitre of the batter was smooth. Alisha's anxious face was almost as pale as Jess's. Her freckles stood out a mile, highlighting the contours of her face, showing Jess how spot on she'd been with her nagging feeling that the cabin crew girl persona was fake.

Quietly, not sure if she was allowed to ask or not, and keeping her back to the action behind her, Jess asked, 'Why are you here?'

Alisha began to test the consistency of the batter, not stopping in her work as she replied out of the corner of her mouth, 'I'll tell you the answer to that when I've worked out it out myself.'

Miss Sarah closed her eyes. The granite floor she'd been staring at for the last 25 minutes was beginning to swim before her eyes, and despite the fact that the punch of the spoon hadn't recommenced against her arse, her butt continued to smart as if every stroke was being studiously reapplied. The towels she lay on were as damp from her sweat as they were hot from the range, and the steam the situation was creating was stinging her dangling arms, legs, and head, and making her eyes water.

Although they were no longer being beaten, the contact against her slick flesh was maintained. Kane's fingers wandered continuously across her shaking legs, his fingers sometimes reaching as far as her inner thighs, sending shockwaves of a contradictory desire see-sawing through her lubricated pussy. The clatter of a metal spoon whisking in a bowl informed Miss Sarah, through her anxious haze, that Jess and Alisha were getting on with their task as fast as they could. Even so, she wished they'd go faster.

Lady Tia's breathing was as vocal as her own now, and Miss Sarah knew that, although the other woman had an additional layer of protection over her chest, she was suffering every bit as much. Perhaps her silver corset is acting as a heat conductor? Suddenly the thought that the woman next to her was being slowly baked, and had actually been tricked into thinking she had the advantage, when in fact that was not the case, lent wings to Miss Sarah's flagging determination.

At last, Jess and Alisha approached the range.

The frying pan was unbelievably heavy as Jess carried it across the room and placed it on the edge of the table next to the range. Risking a covert glance at Miss Sarah, Jess noticed that her mistress's eyes were clamped shut, and there was a glossy sheen of perspiration on her skin, squinting under the glare of the kitchen's artificial light.

'The batter is prepared, doctor.' Alisha half curtseyed, as if she knew she should show deference, but wasn't quite sure what the protocol was.

'Thank you, Alisha.' Dr Ewen picked up the ladle that she'd previously used to buff Miss Sarah's breasts. 'Place it upon the table, and fetch me an extra bowl.'

Moving quickly, Alisha did as she was told.

Pouring a quantity of the batter mix into the new bowl, Dr Ewen dipped the ladle into the freshly decanted mix, and passed it to Kane. 'Time to test if the range has reached the optimum temperature.'

Jess's pupils dilated fast, and yet, despite the lurch of her stomach, and the corresponding convulsing of her channel, she wasn't sure she wanted to see what was going to happen next.

Kane came to the front of the range, and lowered the brimming ladle between the shoulders of the two women. He hovered it over the slim gap in the range top devoid of the fluffy towel barrier. As he tipped the ladle, a tiny dribble of batter hit the metal with a fierce crackle, spitting at the two women, who yelped as they were spattered with microscopic flecks of scone mix. Instantly, the puddle of batter hardened and transformed from pale yellow to a buttercream. Kane's eyes, already dark, hardened as he stared at Alisha. 'Not bad, considering you made this.'

Ignoring Kane's dismissive attitude towards her cook, Elena examined the results critically, acting as though there weren't two vulnerable women cooking alongside the batter. 'Almost perfect, in fact, but of course, once they are in the griddle the temperature will have to be higher.'

Higher! Miss Sarah only just prevented her horror from escaping her mouth as the short gasps of air being exhaled at regular intervals from the unmoving Lady Tia became much louder. Whatever Dr Ewen had planned, Miss Sarah knew that time was running out for her companion's stamina as well as her own.

'Kane, if you will be so kind?'

Alisha and Jess exchanged apprehensive glances as Kane carried the smaller bowl to the rear of the dominatrices, picked up two of the silver spoons that Dr Ewen had laid out earlier, and filled them with batter. The taciturn man passed one to The Retreat's mistress. They stood next to each other, their spoons held aloft. Kane broke his silence. 'Alisha, Miss Sanders, come here, please.'

Sweating nearly as profusely as Miss Sarah, wondering what the hell she was about to witness; Jess followed closely on Alisha's heels, and found herself looking at Miss Sarah and Lady Tia's recently spanked backsides.

'Widen their legs.'

As Alisha approached Lady Tia, Jess, guilt issuing from every pore, took hold of Miss Sarah's legs, and drew them gently apart. Unlike the top of the range, where the padding was generous, there was only a single thickness of towel between her mistress's pussy and the hot metal. And although her crotch was not touching the range, it was only a few searing centimetres away.

Kane, his hoarse voice betraying the arousal his body language did not gave away, issued the next instruction. 'You girls, kneel out of our way, but keep hold of their legs, and keep them up and wide. I trust you'll be able to do at least that task correctly!'

As her legs were lifted higher off the ground by Jess's soft fingers, Miss Sarah gasped. Turning her head, she found herself looking into the clouded eyes of Lady Tia. Neither gloating nor victorious, her expression was filled with a trepidation that Miss Sarah knew she was reflecting back at her. Lady Tia was no defrocked Cinderella now.

They were Hansel and Gretel, and they were perilously close to the witch's oven. Jess was right – this place is one mixed-up, warped fairy tale, Miss Sarah thought. Proctor never did anything without a profitable reason. But fairy tales …?

Her musings stalled as, in one coordinated move, Kane and Elena acted. They tipped their spoons so the cold, gloopy mix landed directly on each dominatrix's cruelly exposed channel. The second it landed, they simultaneously slammed the women's butts forward, so the newly anointed pussies were clamped against the thinly covered range back for a split second, before being withdrawn again.

The results were instant, spectacular, and unified.

Jess wasn't sure who cried out loudest or bucked the hardest, as the conflicting sensations of the icy batter against the women's scalding skin, the sudden dose of extra heat at their pulsating clits, and the discomfort of their roasted, squashed nipples, not to mention their fear at being cooked alive, sent them into juddering, angry orgasmic squeals.

Miss Sarah, her legs and arms quivering, her body blotched with heat rash, her upper legs dripping with cooking batter, didn't wait for permission to stand. She reached out an arm to Lady Tia, who reluctantly took it. Her need for physical support greater at that moment than her desire to maintain her dignity, Miss Sarah already had a renewed glint to her furiously blazing eyes.

Jess was inwardly cowering even before the onslaught began.

'How *dare* you?' Passing Lady Tia's arm to the hovering Alisha, Miss Sarah drew herself up to her full height. Paying no attention to the fact her hair was in disarray, or that her favourite corset was singed and covered in sweat patches that had ruined it beyond repair, she clasped her hands to her hips to disguise their shaking, and vented her displeasure. 'We could have been seriously hurt! We are here to learn from each other, to help you improve life at The Retreat. We are not here to take torment to a level where life and limb is endangered. Miss Sanders!'

Lifting her head, Jess answered, 'Yes, Miss Sarah.'

'We are going home. Go and pack.'

Jess had only moved half a step when Kane's booming Scottish brogue echoed around the room. 'Don't move!'

'Miss Sarah.' Dr Ewen took over, her voice silken compared to that of Proctor's henchman. 'It seems I frightened you with my test. I should assure you that everything was under control, and at no point would any permanent harm have come to you.'

Looking pointedly at her sweat-stained outfit, Miss Sarah risked the wrath of the doctor further. 'And what makes you so sure of that, madam?'

'Tell her, Kane.'

From out of his pocket Kane produced a hi-tech heat sensor which flashed a small, red-lighted digital display. 'If this shows a number higher than six, then you are in danger. So providing I am careful about the exact thickness and placement of the towels – which I always am – and I don't let the number reach more than 5.3, then you will not experience more than the intense heat, and unless you deliberately placed your skin onto the stove top, you'd do no more than sweat out your climax, as if you were being serviced in a particularly hot sauna.'

Kane pocketed the device, and cleared away the towels. 'This session was popular with some of Dr Ewen's more extreme thrill seekers prior to David taking over, and it is a session he wishes to keep in The Retreat's repertoire. Once again, Proctor's claim that you and Miss Sanders could take anything seems unfounded. How is it he put it, Dr Ewen?'

'That they could even cope with the most twisted of our potential clients' darkest fantasies.'

Jess jerked her head up rather faster than normal, making her attention obvious. *Twisted and dark?* It was like the Brothers Grimm had been brought to life and had their sexual peccadilloes let loose.

'Who are these potential clients?' The quivering of her shoulders had stopped now, and although she still looked the worse for wear, Miss Sarah's controlled pose was back in place.

'Proctor has ambitions to take on a company's worth of guests. We expect the first of these potential clients at the end of the week. We are assured that they like their experiences to be memorable.'

Lady Tia, who'd taken longer than she wanted to admit to pull herself together, rounded on Miss Sarah. 'And who are you to be talking to Dr Ewen in that way? Has she not just taught you how to reach a whole new level of self-discipline?'

There was a second's hush, and then Miss Sarah bowed. 'You are correct, Lady Tia, forgive me, but as you'll know from having listened in on the second hidden microphone I am certain I will find in my bedroom shortly, I have only one terror in life, and that is fire. To be placed thus was not easy. But, as you have so kindly pointed out, I am undoubtedly stronger for the experience. Now, if you will excuse me, I would like to change. If you wish me to be of any further use to you today, then I need to make myself more presentable. Do you still require Miss Sanders to help prepare lunch?'

Her usual calm back in place, her expression once more unreadable, Elena smiled her amused smile. 'I would like her to assist Alisha, but Miss Sanders will bring lunch for both you and herself to your room once it is done.'

'Thank you, doctor.'

With as much dignity as she could muster, her anger at being put in such a position raging within her chest, Miss Sarah walked serenely towards the door, before adding, 'Doctor Ewen, forgive my imposition, but on my arrival you indicated that there would be time for me to discuss a few matters concerning The Retreat once I had settled in. I believe it would be of benefit to us all if I understood the rules here. We will do better here if we work as if we are all on the same side, and not rivals in a non-existent competition. May I make an appointment for such a meeting?'

The Retreat mistress's eyes gave nothing away. 'Two-thirty. My study.'

Miss Sarah nodded, and was gone.

Chapter Eleven

LESS THAN 60 seconds later, Jess and Alisha were alone.

Shocked by what she'd just witnessed, Jess threw caution to the wind, and risked being overheard asking questions. She spoke with hushed urgency, whisking the larger, unsullied bowl of scone batter as noisily as she could in an attempt to drown out her words to any hidden camera that might be recording, even though the activity in the kitchen had returned to the mundane. 'What do they want with you here? I'm damn sure it isn't Jason I'm here to teach, and Lady Tia certainly doesn't need any improvement to her spanking technique!'

Pouring some fat into the frying pan, watching it firecracker in the pan as she placed it onto the now towel-free, batter-sprayed range, Alisha answered with equal speed out of the corner of her mouth. 'I came here as a cook, to do the guests' meals, staff food, and organise outside caterers when they are required. As soon as David saw me he liked me.' Alisha blushed as she added, 'And I liked him too. He told me about you and Fables, and what he wanted from some of his staff here outside of the conference season, and it appealed.'

Jess's eyebrows rose. 'You knew you wanted this life?'

'I take it you didn't?'

'I had no idea. My experience wasn't vast before I met Mrs Peters.' Jess passed the ladle to Alisha as they huddled close enough to appreciate how hot the women

134

must have been as they lay across the cooker. 'I couldn't go back now.' Her voice lost its surprise and became deadly serious. 'You do understand that, don't you? Once you're in, there is no way out. Your body would never forgive you. I positively ache if I'm left unsatisfied for too long.'

Alisha glanced at the wall clock, and then down at the fast-cooking scones. 'We don't have long. Can you put the kettle on for me?'

Jess was about to head toward the sink when Alisha caught her arm, causing sparks of longing to shoot from one girl to the other. 'I *have* to talk to you – I want to be like you. I *have* to learn how to let go. I can't let go when I'm supposed to. If I can't learn how, they'll get rid of me. And I really want to stay.'

Speaking over the gurgling of the huge kettle, Jess frowned. 'And what about Jason? He is a born sub. And despite David telling me he's new, I don't think he is.'

'Jason loves it. He is newish here, but he's had training somewhere else, I'm sure. But The Retreat needs a female submissive as well. And I want it to be me. Will you and Miss Sarah help me?'

'These are delicious, Miss Sanders,' Miss Sarah said. 'Perhaps Mrs Peters should put you to work in the kitchens at Fables?'

Jess poured a second cup of coffee for the freshly corseted Miss Sarah, before taking a seat amongst the wreckage of fallen books in their bedroom to eat her own lunch. 'Alisha made them, ma'am, I merely assisted. Cooking is not my strong point.'

'I trust you listened and learnt while she worked?'

'Yes, ma'am.'

'Taking care not to be overheard?'

'I did my best, but I cannot promise. Proctor is clever.'

Thinking of the second microphone she'd located

behind another row of books, Miss Sarah agreed. 'He most certainly is, Miss Sanders.' She gestured to the literary chaos in which they sat. Books littered the floor, the bed, and the desk. 'You will see that I discovered another bugging device while you were otherwise occupied. I have also conducted a thorough search to ensure that there is not a third camera hiding anywhere.' Tidying the closest books, which Jess recognised as the Grimm fairy tales she'd spotted when she was exercising the night before, into a stack Miss Sarah continued, 'What was the sub like?'

'It wasn't Alisha. It was a gentleman referred to as Master Jason Richards. I'd estimate he is about 26 years old; he's obviously a worker on the estate. He is blond, has blue eyes, is very fit, very willing, and I would venture is already well disciplined. Lee, back at Fables, would not have withstood what he had to contend with any better.'

Miss Sarah sipped her coffee thoughtfully. 'I trust you implicitly in this matter, Miss Sanders. After all, you have proven on many occasions that you know your business, and are sensible enough to always remember your place.'

Blushing, her head lowered, Jess murmured, 'Thank you, ma'am.'

'And Alisha? Is her situation as uncertain as we predicted?'

Jess recounted what the would-be submissive had told her, including how Proctor and Dr Ewen were after a female submissive whose obedience could always be relied upon, as well as a male one, word for word.

Miss Sarah gave a knowing smile. 'So that's why we're really here. To teach Miss Alisha the art of letting her brain allow her body to experience what it wishes to experience.' She paused. 'Although I bet there is more to all this than that.'

Jess continued to eat. The patch of skin on her arm that had experienced Alisha's urgent, yearning touch before she'd left the kitchen still keenly registered her presence. 'She wants our help. If we can't train her up soon, they'll have to look for another female sub. I got the impression that time was short.'

'I'm very sure time is short. The Retreat will have to open its doors soon so it can pay its way. When it does, they'll need a complete willing and compliant staff to attend to David Proctor's guests.'

A shudder of cold passed over Jess. 'You don't think …?'

'You belong at Fables, Miss Sanders. Mrs Peters would not let them keep you.' Saying nothing more for the moment, her fingers caressing the spines of the fairy tale books, Miss Sarah wished she felt as certain as she sounded. 'I am also curious as to how Dr Ewen knows Mrs Peters. Have you overheard anything that could shed some light on this relationship?'

'No, ma'am.'

Standing up decisively, Miss Sarah gathered their lunch things onto the tray Jess had carried to their bedroom. 'I think I will take these back to the kitchen before my meeting with Dr Ewen.'

'Surely I should do that, ma'am?'

'Normally you would. But I wish to observe Alisha alone for a moment. And you are going to put all these books back on the shelves. While you're at it, have a good look at these fairy tales. See if you can work out if there is more to the recurring theme within these walls than a whim following on from the "happy ever after" look of the castle. I don't mind having to strut about looking like a slutty version of Sleeping Beauty, but when someone tries to literally bake me into the story of Hansel and Gretel I want to know why.'

Grateful that she had not encountered anyone on the walk from her room to the kitchen, Miss Sarah eased the sturdy oak door ajar as quietly as she could. The scene that met her eyes didn't shock her at all.

Sliding the tray onto the worktop beside the door, the sound drowned out by the kitchen radio playing in the background, Miss Sarah silently observed Alisha. Her naked body was quaking with the clear signs of climactic desperation. Bent over David's knees, she was having her backside roundly spanked with a paddle expertly wielded by a refreshed and supremely confident Lady Tia.

'How many times do I have to tell you, girl!? You come when I say you can, and then you say *thank you.*'

'Sorry, Lady Tia, I …'

The woman swung the red leather weapon high into the air, and Miss Sarah was able to see that it was noduled for greater discomfort on impact. 'When I tell you to beg me to send you over the edge, to hit you, or to kiss your nipples, then that is *exactly* what you are going to do. Do you understand?'

'Yes, Lady Tia.' Alisha's voice was small, and although Miss Sarah was unable to see her face as she hung over David's motionless lap, she was sure the conflict on it would speak volumes. Jess had been right. Everything about Alisha told Miss Sarah's practised ears that she wanted to obey, but the switch in her brain that controlled her humility hadn't been clicked into the correct position, so the satisfaction she so badly wanted was being denied her largely by her own subconscious.

'If you don't put more effort into this, girl, then I will have to proceed with David's plans to replace you. A candidate is already lined up. This is not something that would please me. I heartily dislike the girl, not to mention the way in which she has been trained, or her trainer. '

The concerns Jess had expressed in their bedroom replayed themselves in Miss Sarah's head as she continued to observe the tableau before her. All the time she spoke, Lady Tia brought her palm down onto the girl's arse. Miss

Sarah was impressed by Alisha's lack of movement, noting as well that the few gasps that did break from her lips were soft and controlled, rather than shocked and noisy, as they would have been from most people. There was definitely a submissive skill there worthy of development.

'Please, Lady Tia! Please, David. I want to stay here with you.'

Joining in the conversation for the first time, David spoke curtly. 'What you want isn't going to hold any sway with the guests from Fairtasia, is it?'

'No, David.'

Ensuring Alisha was safely balanced on top of David's lap, Lady Tia raised her hand high in the air to slap the glowing cheeks again, while David freed his length from his trousers, announcing, 'You can think about the importance of obedience while you suck my cock.'

As Lady Tia abandoned the paddle, and grabbed a handful of Alisha's blonde curls to steer her head into place, Miss Sarah backed out of the room. Stopping a few paces along the corridor Miss Sarah thought fast. Fairtasia? That was not a company she'd heard of, but she did know that Proctor had a finger in a vast number of business pies.

Although she hadn't had the opportunity to talk to Alisha she'd hoped for, now that Miss Sarah had seen the girl alone with David, she could clearly see her desire to stay at The Retreat as a full-time rather than occasional culinary member of staff. Although the idea she'd had on the aircraft about the girl being a gold-digger could now be dismissed, the fact that this attractive young woman, for reasons Miss Sarah had no inclination to fathom, had formed an attraction for Proctor was probably what was standing in her way of full submission. It was also very likely the reason she'd been given so many second chances. David was no fool. How could he fail to notice that this beautiful young woman wanted him to be her master, and hated herself for not being able to let herself please him?

Wondering if either Alisha or Proctor had worked that out for themselves yet, Miss Sarah checked her watch. She had 20 minutes before her meeting with Dr Ewen. Just enough time to explore a few of the other rooms in The Retreat.

Elena closed the old diary she'd been reading with a thump. That had been then. Were things that much different now? She wasn't sure. Both she and Laura had pursued rewarding careers in hotel management since their time together at university. Although Laura had branched out into their current realm of employment before she had, Elena had no doubt she was every bit as skilled as Laura. After all, they'd learnt everything they knew from the same woman; a very unusual and perceptive tutor called Ms Webster.

Ms Webster had known she and Laura had plans to go into the management of hotels, and saw something in both women that caused her to teach them as much about the benefits of what she called "the incentive entertainment industry" as standard customer service and reaching business targets.

Shutting her eyes for a moment, Elena could see her younger self, so earnest, so ambitious, although never as ambitious as Laura – or so she'd believed at the time. And then there had been David Proctor, always hanging around them, but they'd been too strong for him; too clever. He'd needed submissives to boost his ego back then, just as he did now.

'What time is your meeting with Miss Sarah?' The door opened, and David marched in without so much as a knock, not even bothering to close it behind him. He slammed his hands down flat on the desk that separated them.

'In ten minutes, as you well know.' Elena looked over the top of her glasses.

'A quick summary of your thoughts so far?' David's hectoring tone was not appreciated, but Elena disregarded it for now.

'I think Miss Sarah's wish for their bedroom to be left unbugged is fair, and I think it should be a courtesy extended to all the staff rooms.'

'Is that so?'

'Yes. It is. I think some private time will enhance public performance. Also –' Dr Ewen continued before David could give an opinion '– it has already done Lady Tia some good to witness a different style of discipline. Her techniques are good, and precisely what you'd expect from someone trained in one of the most exclusive BDSM clubs in London, but a little refinement wouldn't go amiss.'

'I wasn't interested in your views on Lady Tia. The little matter of our female sub has to be settled ASAP. The party is only a week away now.'

Exasperated, Elena said, 'Only your unwillingness to admit that Alisha is not going to fulfil that role has delayed this process. We have an excellent male submissive in Jason. It is, in my opinion, time you let Lady Tia and Jason work together in preparation for the Fairtasia guests. I am sure Miss Sarah would tell you the same if you'd allow me to let her see Alisha in action. I think it's only the fact you have formed an unwise personal attachment to the girl that has kept her in a function beyond that of cook and waitress for the past weeks. Keep her on as an extra help by all means, but she's not going to be ready as our female submissive before next week. If you'd allow me to advertise for a new sub, an appointment could be made quickly.'

Through clenched teeth, David hissed, 'I take your

comments on board, and of course I respect the fact that you have the final word on staff appointments, but in this case, Dr Ewen, I think we can assume our female submissive has been found. You know as well as I do that we asked the Fables women here in case Alisha didn't make the grade, not to teach her. It's far too late in the day for any proper training to make a difference. If Alisha cannot do as she is told, then the need for an instant, and well trained, submissive is imperative. So much depends on that party going according to plan.'

'So while the Fables women *are* here, and they are clearly every bit as good as I'd expect anyone working for Laura Peters to be, why not let them do what they think they are here to do? It is not too late, but you are going to have to allow them to help, and trust *me* to provide an opening party that will ensure Fairtasia have an evening of dark, fantasy fairy tale entertainment they will never forget.'

'I'm not going to say this again, doctor.' Proctor all but growled his response. 'The future of The Retreat rests on this. If I fail, then you fail as well. And if Alisha isn't up to scratch by next Friday night, Miss Sanders will have to consider herself the proud owner of a new place of employment. End of story. Or in this case, end of fairy tale!'

Frowning, Miss Sarah backed away on her bare feet, into the nearest bathroom. Her mind was processing everything she'd accidentally overheard as she'd waited outside the study's open door, a few minutes too early for her appointment.

Running her hands under the tap, so that if anyone came in it would look as if she needed to be there, Miss Sarah knew she had to talk to Jess, and fast. First, however, she had to meet Dr Ewen as she was meant to, and it was imperative she didn't act as if she knew any of Proctor's plans.

Chapter Twelve

'IN FIVE DAYS' time?' Miss Sarah's voice dripped incredulity. 'This weekend?'

'Yes.'

'And yet we haven't even begun to do what we were brought here for.' Miss Sarah stood before Dr Ewen's desk, on the exact spot where she'd been manhandled to a climax on her first visit to the room.

Responding serenely, The Retreat's mistress said, 'I realise that.'

Miss Sarah crossed her arms as she went on with her line of enquiry. 'This makes me think that Proctor has brought us here under false pretences. And so, the real question is why are we here?'

Without asking for permission, Miss Sarah pulled out a chair and sat down, keeping her eyes level with Dr Ewen. She continued, 'Miss Sanders tells me you already have a well-trained submissive. Therefore, Kane was lying when he told us that you needed our assistance in that area.'

'You trust the word of your submissive.' It was a statement not a question, and Elena wasn't surprised when Miss Sarah continued to speak without giving a direct reply.

'If, on the other hand, I am here to train up this submissive, one Master Jason Richards, then I'd have assumed I would be introduced to him without delay on my arrival. So I'm obviously not here for that purpose.

And now you tell me that The Retreat has a very important group of guests coming on Saturday night, which Miss Sanders and I will help entertain.'

'Yes.' Watching her companion very carefully, Dr Ewen said no more.

Miss Sarah, her eyes calculating, added, 'With respect, doctor, nothing about our presence here rings true. I have never trusted Proctor. He knows that, and we have developed a mutual dislike over the last year that allows us to function profitably around each other when we have to. I have no idea what role the monosyllabic Kane is playing in all this, but I suspect it is a greater one than we have been allowed to think so far. Frankly, at the moment, I don't care.

'I'm disappointed that it appears I cannot trust you. Mrs Peters is devious, but she does not lie to the staff to the detriment of the business. If the manageress of the establishment cannot keep her staff safe, and her guests satisfied, then she is not doing her job.'

The second she'd spoken, Miss Sarah knew she'd gone too far. Dr Ewen's face went from its usual pallor to a dark crease of displeasure. Reasoning that as she'd already pushed her luck, she might as well keep pushing, Miss Sarah was about to demand some answers when Elena shot around to the other side of her desk, and grasped her chin in her bony fingers.

'Get one thing absolutely clear, Miss Sarah. I gave you permission to ask me questions. I made no such promise about answering them.' Her free hand drew the basque forward so she could view Miss Sarah's breasts, 'Still tender, I see.'

The dominatrix didn't even blink as the steel eyes grinned at the remaining blotches of bruising from her encounter with Lady Tia's tape measure.

'I have already told you more than I intended.'

'I have one more query.'

'Are you really are as brave as Proctor told Kane you were? Or perhaps you are developing a taste for a more submissive life yourself?'

Managing to withhold the wince of discomfort as Dr Ewen snapped the front of her corset back in place, Miss Sarah responded with more calm than she felt. 'Is your desperation for a female submissive so great that you have begun to con yourself I could fulfil that role myself, and attempt to taunt me in to the bargain?'

'Was that your question?' Elena sat across Miss Sarah's legs, pinning her to the leather-cushioned chair with her bony backside.

'No, that was merely an observation. My enquiry concerns Alisha.'

A possible flash of concern about being found out crossed Dr Ewen's face as she snaked a hand between Miss Sarah's legs, drumming a steady rhythm against the satin-covered mound with her fingers.

'I wish to know why Alisha isn't being properly trained as a submissive. She is plainly keen to adopt that lifestyle. It wouldn't take much to form her into the creature Proctor wishes her to be.'

'We have tried, repeatedly. She cannot fulfil the role.' Frustration at her staff's failure to train the girl translated itself to an increase in pressure between the dominatrix's legs.

'Because Lady Tia couldn't do it does not mean that I cannot. Although we have already lost precious training time.'

'Arrogance does not become you, Miss Sarah.'

'Not arrogance. Professional pride in my abilities. I could teach Alisha so that she'll be a good enough submissive to get through the party. After that, Miss Sanders and I will leave, and Lady Tia can refine the girl's skills.' Miss Sarah felt her channel muscles clench as the older woman continued to display the subtleties of her skill against her mound. 'How has Lady Tia tried to train her?'

'She has been spanked, tied, caressed, and yet she shows no ability to control her climaxes.'

'You mean she has been bullied – pleasurably, I have no doubt – but bullied nonetheless. Has her stamina been tested? Has she had stimulation denied her for long periods? Has Lady Tia stimulated Alisha visually as well as physically, so that her strength of will has been strengthened? Or has it all been rather bull in a china shop?'

Changing the angle of her hand so she was now squeezing Miss Sarah's pussy in time with each of the damningly true words, Dr Ewen spoke with resigned patience. 'Very well. I will give you Alisha for the next five days. The party is in six. But if you do not succeed, there will be a price.'

'And the price is?' Aware that her pussy juice was staining her satin thong, and spreading its way onto the manageress's hand, Miss Sarah experienced a cold rush of apprehension. She already knew what the answer was going to be. This had been the plan all along. Damn, she'd played right into Dr Ewen's hands!

'Miss Sanders will remain here as The Retreat's female slave.'

'As Proctor was planning to trick Jess into staying anyway, that is a condition I am happy to agree to. For, make no mistake, I will ensure she comes home to Fables with me.'

'You are so sure you will succeed where Lady Tia failed.'

'Yes.' The steadily unravelling knot of a climax bubbled in Miss Sarah's belly as she continued to lock eyes with Elena. 'I will require the use of the conference room, Miss Sanders to help me, and, if possible, I'd like Master Richards to assist as well. It would be useful to learn about the man Alisha will presumably have to

146

interact with for your clients.'

'Jason and the conference room you may have, but not Miss Sanders. Mr Proctor would not thank me if she knew about our agreement.'

'Without Miss Sanders' help I will not be able to give you the submissive you want. Plus –' her tone was laced with determination '– this is *not* my agreement, I am merely accepting the underhand plan you and Proctor had already made, and am doing my best to make sure that it does not take place. Jess will assist me. I give you my word that I will not speak of this conversation with her. It will not help either of us if she knows that she is in danger of being held here against her will.'

Feeling rather than seeing the orgasm build within her companion's body, Dr Ewen snapped, 'And why would I trust that you'll keep quiet?'

'Because although I withhold information from time to time *I* do not lie.'

Concentrating the pad of her thumb over Miss Sarah's slit, Dr Ewen inclined her head. 'You know, of course, that if I discover you have betrayed my trust, there will be consequences. So far I have kept a strict eye on Lady Tia. She does not like you being here, and resents that I have not let her off the rein to display her irritation.'

'Understood.' Miss Sarah knew she had around 30 seconds before she came. 'Miss Sanders is no fool. I should warn you she already suspects that Proctor has some ulterior motives for our presence here.'

Dr Ewen changed the pressure of her thumb from continuous to repetitive light flicks, and leant back a little so see could see the snatch she was caressing. 'Then you must reassure her that her suspicions are unfounded.'

Digesting this information while keeping every trace of emotion from her voice, Miss Sarah gestured towards the deliciously moving hand with a flash of her eyelashes. 'May I?'

'You may.'

With a protracted sigh, Miss Sarah let out a gentle whistle from between her composed lips, her pussy quivering against Elena's hand for a few moments before the outwardly low-key climax passed.

'Thank you, Dr Ewen. I see you are very skilled.' Thinking a little extra flattery might be wise, she added, 'I usually require at least minimal penetration before I come.'

Backing off Miss Sarah's lap, Elena, unimpressed by her sycophancy, added, 'If you disappoint me, you will see *exactly* how skilled I am. Mrs Peters and all the toys in her dungeon would be nothing by comparison. Understood?'

'Understood.'

'Miss Sanders!' Miss Sarah strode into her bedroom. Her submissive was busily stacking books back onto the shelves.

'Yes, ma'am.'

'Leave what you're doing and come with me. We have a submissive to train.'

'Miss Sarah?'

Walking quickly along the stone corridor with Jess trailing behind, the dominatrix issued her instructions. 'Go to the kitchens. Tell Alisha her request for help has been granted. She will report to me in the conference room in 15 minutes. Then find Master Richards. Bring him to the conference room as well. There is little time.'

'Yes, ma'am.' Jess had no idea if there was little time to get to the conference room, or little time left to them at The Retreat, but something about the vibe Miss Sarah was giving out did not invite questions. As she rushed off to the kitchens to find Alisha, Jess hoped the cook would know where to track down Jason, and for the first time since they'd arrived, she wished mobile phones were allowed here.

The conference room had once been the great hall of the castle. A long, highly polished mahogany table was placed centre stage, with 16 matching chairs neatly tucked in around its sides. Windows, which had been added by the Victorians, and not the more security-conscious medieval occupants, flooded the light of late spring into the castle, affording the room a stunning view over the loch and beyond to the mountains and forest. This place really could have come from a fairy tale.

Miss Sarah knew exactly what she had to do. Until she'd had the chance to get to know the triggers and workings of Alisha's body, she wasn't sure if she'd be able to fulfil her promise to Dr Ewen, or if she'd have to start thinking of an escape plan for herself and Jess.

Examining the slim stone pillars that, at 12 feet intervals, held up the ceiling, she could easily imagine them being utilised during the party on Saturday night, but was loath to introduce them to Alisha's training until the young woman was truly ready.

She wouldn't have been surprised if Proctor had already taken the young woman while tied to such a post. The man always wanted to run before he could walk. Miss Sarah cursed. If Lady Tia had only had the sense to explain the problem of the female submissive from the moment they'd arrived, they could already have had a day of training completed by now. Miss Sarah hoped Alisha already had the built-in level of fitness and stamina that was required for this lifestyle, because there certainly wasn't time to develop the type of exercise plan that had worked so well as the basis for Miss Sanders' training.

Opening the door, Jess quietly crept in. Crossing the rug-covered stone floor on her bare feet, she kept her eyes lowered, her whole body adopting a position of meekness. She had a feeling she was supposed to be out-submissiving everyone else. A keen but apprehensive Alisha and a wary

Jason followed her into the old hall.

Not turning round at their approach, Miss Sarah observed, 'Beautiful out there, isn't it, Miss Sanders? We must take the opportunity to explore before we leave.'

'Yes, Miss Sarah.' Jess knew her mistress was only making small talk to enforce a wait upon the other members of the room.

She felt alert and sensitive at the prospect of what was to come. The memory of the almost singing touch of Alisha's hand against her arm had had Jess longing for her touch to go somewhere entirely more intimate ever since. This, combined with images of Jason's body, solid, toned, and equally as subservient as her own, made her mouth water.

As she continued to stare out of the window, Miss Sarah addressed the group behind her. 'We are here to train Alisha to become the submissive she wants to become. From the little I have witnessed, I'd say it isn't her body that needs training, but her mind. Her inability to let go and allow herself to let go at the will of others is the issue. Would you agree with that, Miss Alisha?'

Feeling rather uncomfortable at being spoken of as if she was a mere thing and not a person, Alisha muttered, 'Yes, Miss Sarah.'

The dominatrix spun around on the balls of her feet. Her expression could have frozen an ocean. 'This is very important. Do you, Miss Alisha, truly want to learn this skill?'

'Very much, Miss Sarah.'

There was a drawn-out silence. Alisha couldn't help but lower her gaze as the dominatrix's eyes assessed every curve and line of her body as if her apron, jeans, jumper, socks, and trainers simply were not there.

Eventually, long after Alisha's feet had begun to fidget nervously on the floor, and Jason's breathing had started to become audible, Miss Sarah clapped her hands together in an unnecessary move to grab their attention. Pulling out one of the room's many chairs, she sat down. 'As you may or may not have been informed, in six days' time there is to be a party here. A celebration to launch the beginning of a change in direction for The Retreat, under the ambitious ownership of David Proctor.'

Miss Sarah ran her eyes over the three faces before her. If they knew any more than she did about the party, it didn't show.

'Miss Sanders has spent some time this morning searching through books concerning Grimm's fairy tales, in the hope she could discover why so much of the activity here is based loosely on those stories. Did you find anything?'

'A little, ma'am. A few Post-it notes on the pages, highlighting episodes from the tales which, I am guessing, could be used here as the basis for guest sessions. Like Hansel and Gretel's oven, Red Riding Hood's basket, and Snow White's mirror.'

'Any episodes we have yet to experience?'

'Not that I saw, but I haven't finished looking yet.'

Miss Sarah nodded, and crossed her long, shapely legs. 'I have found a reason behind this obsession with this particular brand of fantasy. Something that, in all the time I have worked with Proctor in Oxford, I have not seen him demonstrate. As ever, it is to do with money.' Conscious of wasting time talking, and seeing no light of recognition in the eyes of her three companions, Miss Sarah decided to press on. She pointed to Jess. 'Miss Sanders, I wish you to stand in front of Alisha. Master Richards, you will stand next to her. Close, but not touching.'

The submissives moved quickly. 'Alisha, you will note that neither of your comrades queried what I asked of them. I do not know Master Richards, but I can tell you with certainty that Miss Sanders did not even stop to question why I was asking her to move before you. That is the level of obedience Mr Proctor requires of you, Alisha.'

Alisha whispered, 'Yes, ma'am,' acutely aware that she'd been privately taking issue with everything Miss Sarah had said since she'd walked into the room. She felt a niggle of panic start in the wriggle of her toes, climbing up her body, and threatening to overtake the desire to become the plaything she wanted to be for David.

'In the time we have been given, I do not think this will be possible. What *is* possible is learning to overcome the barrier in your psyche that stops you reaching your goal. Tell me, Alisha, what happens when you are told you can climax, or you're told not to climax?'

Wiping her hands nervously on her apron, Alisha felt stumped. This was not what she'd expected. Lady Tia and David had been solely hands-on with their teaching techniques. Not once had they asked her what was stopping her complying, but merely shouted at her, or beat her harder – which she loved, but only resulted in her being turned on, disappointed further, or made to feel a fool who was frightened of losing her job.

'Well, Miss Alisha?' Miss Sarah's tone advised that she should begin to speak, even if what she said made no sense to anyone but herself.

'I want to do as I'm told, and I often do manage to hold off my orgasm for a while, although not always for long enough.'

'That is something that can be taught. We are all like that in the beginning. Single-mindedness will be your friend there. It is your failure to let go once permission had been given that I am interested in. What goes through your mind after you have held back your own satisfaction successfully, and you are finally granted what your body wants, when you find you can't respond as you and your master wish?'

'I ...' Goosepimples spread up Alisha's arms, even though they were well protected against the air of the room, which, thanks to the sun streaming through the windows, was not as cold as normal. Her voice was wretched as she tried to explain. 'It's as if because I've been keeping my body on hold for so long, focusing on not letting David down, the barrier I create to stop me climaxing becomes stuck. When the time comes, I can't shift it. All the excitement fizzles away and I have to go without.'

'I see.' Noting the sad expression that had clouded the girl's face, Miss Sarah stood and moved directly behind her. Taking the cook's hands, she placed them on top of her blonde locks. 'We will tackle this issue one step at a time.' Reaching around the curvy body, Miss Sarah undid the apron, and placed it to one side.

Stepping away from the tableau of submission, she gave her first instruction. 'Miss Sanders, undo the top button of your shirt.'

Jess's insides were churning with anticipation. Something about the erotic static in the room, and the relief of being in a position that she understood for the first time since her arrival in Scotland, had topped up her usual constant state of arousal to the point where Jess knew she'd have to be careful not to disgrace herself by coming before anyone else.

The dominatrix turned to the mute, ever-watchful Jason. 'Master Richards, remove your shoes and socks.'

Keeping her eyes reverently dipped away from Miss Sarah, Alisha let them stray over Jason's bare feet, and on towards Jess's naked legs, miniskirt, and tight-fitting buttoned blouse. Alisha's shoulders were already aching, and she found herself looping her fingers together through her hair to prevent herself from reaching forward to hasten the process of her colleagues undressing.

The next set of instructions came from Miss Sarah, delivered in a brittle tone. 'A second button, Miss Sanders. Your jumper, Master Richards.'

This was agony. Nothing had happened. For goodness' sake, they're only taking off their outer garments! Alisha could feel Miss Sarah's eyes boring into her as she watched everyone in the room, noting every reaction. A treacherous voice at the back of her head told her that Lady Tia would have stripped her naked and initiated a comfortable bruising by now. This lack of activity, this hiatus before any action, was something new.

Alisha gulped. Jason's work-honed torso seemed to be calling to her restless fingers all on its own.

'How wet are you, Miss Alisha?' The practical tone of the question jarred the tense atmosphere as Miss Sarah's query wrenched the cook out of her lecherous contemplations.

'Very.'

The mistress reprimanded her sharply. 'That should be "very, Miss Sarah" or "very, ma'am".'

'Yes, Miss Sarah.' Alisha's face flushed. She felt ashamed to have made such a rookie mistake, and again it occurred to her that this was not a sensation she experienced when she was with Lady Tia.

Keeping up the teasing torture, Miss Sarah said, 'Take off your top, Master Richards.'

Jason moved fast, his sapphire eyes blazing with a stronger glow than they had before, but otherwise his composure was faultless, if you overlooked the matter of his dick bulging with evident urgency beneath the safety of his denims.

Working as if she was a director in a play, Miss Sarah wove the strands of the training session together. 'Miss Sanders, use Master Richards' T-shirt to tie his hands behind his back.'

The level of disappointment that hit Alisha at the thought that perhaps Jason would not be permitted to undress any further lumped unexpectedly in the back of her throat. The resulting cough earned her a stern stare from Miss Sarah that sent a new shot of anxiety on a collision course with her neglected pussy.

'Another button, Miss Sanders.'

Alisha was almost afraid to look. Now that Jess's nimble fingers had popped open another of the little fasteners, only one button struggled to keep her shirt closed over her ample tits.

Ever since Alisha had clapped eyes on Jess in the plane, she'd fantasised about being ordered to have sex with the submissive. Now, as the semi-flapping shirt revealed a shapely chest covered in a plain black satin bra, Alisha knew she'd never wanted to touch anything so much in her life.

A minor shift in Alisha's stance told Miss Sarah that her lesson was having the required effect far quicker than she'd expected it to. It was time to make the cook rein in her desires for a while, to help teach her how to stall her climax, yet be able to maintain the ability to come when asked. Adopting her harshest voice, she cut the air with her words. 'I did *not* instruct you to keep still, Alisha. Nonetheless, I thought you'd have learnt enough from Lady Tia to know that *is* what you should be doing. That minor movement of your right foot a few seconds ago did not go unnoticed.'

'Sorry, Miss Sarah.' Alisha felt as if every part of her being had been set alight. No one had touched her, all her clothes were in place, and yet Alisha had never been so aware of herself. Every part of her felt as if it had been morphed into an erogenous zone, not just her nipples and her clit, but her neck, her feet, even the back of her knees. If she was ordered to come now, Alisha thought she probably could do so without anyone doing more than say the words.

Coming to stand behind Jason, Miss Sarah shook her head, undid his hands, and gestured for Jess to do up her shirt. 'Sorry is not good enough, Alisha. We will do this again in three hours' time, at four o'clock. I hope we get further before you let yourself down. In the meantime you will not masturbate. None of you will. If you do, I will know.'

'But I …' Alisha felt like bursting into tears. How could they leave her now? For three hours! What if she failed again? Would she be left for another three hours after that, and then again, and again? 'Please Miss Sarah, I …'

'Not another word, Miss Alisha.' Cutting through the cook's muttered protest, Miss Sarah snapped, 'You are dismissed. I will see you, dressed as you are now, at four o'clock. Do *not* be late.'

Spinning on her heels, Miss Sarah addressed Jason and Jess. 'I will also require your presence. In the meantime, Jason, you have work to do outside. Miss Sanders, come with me.'

Chapter Thirteen

ALISHA'S CONCENTRATION HADN'T so much been shattered as splintered. *I will not wank.* She repeated the phrase over and over again in the privacy of her head as she stood in her kitchen, a list of the culinary requirements she needed to order in readiness for the fast approaching party clutched in her hand.

She'd read the list three times already, but Alisha's eyes had registered none of the ingredients she had to make sure were in stock. Her heavily dilated green eyes stared at the larder shelves as if they were completely blank.

A confused anger welled within her. Her every instinct had been focused on obeying Miss Sarah while they were in the conference room. She'd tried so hard. Railing her annoyance at the lines of plastic containers before her, Alisha spoke through gritted teeth. 'All I did was shuffle one foot, for fuck's sake!'

Although Alisha had always relished being at Lady Tia's mercy during the sessions David had set up for her since she'd confessed she harboured subservient urges; there had often been the urge to giggle, as if it wasn't real somehow, and The Retreat's dominatrix was just acting.

With Miss Sarah everything was very real, and the temporary sense of deprivation Alisha generally felt when she failed to live up to Lady Tia's expectations was nothing to the sensation of loss and neglect that swamped her body even though an hour had passed since her training had been curtailed. The minutes until four o'clock seemed to move with paralysing slowness.

Talking to the catering packs of sacks of flour in front of her, Alisha attempted to pull herself together as she tried to put into perspective the feelings that rushed around her system. The closest comparison she could make was like being treated if she was the new girl at school, rather than an established pupil who'd decided to take on a new course. The cook muttered to herself, 'Face it, this is what you wanted. This is what it feels like to be a submissive. This is what you wanted to feel. Fuck, I have *got* to come!'

Forcing her eyes to move from the flour to the sugar, gauging how much she had left in stock, Alisha listened to the voice at the back of her head. Jess was right, it said. Once you start this life, you can't go back. Why do I see that now, after only a few minutes with Miss Sarah, and not before?

With every thought of Miss Sarah, the potential nakedness of Jess and Jason, and what they might be asked to do, a fresh gush of pussy juice flooded her knickers. The urge to give herself some relief was growing stronger with each tick of the kitchen clock, but that would have meant disobeying Miss Sarah, and Alisha had believed the mistress when she said she'd know if Alisha had wanked. 'But how would she know? If I was in the main kitchen she'd know, but in the larder? There are no cameras in here, and I am supposed to be here, so my lingering can't be seen as wrong.'

Gripping her pen in trembling fingers, Alisha tried to dismiss her thoughts and wrote a note to order more icing sugar. Then, examining the rows and rows of herbs and spices in the rack on the back of the larder door, she hunted down the jar of ginger powder to see how much was left.

The remaining contents of the pot reminded her of the

colour of Jess's hair, and Alisha couldn't prevent herself from speculating how the tresses, cut so neatly into the back of her neck, would feel if she ever got to run them between her fingers. The involuntary shiver of wistfulness that kept pace with the nerves that were doing the conga around Alisha's veins was causing her body to feel heated and chilled at the same time.

She took a deep breath and, continuing to chat to the produce before her, asked the bottles of food colouring, 'And how am I supposed to control myself next time? How the hell can I keep so motionless that not even a toe or finger moves?'

It suddenly struck Alisha that the problem which had been preventing her from becoming the obedient servant she wanted to be for Proctor's Retreat team had shifted so quietly, and with so little fuss, that she hadn't even noticed. The issue was no longer that she couldn't let go when she was ordered to, but holding on to her climax for long enough to at least become naked!

With a genuine sense of surprise, Alisha found that her right hand, still holding her pen, was snaking its way to the zip fly of her jeans. The feel of the writing implement as she slid it between the freshly opened gap was at once tantalizing and frustrating against her white cotton knickers. With her hand seemingly moving of its own free will, her eyes took in the large squeezable tube of chocolate cupcake topping. She picked it up with her left hand to weigh how much was left inside. It was virtually empty. Alisha's right hand, without bothering to engage her brain first, conscientiously placed her pen on the shelf before dropping her denims and knickers.

Alisha wasn't thinking at all as she screwed the cap back on the icing tube. The only factor that registered was that it had to be thrown away anyway. That, and it was a thick, long, and clean packet.

Kicking her clothes to her ankles, Alisha bent her knees

and squatted as far as the larder's limited floor space would allow. Then, with the cold of the granite wall against her exposed butt tingling the healing bruises left by Lady Tia's palm, she slid the tube up inside her channel before she'd even considered that she might not be wet enough to accept its thickness.

Sinking further to the floor, her knicker-tethered ankles forcing her to widen her knees, Alisha let out a happy, guilt-ridden whimper as she worked the tube, its tapering shape adding to her pleasure.

Tears dotted at the corners of her eyes as her gaze again fell upon the jar of ginger powder. A wave of guilt hit her. She was breaking Miss Sarah's rules. But surely they'd known she would. How could they expect her not to?

As she continued to ease the tube in and out of her pussy, Alisha's free hand came to her hair. With her eyes focused on the ginger, and her mind teeming with images of Jess and Miss Sarah making love to each other before her, torturing her by not allowing her to join in, Alisha came in a quiet, trembling heap of liberation. The muscles of her channel manipulated the used-up carton so violently that the cook could hear the plastic sigh in time to her climax.

Shame engulfed Alisha. She was sitting, her butt on show, her pussy dripping, a sticky chocolate icing tube by her feet, and her breasts so taut beneath her clothes that she could hardly inflate her lungs. The knowledge that she'd broken every hygiene rule going, not to mention flouted Miss Sarah's order, therefore potentially incurring the wrath of David, Dr Ewen, and Lady Tia, made panic clutch at her chest.

Hurriedly standing, dressing, and disposing of the tube in the nearest bin, Alisha scrubbed her hands under the kitchen tap. Her pulse hammered in her wrists as the water got hotter and hotter. As the heat got too much, the cook grabbed a towel and glanced at the kitchen clock. There was an hour to go. It might as well have been an eternity.

'Jog faster.'

Jess feared her chest would break out of its bra all on its own if she wasn't permitted to take it off soon.

'Keep those knees up.' Miss Sarah sat back against the headboard of her bed and watched as her submissive's breasts flopped up and down within the black underwear. 'That's better. Your level of fitness continues to impress, Miss Sanders. Unless I'm much mistaken, it will have to be at its peak for the party on Saturday. An increase in your exercise regime would be wise.'

Jess could feel the muscles of her thighs begin to burn as she continued to jog on the spot. The room was tidy once more, and her mistress sat on the bed with the fairy tale books, their pages marked with bookmarks, scattered around her. Jess was getting to the stage where her breathing became laboured, and gasped out her words rather than spoke them. 'Yes, Miss Sarah.'

'Now do 20 star jumps. Begin.'

Containing her groan, Jess rolled up the hem of her miniskirt so it wouldn't interfere with the movement of her legs as she jumped. She wondered how Alisha was. Jess doubted she was suffering the confusion she herself had in the early days of her employment at Fables. After all, Alisha had asked for this training, whereas her own had been somewhat thrust upon her. Yet the shocked look in the cook's eyes as the session was abruptly curtailed and she realised she wasn't going to receive any stimulation, be it visual or physical, until the next lesson had appeared genuine.

Counting down in her head as she threw her arms and legs out into an airborne star shape, the incentive of discovering what would happen kept Jess going. She found herself hoping that Alisha would manage to keep still for longer this time. For a lot longer. It seemed ages since she'd had a climax herself, and Jess knew the idea of receiving one before Alisha, or even better, with Alisha, was something her body was very keen to experience.

Lowering her arms, Jess caught her breath as Miss Sarah continued to examine the pages spread before her. Allowing a few seconds for her lungs to inflate properly, Jess asked, 'Do you know what is expected from us at this party, ma'am? It seems to have been sprung on us, yet I have no doubt Proctor has been planning it for some time. '

Closing the nearest book with a snap, Miss Sarah looked up at Jess with an expression that was almost in danger of displaying some of the affection she felt for the girl. Swiftly wiping all emotion from her features, keeping in mind her promise to Dr Ewen and knowing how ill-advised it would be to say anything to Jess about her potential imprisonment here, she said, 'I am not in a position to give you much information, and I must insist that you keep what I'm about to tell you to yourself in case Alisha and Jason are unaware of the situation. The party is an incentive to a very influential business known as Fairtasia to sign a contract with Proctor. Quite a lot of money is at stake, and much will ride on our performances. And, in particular, the performance of Miss Alisha.'

'And if Alisha does not please Mr Proctor?'

Ignoring Jess's worried query, Miss Sarah passed one of the leather-bound volumes to her submissive. 'How well do you know *Snow White*?'

Alisha wasn't sure whether she felt more sick or excited as she stood, her backside propped against the conference room table, at five minutes to four. She'd been so worried about being late that she had arrived early. Now she was worried that being early would be as much of an error as being late, and that she should have turned up precisely on the dot of four.

No one else had arrived. As Alisha stared through the window, the brilliant spring sunshine shimmering across the surface of the loch, a feeling of foreboding crept up her spine. What if they weren't coming? Was this all a trick; another way of making her wait? A cruel method to ensure that, by the time she did get to see Miss Sarah again, she was so desperate she'd capitulate to anything?

The creak of the conference room door made Alisha jump. All three of her previous companions walked in together.

'I told you to be here at four o'clock. It is exactly four o'clock now. You were not permitted to be here prior to that time.'

'Sorry, Miss Sarah.' Alisha bit her lip, recalling the withering tone in which she'd been told at their previous meeting that sorry wasn't good enough. She could feel her complexion blanch, and the thought that she'd disappointed Miss Sarah already, as well as indulging in a secret masturbation session, made her feel as though she had "guilty" tattooed across her forehead.

Only the knowledge that time was short stopped Miss Sarah from making the cook delay another three hours for any fulfilment as punishment for her lack of punctuality. Instead, her voice laced with the cut-glass vowels Jess was used to hearing her mistress use with her clients at home, she ordered, 'All stand as you were before.'

All three sets of feet moved quickly, and Miss Sarah began to repeat the requests she'd made of Jess and Jason during the previous session. In minutes, Jason's socks, shoes and T-shirt were off, and Jess was securing his wrists behind his back with his own top. Jess's chest was only partially covered by the stretch of her cotton blouse, kept in situ by one secured button.

Alisha, her hands back on her head, her eyes hungry, but lowered enough to show some reverence to the

163

mistress, was finding it difficult not to work moisture into her fast-drying lips. The last three hours had taken for ever, but now she was finally here, she was having trouble holding on to each moment. Her yearning for things to go faster, to be able to see and feel the flesh of the man and women before her, and to be touched herself, was overwhelming.

'Take off your jumper.'

The instruction felt like an invitation to heaven. The woollen layer had been mercilessly adding to Alisha's rocketing body temperature.

'Miss Sanders, you will unfasten Master Richards' jeans and roll them to the floor.' The dominatrix then addressed Jason himself. 'You may kick your trousers from your ankles.'

There was no moisture left in Alisha's mouth to moisten her lips with, even if she'd wanted to risk making the minor movement in front of Miss Sarah. The black boxer shorts on the man before her were tenting to the extreme as they strained to contain the cock within. Although she'd seen Jason in action at The Retreat many times, Alisha had never been permitted to suck him off before. Now it seemed the most desirable idea in the world.

Producing a short white cane from its hiding place in her left boot, Miss Sarah held it in both her hands at once, but refrained from mentioning its presence in words. Just a glance at Miss Sanders' face told Alisha the fact it was there was enough to get her submissive companion's imagination racing.

'Alisha, I wish you to observe.' Adopting a kind tone that wasn't fooling anyone, Miss Sarah took hold of Jess and steered her closer to Alisha. So close that it would have only taken a single step and the two women would have been touching, covered nipple to covered nipple.

Reaching a hand between the two women, Miss Sarah

flicked the last button of Jess's blouse open. 'I don't have to ask how badly you want to touch Miss Sanders, Alisha. Every part of your body looks as if it is ready to pounce. And yet you will not pounce. You will wait.'

Miss Sarah trailed the end of the cane over Jess's nipples, interested only in Alisha's reactions and uncaring for the effect she might be having on Jess herself. Pulling a condom packet from her other boot top, the dominatrix said, 'In a few moments I am going to give this to Master Richards. Then, and only then, I will allow Miss Sanders to strip.' Twirling the cane between her fingers, Miss Sarah went on, 'If you tell me the truth, I will let you watch them fuck. However, if you lie to me during the course of the next conversation, this will not happen. A fact which I don't think either of your colleagues here would thank you for.'

How did Miss Sarah know? She couldn't be sure – could she? Trying not to let her expression give her away, Alisha braved herself for the forthcoming inquisition.

'Where did you bring yourself off?'

The question wasn't the one Alisha had expected. She'd been swaying back and forth in her mind as to whether she should confess she'd masturbated, but Miss Sarah had already taken that fact as a given. 'In the larder.'

In response, the dominatrix gestured to Miss Sanders to take off her clothes.

Alisha didn't know where to look first. The pale legs, the sweet, heart-shaped shaved pussy, the curve of the feminine belly, the nut-brown nipples that topped off Jess's appealing breasts, the neck that was partly shrouded by a curtain of neatly cut red hair ...

Such was Alisha's absorption in the vision of a naked Jess that she missed the next instruction Miss Sarah aimed at the Fables submissive, who was now plucking the condom out of Jason's tied fingers.

The rip of the condom packet brought Alisha to her

senses. A shot of panic poured through her, followed by a rush of relief. She'd been lucky; she hadn't missed an order directed at her. I must keep focused, she told herself.

'Alisha.' Miss Sarah stood behind her. She was so close that the patterned embroidery on the front of her burgundy basque buffed up against the cook's cotton-covered back. 'How did you pleasure yourself?'

'I …' The presence of Miss Sarah's chest against her back, pushing with a subtly increased pressure against her, made Alisha stumble over her words. Her cheeks burnt every shade of red as she realised she was going to have to publicly confess that she'd fucked herself off on a tube of chocolate frosting.

Miss Sarah took a step backwards, causing Alisha to instantly miss the contact. 'You were saying, Miss Alisha?'

Mumbling her words, Alisha said, 'I used a tube of icing.'

As soon as the cook had answered, Miss Sarah returned to her previous position, this time rubbing herself ever so slightly against the T-shirted back. 'And how did you move the tube once it was in place?'

'I pulled it in and out.' With the mistress behind her, Alisha felt it safe to lick her dehydrated lips, while her eyes remained fixed on the nude torsos before her. She could have sworn that Jess's tits were swelling as she watched her. The other submissive's obvious lack of shock at her confession encouraged Alisha to go on. 'I sat on the floor, with my backside exposed.'

With a hand signal that Jess knew well, Miss Sarah indicated that the condom should be rolled onto the saluting dick. 'Miss Sanders was correct in her report to me. Master Richards, you are indeed experienced. I must commend your silence and your composure.'

Rather than responding verbally, Jason bowed low, his beautiful penis vibrating with impatience. The sight caused

Alisha to speculate about what might be going on in his head.

Waving her hand in an almost regal manner, Miss Sarah indicated to Jason to sit on the nearest chair. With his arms behind his back, he had no choice but to sit at an awkward slope, his arse perched on the edge of the seat, his back at an angle so his neck was resting against the top of the chair back, and his cock stuck out at 90 degrees from his lap.

Switching from commendation to disapproval, Miss Sarah moved her attention to Alisha. 'I told all three of you *not* to wank. Miss Sanders did not. Master Richards did not. You did. Tell me, Miss Alisha, what made you think my rules do not apply to you?'

Alisha didn't know what to say. She hadn't thought that the rules didn't apply to her. She'd been so desperate to come; to have her head cleared of its clamouring for sexual release.

'Miss Sanders will sit astride Master Richards as soon as you tell us why you consider yourself above my rules. If you do not, then you won't see them perform together.'

Alisha wasn't sure why that sounded unthinkable. It was illogical. Surely having her needs withheld would be a greater punishment than being forbidden to witness the pleasure of others. Yet every cell of Alisha's brain told her she wanted to witness the solid penis disappearing inside Jess's channel.

'Truly, it wasn't that I thought the rules didn't apply to me. I was so desperate. I'm sorry.' Alisha's words came out in a rush, her shame flaming deeper in her face, but she kept her eyes on the two figures before her.

Having loosened the top two laces of her own corset, Miss Sarah grabbed hold of Alisha's hands. Placing them at the cook's sides, the dominatrix yanked off Alisha's top, then replaced the arms on top of the cook's head.

Coolly regarding Alisha's staged pose, Miss Sarah

decided that before she left The Retreat she must pass on her specialised training exercise routine to Dr Ewen. She could see this girl was willing, but as yet, her body wasn't as highly tuned as it should be. 'The removal of your top was your reward for honesty, Alisha. Learn from it!'

Walking to Alisha's side, she smiled sardonically. 'And this is your punishment for defying me.'

The inflexible cane flew onto Alisha's denim-clad backside, making her yelp as Miss Sarah pointed to Jess and Jason. 'You will watch them. No one will touch *you*. After all, you have had *your* climax today, haven't you?'

Alisha longed to protest. She wanted to yell that it wasn't fair, that she'd only sorted herself out because Miss Sarah had left her hanging. She wanted to scream that she hadn't understood the rules. But she wisely clamped her lips together, feeling the heat of frustrated need trip through her body, and unbidden tears gather at the corners of her eyes. Her chest felt as swollen as Jess's looked, and her crotch prickled with a heat that could have rivalled Miss Sarah's when she'd been laid upon the range.

'Miss Sanders, you may work yourself off on Master Richards.'

Not waiting to give her mistress the chance to change her mind, Jess straddled the sides of the chair upon which Jason sat before fixing her hands on the silent man's shoulders.

As Jess sank onto his pole, Alisha thought she could hear the sounds of relief that neither of them actually made. She wondered how badly Jason wished his hands were free so he could cup Jess's breasts as they bounced with delicious abandon, making tiny slapping sounds as they hit each other and her flesh beneath.

The hair beneath Alisha's palms felt greasy with sweat as the need to touch Jess's swaying tits began to consume her. The pictures that had danced around her psyche as she'd screwed the frosting tube in the larder taunted Alisha as the faces of her lucky companions creased up in the expression of ecstatic contemplation that only comes with having sex.

So absorbed had she been in the vision before her that the sound of Miss Sarah suddenly talking made Alisha jump. 'You will observe how charmingly Miss Sanders' breasts move when unfettered. I am sure you are also appreciating that Master Richards is doing well not to beg for me to allow his hands the freedom they want. Only a minor clenching of his fingers gives away his secret wish to hold them, to feel Miss Sanders' nipples push against his palms, to flick her tips between his teeth.' Miss Sarah paused, knowing her words would be speeding up the arrival of the climax that was about to trigger before her, as well as enflaming Alisha further. 'I suspect you'd like to do all of those things as well, wouldn't you?'

'Yes, I …' Alisha snapped her mouth shut, the realisation that she hadn't been supposed to speak catching up with her.

A smile curled one corner of Miss Sarah's mouth. 'Good girl, you're learning. You have permission to answer me.'

'I want to touch her so badly. I swear I can taste her nipples.'

Moving swiftly, the dominatrix said, 'Like this, you mean?' Undoing his hands with one tug at the T-shirt tie, Miss Sarah nodded to Jason, whose palms were on Jess's tits in less than a second.

Jealousy shot through Alisha in a tidal wave of passion that made her whole frame shake. She found she was panting, her body reacting to the voyeuristic display more violently than in all the times she'd witnessed David, Lady Tia, or Dr Ewen administering to each other.

The dominatrix continued, her voice remaining as calm as if she were a maths teacher expounding the finer points of algebra. 'And I suspect that once they are done, you'd like to lick Jason back into shape?'

'Yes, Miss Sarah.'

'And perhaps be allowed to form a threesome?'

'Yes, Miss Sarah.'

'Thank you, Miss Alisha. You may be quiet again now.'

The sound of the chair scraping against the stone floor swung Miss Sarah's attention back to the rutting couple. 'You may both come.'

A mutual cry ricocheted between those assembled as Jess increased her pace. Her thighs pumped against the chair as Jason pinched her nipples, making them pink and tight. Then, in a unified rush, they slumped together in a judder of a climax which shook the chair beneath them, and sent a sympathetic flush of juice gushing from Alisha's pussy, flooding her already wet knickers, and producing a damp patch through her jeans.

Jess and Jason hadn't finished coming when, with her expression switching from veiled approval to one that only a fool would disobey, Miss Sarah twisted abruptly towards Alisha, and barked, 'Beg!'

In that unexpected second, Alisha had no idea what she was meant to be begging for. Forgiveness for wanking? To be allowed to touch Jess's chest? To be given the chance to suck Jason back to solidity? To have a three-way fuck? The conflict of indecision on Alisha's face made it redder than ever as she flicked her eyes from face to face, frantically searching for any indication.

'I told you to *beg*, Miss Alisha. Common sense is surely telling you not to keep me waiting.' Miss Sarah's tone was quieter now, and felt infinitely more dangerous as she directed her words to Jess. 'It appears, Miss Sanders, that Miss Alisha doesn't wish to touch you after all.'

Chapter Fourteen

'NO!' THE FORCE behind her protest took Alisha by surprise, yet she found she was unable to stop her outburst from continuing. 'I didn't answer because you told me to keep quiet. I thought I'd be in trouble if I spoke. Why are you trying to trick me? David and Lady Tia never did that!'

'David Proctor and Lady Tia have consistently failed to satisfy you.'

Jess winced as Miss Sarah's reply left an aura of anger at Alisha's ingratitude in the air. There was no time for her to consider the cook's disappointing outburst, for Miss Sarah was pointing to the two piles of clothes on the floor, indicating that she and Jason should dress.

As she eased on her clothes, Jess kept one eye on her mistress, hopeful of seeing her open her corset further, while simultaneously bracing herself for a tirade of verbal abuse aimed towards Alisha.

Miss Sarah, however, rather than burst into the threatening full-on anger that Jess had feared, spoke with resolute calm. 'Of course it's a trick. But it's a trick that will help you become what you maintain you wish to become.'

Alisha, with her fingernails digging into her scalp for all they were worth, and her eyes darting between the three people before her, felt confused. She'd been so sure she wanted their help. But this wasn't help; this was a torture of inaction.

'Miss Alisha, you may take your arms down.' Miss Sarah continued in her no-nonsense manner. 'Miss Sanders, Master Richards, you will dress and report to Dr Ewen's study. She requires your help in getting this facility ready for the party.'

Only the sound of the door to the conference room closing told Alisha that she was now alone with Miss Sarah.

As she obeyed the dominatrix's instructions, every muscle in Alisha's arms creaked as they were lowered into a more natural position. Managing to resist the temptation to rub them better, Alisha kept her eyes on the mistress's semi-open basque, her thoughts racing in ever-decreasing circles. Were they helping her or not? Or was this how they got their kicks? Did they really want The Retreat to fail so Fables' reputation for being the best was kept intact? Or perhaps this really was how she could learn to let go? She couldn't deny that trepidation at what would happen to her at Miss Sarah's hand if she'd climaxed alongside Jess and Jason had stopped her from allowing the sodden presence of her panties against her clit to send her into a lower level of bliss alongside them. Not her inability to let go.

Breaking through the cook's conflicting thoughts, Miss Sarah asked, 'Am I correct in assuming you would like to undo the remainder of my corset for me, Miss Alisha?'

Wrong-footed, she decided that trying to second guess what she was supposed to say was pointless. The dominatrix seemed to have decided what the correct answers to her own questions were anyway, so Alisha thought she might as well be honest in the hope that she would at least be respected for that. 'Yes, ma'am.'

'The party for David's special guests is only days away. It is supremely important for the future of this establishment that you perform well. Because of that, and most certainly *not* because you deserve it, I will allow you to unfasten my corset. It is important to your training that you can carry out this simple task without error.'

Alisha hadn't considered that there could be a wrong way to unlace a corset in the quest to reach the chest beneath. But now, as she approached Miss Sarah, what had felt like a minor victory became a minefield of potential disaster.

The older woman smelt of expensive moisturiser and sex; Alisha trembled as she reached out to the thin ties. The feline glare to Miss Sarah's eyes as she peered down her nose robbed Alisha of her last ounce of confidence as she started to undo the corset with clumsy fingers.

As Alisha brought the dominatrix's porcelain tits slowly into view, Miss Sarah explained some of what lay ahead. 'During the party you will be expected to serve a large number of people, whether you find them attractive or not. Sometimes you may have to help more than one guest at a time. Obviously the requirements of sexual health will be observed, and every male will be issued with condoms on arrival. Beyond that, you will do whatever is asked of you.

'It is very important that The Retreat impresses this first delegation of visitors, or Mr Proctor will lose a very important contract for his PR business, as well as a steady supply of trade for Dr Ewen.'

The corset was only hanging together by one looped tie now, and Alisha's pupils dilated wider as she visually devoured the small round globes before her. Delicate yet firm, and just ripe for exploration.

'I would like you to pretend I'm one of the party guests, Miss Alisha. I have ordered you to pleasure my breasts. You are only to use your tongue. You are not to come yourself. Show me how you would do this.'

Diving forward, Alisha planted her hands beneath Miss Sarah's breasts, supporting their pleasing weight as she wrapped her tongue around the right nipple.

Disguising her mew of delight at the gentle touch with a tut of annoyance, Miss Sarah said, 'I said your mouth only, yet you have your palms upon my flesh.'

The cook clasped her hands behind her back, not willing to risk accidentally disobeying further.

Miss Sarah's chest tasted divine; her china skin was in stark contrast to Lady Tia's in every possible way. With each lap and pinch of the almond nipples, Alisha wanted to be able to feel the flesh beneath her fingertips as well as in her mouth. She was shocked by the strength of this sensory deprivation.

The only indication Alisha had that Miss Sarah appreciated what she was doing to her was the continuing tautness of her breasts. No sound came from her mouth, nor was there any discernible increase or alternation in her breathing, but Alisha didn't dare stop. She didn't want to stop.

Her head spun with images of Miss Sarah sat next to Lady Tia; both naked, one chocolate tit jammed up next to one creamy tit, while her tongue switched from one to the other. Her imagination savoured the would-be flavours, textures, and taste of each woman as she visualised them ordering her to bring them off, both pleading with her to rub their clits as she feasted on their tits, repeating over and over again that she was the best submissive they'd worked with, both saying …

'Miss Alisha!' Miss Sarah's voice bristled with sharp edges. 'I told you to stop. What hope have you in fulfilling this role if your concentration is so easily fractured?'

Dropping the mistress's right tit from her lips with extreme reluctance, Alisha lowered her eyes to the floor. She couldn't believe she'd let her mind wander like that, but it had all felt so good.

'If you get carried away by your own fantasies then this is never going to happen for you.' The dominatrix brought her face so close to Alisha's that for a moment the cook thought the woman was going to kiss her, and felt a stab of disappointment when she found that this was not to be the case.

To her surprise, Miss Sarah whispered to her instead, 'Keep your face neutral while I speak, for I am not supposed to tell you this.' Muffling her speech by nipping Alisha's neck with the tiniest of nerve-sparking bites, Miss Sarah walked slowly forward as she muttered, 'If you don't perform well at the party, Alisha, you are to be dismissed, and Miss Sanders will be kept here in your place.' She grazed Alisha's neck again, impressed by how little visual reaction the cook gave, although she could feel the increase in her anxiety through her pulse rate.

Enjoying the gentle nibble against her neck, allowing herself to be forced against the tapestry-covered wall as Miss Sarah coerced her into moving, Alisha hissed out her concern. 'I don't want to leave here.'

'I know.' Continuing to smother Alisha's body with her own, taking a private thrill from the heat of the hungry form against hers, Miss Sarah unhooked the girl's bra, and tapped the ends of her nipples with steady slaps of her fingertips.

Alisha gasped, her eyes blazed, and her pussy spasmed uncontrollably. She didn't dare speak in case the words that came out were pleas for a climax that would make Miss Sarah cross and therefore stop what she was doing.

'And I want Miss Sanders to come home with me. She belongs at Fables.'

'And you love her.'

This time the words left Alisha's mouth before she'd stopped to think about what she was saying. The smack that flew towards her chest as Miss Sarah magically produced her cane from her boot, swinging it across both teats in quick succession, was more agonising in its precision than anything Lady Tia had ever administered.

175

Gasping, automatically reaching up to protect her nipples, Alisha found herself again sandwiched between Miss Sarah and the wall.

'Miss Sanders is my submissive. I have the utmost respect for her and her abilities. She is ten times the sub you will ever be. Our relationship is based on professional understanding. Yes?'

Alisha's reply came out in a hasty squeak. 'Yes, Miss Sarah.'

Standing back, Miss Sarah rapped the cane again, but more lightly this time, landing it between Alisha's nipples. 'You have adequately proved you can take pain. Lady Tia's training in that area cannot be faulted. And you like it don't you. The pain?'

'Yes, ma'am.' The words were barely a whisper.

'But pain alone is not enough, is it?'

'No, ma'am.' Alisha's brain tried to grab hold of that fact. It was obvious. That had been the problem. For Lady Tia it was enough – but not for her. Although Alisha knew she loved the bloom of a smack, the heady ache of a strike to her backside as it spread to her pussy via every nerve in her body, she needed something more. Only now did she see that, for her at least, discomfort was only half of her sexual requirements.

'Beg, Miss Alisha. Beg me now.'

This time there was no hesitation. Pleading words flew from Alisha's mouth. 'Please let me come, Miss Sarah, please! I'm sorry I failed before. Please hit me again!' Her words became punctuated by anguished pants. 'Please let me fuck you, please touch my pussy, please kiss me while it hurts, please ….'

A carefully regulated hit of success fluttered through Miss Sarah as, with a rapid jerk of her knee, she pressed the girl's mound hard through her sodden denims while pushing her palms over Alisha's naked, freckle-spotted breasts.

The strength of her orgasm made Alisha gasp as she cried out her coming, tears of liberation streaming down her face. 'Thank you, thank you, ma'am, thank you, thank you … I …'

As Alisha's limbs sagged into the warm limpness of accomplishment, Miss Sarah pulled away, her thrusting hands becoming supporting ones, as she steered the cook to the table so she could lean against it.

'You will return here at 10 o'clock tomorrow morning, and again at 2 o'clock tomorrow afternoon, and then at the same times every day until the party. In between, you will see to the list of tasks I am sure require your culinary talents. You will not indulge in any solo pleasure, whether in the larder or elsewhere. Understood?'

'Yes, Miss Sarah.'

Lacing up her corset, the dominatrix added, 'In addition to your self-restraint, a toughening of your stamina is required.'

Alisha's imagination was already jammed with a host of impossible scenarios that Miss Sarah might have planned. She swallowed hard.

'Walk this way, please.' Miss Sarah approached the nearest granite pillar, and stroked the cool surface.

Already confident she knew what was about to happen, Alisha felt her skin bump with apprehension, but kept her mouth closed.

'I have no doubt you've been secured to a post such as this before. Yes?'

'Three times, Miss Sarah.'

'And each time you were spanked until you almost climaxed, but then did not?'

Her eyes dipped to her feet in shame. 'That is correct, Miss Sarah.'

'And the weapons used were …?'

'David used his hands and a paddle. Lady Tia favoured a cane or a whip on these occasions; usually she only uses me when she needs to practise with any new toys she may have. Dr Ewen has only watched me against the pillar; not joined in.' The memory of her deliciously enticing past experiences, giving her the stimulation of pain she so enjoyed, yet stopping short of gratification, made Alisha both re-aroused and defeatist.

'Were more gentle applications of pressure and stimulation used in conjunction with those tools? Kisses, strokes of the fingertips, the brushing of the palms over the nipples?'

The cat-like purr vibrating through those words was enough to push Alisha from thinking another climax was merely desirable to it being essential. Careful to keep as much of her craving from her voice as possible, she replied, 'No Miss Sarah, none.'

'I see.' Circling the post, Miss Sarah came to a snap decision. 'Remove all your garments.'

Alisha swiftly did as she was told.

'Umm ... you have a good overall shape. Slim, but curvy. My manageress at Fables, Mrs Peters, would be impressed.'

Not sure if she was supposed to say thank you for this compliment or not, Alisha remained quiet.

Deep in thought, the dominatrix continued to pace around the cook and the post. Finally she came to a decision. 'You will stand with your back to the pillar. Make sure your feet are together, and your buttocks are firmly against the stone.'

Alisha backed herself onto the cool stone column, wondering if Miss Sarah kept cuffs or other restraints along with her cane and condoms in her thigh-high boots. Clenching her backside as it hit the aged granite, she adjusted her stance so that her ankles rubbed together, and her heels touched the pillar.

'Excellent.' Miss Sarah reached for Alisha's right arm, but rather than wrap it around the back of the stone cylinder as she had expected, she examined the watch strapped around her wrist. 'A fine timepiece. I suspect the stopwatch setting is essential for making sure your cakes do not overcook in the range.'

'Yes.' Alisha was confused. 'I use it all the time.'

Taking the watch from the girl's wrist, Miss Sarah laid it two inches in front of her bare feet. 'Bend at the waist, touch your toes, and let your fingertips brush the floor either side of the watch.'

Gulping, not sure she'd be able to hold the position for more than a few seconds, Alisha did as she was bidden. Her hair flopped over her shoulders, forming a curtain through which she could only just see the face of the watch.

'Good.' Miss Sarah sat cross-legged in front of the trainee submissive. 'I'm setting the stopwatch to run for 60 seconds. Once it has reached zero, you may stand.'

Wishing that she had taken more time to exercise in the past so she didn't feel the strain in her arms and thighs already, Alisha didn't waste breath replying, but fixed her eyes on the countdown.

'And zero. You may stand.'

Rising slowly, aware that the blood had rushed to her head, Alisha was about to ask why that had been necessary. Miss Sarah stopped her query in its tracks by placing the flat of her hand against her pussy.

'Before each and every session, you will place your watch where it is now, and repeat that exercise.' Miss Sarah gently compressed the handful of mound, making Alisha's lips part with the intense pleasure. 'With each bend you will add an additional 30 seconds to the time you spend in that position.'

Alisha groaned out loud, but only partly at the prospect of having to repeat the exercise so often and for so long, for Miss Sarah's free hand was stroking her hair while she continued to flex her grip over her pussy.

'When training Miss Sanders, I found a regular, invigorating keep fit routine improved her stamina and the capacity to put off her climax without it losing any of its intensity. '

Nodding, unable to speak, she blew tiny pants from her lips. Alisha's chest rose and fell of its own accord as the digits resting on her pussy began to treat it like a drum.

'Once we have finished our training each day, you will repeat your bending stretch, but for only 30 seconds.' Miss Sarah moved her hand so that a fingertip hovered over the top of Alisha's clit. 'It will be at that point that I decide if you have earned a climax or not.'

Thrusting one finger onto the girl's erect nub, Miss Sarah gave a half smile as Alisha bucked between her hand and the solid pillar behind her. Her head thrown back, Alisha's eyes slammed shut as her forehead creased in ecstasy.

The moment Alisha had stilled, Miss Sarah slipped a hand to her elbow to help support her while the world stopped spinning. As she waited for the girl to recover herself enough to move, Miss Sarah spoke, her tone deadly serious.

'If you continue to do as I say, Miss Alisha, there is a chance you will make Proctor happy enough to make sure he keeps you on. If not, he will try to keep Miss Sanders. That would make me very unhappy. And that, I have to tell you, is not something I would advise anybody to do.'

Chapter Fifteen

WITH THE PARTY only 24 hours away, David stood with Dr Ewen in her study, leaning over the laptop on her desk. He looked stunned as he watched the live action of Alisha's final training session with Miss Sarah via the webcam. 'I'm not sure I believe what I'm seeing. It could be fixed.'

Alisha stood, naked and unbound, against the picture windows. For the past ten minutes David had observed her budding arousal as Miss Sarah tickled the underside of Alisha's tits with a dyed pink feather.

The girl, although her body occasionally quivered with the build-up of desire, did everything that was asked of her. When the dominatrix told her to stand upright, David could see the liquid that had wept from her vagina glisten against her bare thighs. His eyes widened as, with the words "you my come now", and a soft, glancing touch to the girl's clit, Miss Sarah produced a climax from Alisha exactly on cue.

Dr Ewen, who wasn't sure if she should feel vindicated or annoyed by the fact that Miss Sarah had achieved so much so quickly with Alisha, when Lady Tia had not, knew this was not the time to mince her words. 'Of course it isn't fixed, man! You saw the evidence with your own eyes. In only a few days, Alisha has been taught more self-restraint, control, and patience than I would have thought possible.'

Crossing her arms, Elena studied David carefully before adding, 'You did want Alisha brought up to speed, didn't you?'

Proctor didn't reply for a moment, rubbing a hand over his chin. '*I* did, yes.'

Picking up on the inflection, Dr Ewen asked, 'But someone else did not?'

'All I can say is a discussion with a representative from Fairtasia has revealed them to be less than impressed with Alisha. She has been pretty much written off as a viable proposition when it comes to working as anything but a cook within The Retreat.'

Taking in a sharp breath, the manageress perched on the edge of her desk. 'And this representative is?'

'Influential.' David spoke the word with a finality that clearly stated no further questions should be asked. Dr Ewen ignored the implication.

'And your representative would rather have Miss Sanders here for the party and beyond, should they patronise The Retreat again?'

'Let's just say that to help me secure the contract from Fairtasia, Alisha will have to do better than that, for a hell of a lot longer than that, on Saturday night.' Concern wrinkled David's face. 'Tell me honestly, doctor, do you think she has what it takes?'

Tilting her head to one side, exposing Proctor to one of her most critical stares, Dr Ewen said, 'I regret that I allowed Lady Tia to undertake her training when you first told me of her request to join the entertainment staff. If I had trained the girl personally we would have an able and obedient submissive by now. One every bit as good as any creature Laura Peters could produce.'

David didn't demand why that hadn't happened. He knew why. He'd handed Alisha over to Lady Tia, and made it very clear that she would be the one to train the girl up. After all, Lady Tia had taught Master Richards to perfection. But then he was a natural slave, whereas Alisha thought too much. She had an imagination and a constant stream of queries running around her head. David was struck with how similar to Jess Sanders that made her. 'Even if Alisha does pull off a miracle and impress everyone, I remain reluctant to allow Miss Sanders to return home. She would be an asset here.'

'So, your representative from Fairtasia does prefer Miss Sanders, then?'

Not bothering to argue, David lowered his eyes to the laptop screen. The camera now showed Alisha on her way to her room, presumably to shower and change. He felt his cock stir in his trousers. There was something about that girl. He wished it didn't feel quite so dangerous.

Elena nodded to herself, before bravely stating the obvious. 'You know why you are so undecided about Alisha being our submissive, don't you?'

David raised his chin, challenging the manageress not to utter the words he could see preparing themselves on her lips.

'I know you don't want me to say this, but until someone does this issue is going to continue to go around in ridiculous, time-wasting circles. And, as you have frequently made clear, we don't have time to waste if we are going to impress these demanding clients of yours.'

'I strongly advise you ...'

Dr Ewen had had enough. Hands on her hips, she pushed David into her chair and spoke down to him. 'No, Mr Proctor, I strongly advise you! You took over this business; my business. It was successful, and I had many contented clients. Then you swept in and suddenly the cook is offered a promotion to a sexually demanding job she didn't have the skills for; although now I suspect she does. Don't you dare blame anyone else for the fact that we are not ready for this weekend. You set the date. You have been relying on a girl you've fallen for. And plainly,

183

even if only subconsciously on your own radar, you are unsure if you can bear to share her. You're …'

'Enough!' David didn't shout, but the word was all the more menacing for it. 'Go fetch Miss Sanders.'

'I beg your pardon!'

'I said go fetch Miss Sanders.' As he stretched himself up to his full height, which left him a head shorter than Dr Ewen, David's thunderous expression made up for his lack of stately presence. 'As you said, I am your employer. Bring her into the entrance hall. I will meet you there.'

Pausing, Elena moved away from him. 'You can get Lady Tia to do that.' Then she walked to her study door, and remaining inside the room with David, twisted the key, locking them inside.

'Before you leave, you are going to tell me the agenda here. *The real agenda.* What do you really want for Alisha? Because I am beginning to think you don't want her trained at all. And, more importantly, what exactly do Fairtasia want with The Retreat?' Elena gripped the key in her hand, and pressed her back against the door, every inch of her showing she had the patience to stand there her entire life if she had to. 'Until you tell me the entire agenda, we are going nowhere.'

'How dare …'

Dr Ewen broke in before David had the chance to explode. 'You may own my business now, but I think you are forgetting that I *am* the manager here, *and* how well I know you, David Proctor. Now talk.'

'This is a strap and harness suit, Miss Sanders. Have you ever worn one?'

'No, Lady Tia.'

'And there I was being led to believe that you were a perfect submissive! If you aren't familiar with life in a strap suit, I can't see how that can be the case.'

Coated in a fine layer of flour from where she'd been

helping Alisha catch up on her cooking duties prior to the party, Jess fought to calm her ever-alert body. Standing in the centre of the castle's entrance hall, she saw that the tartan-clad furniture had already been moved to the sides of the room in preparation.

Keeping the thought that Lady Tia was surely experiencing a helping of sour grapes to herself, Jess watched as the large dominatrix gestured to the ever-mute Jason to help her untangle a collection of rope coils.

The only other person present was David. Covertly glancing at his face from her lowered gaze, Jess felt a confusion of emotions. She was partly relieved that he'd stopped pretending to be nice, and was back to the honestly unpleasant man she knew from life at Fables. The rest of her was fizzing with apprehension. If David had dreamt up what was about to happen, the chances were that it would test her to the extreme.

No one had spoken yet. Jason stepped forward, lifting Jess's breasts so that Lady Tia could slip a thick hemp ring around each of them. Then, coming up behind Jess, David attached some shoulder straps to the growing harness. Securing a single rope from the top of the right breast loop, he ran it under her right arm, around Jess's back, over her left shoulder, and under her other arm, before attaching it to the underside of her encased left tit.

As more skeins of rope were produced, Jess saw that it wasn't only her upper body that was going to be suited. An inflexible rope figure of eight was passed over her feet, and shoved up her legs. The knotted cross in the centre of the shape was placed over her clit, so Jess's legs were kept a fixed distance apart, while keeping her continually stimulated.

Threading one of the leads from the front of Jess's right leg hoop up to the base of the right tit loop, Jason then copied the movement on her left side. Moving behind her, Jason did the same there, running both rope strips over her buttocks, so the chafe of the rough hemp irritated Jess's rump.

'Now, here comes the clever bit.' Lady Tia held up eight much longer straps, leather this time, which she again passed to Jason.

Jess felt his fingers deftly working at the backs of her legs, before Jason came to her front, and knotted a further strap under each breast, two more around each wrist, and the final two at each of Jess's ankles.

Her pulse thudded so loudly, as Jess saw what they'd done to her, that she was sure it was audible.

Telling Jason to keep hold of the leather straps attached to the rear of Jess's legs and go and stand behind the bound submissive, Lady Tia gathered up the remaining hanging leads. 'As I am sure you have worked out, Miss Sanders, you are now no more than our puppet. Allow us to demonstrate.'

Passing the leads that had been fastened to Jess's right-hand side to David, Lady Tia kept the left-hand leads to herself. 'David, if you would?'

'Certainly.' With barely a movement on his behalf, David tugged the strap fixed to Jess's right leg.

'Oh!' Jess couldn't prevent the exclamation that blurted from her lips as the rope figure of eight was jerked towards David a fraction, making her take a small step that stretched her legs and caused the rope to dig into her upper thighs.

Copying the gesture on the left side, Lady Tia hauled on the front leg rope, widening Jess's stance further and opening her pussy to any attention they should decide to inflict upon it.

As Jess was taking in what was happening to her, Lady Tia spoke, her voice like treacle, 'You make a very pretty marionette, Miss Sanders. A mannequin on a string.' To emphasise her point, she jerked one of the leather lengths fastened beneath Jess's chest, making her gasp anew as the delicate underside of her globe was lifted and exposed.

She wasn't physically bound to anything, and yet Jess had never felt so imprisoned or helpless.

Wrapping the strap tied around Jess's left wrist around her hand, Lady Tia smiled as she moved her hand here and there, watching Jess's arm dance in any direction she liked. Then the dominatrix sedately walked from left to right, so that Jess's arm swayed back and forth, as if she really was a puppet.

'If you recall, Miss Sanders –' Lady Tia's smile left her eyes, lingering only on her pouting lips '– I owe you a punishment from your lapse in the turret room.'

Jess looked blank. Surely whatever she'd done to displease on that occasion had been equalled out with the tape measure chastisement?

'Do you want me to show you how much of a Wicked Queen I can be, Miss Sanders?'

Jess groaned. She'd forgotten about her accidental slip of her tongue when Lady Tia had been testing Miss Sarah against the mirror. The slight twinge of apprehension that had been accelerating up through her nervous system as she spotted the other object Lady Tia brandished in her hand moved into top gear.

The older woman was holding the glass dildo and pocket vibrator that Jess had added to her luggage before leaving her room at Fables. It appeared Miss Sarah's suspicions had been correct; their possessions had been searched.

'What could we possibly do with these? How thoughtful of you to bring me new toys to play with. I'm sure Alisha will have told you how much fun I get from testing fresh equipment.'

'Perhaps we should see how powerful the battery is in the vibrator.' David spoke lazily, as if he had every intention of this show going on for a very long time. 'I wouldn't be surprised if the little tart has worn it right down.'

'An excellent suggestion.' Lady Tia, towing Jess's arm with her as she moved, yanked on the tit harness. She lifted Jess's breast, which had already begun to swell beyond its confines, so that the hemp chafed and cut into her flesh. Then, clicking on the switch, the dominatrix ran the buzzing tip of the two-inch long cylinder across the undersides of Jess's left tit.

Gritting her teeth, desperately trying to deflect the feeling that she was being wanked by a lump of rope while her chest was caressed to a point beyond comfortable stimulation, Jess tucked her fingers into the palms of her hands.

'It looks as if the battery was recently replaced. Still plenty of zip in it.' David pulled out a wooden chair, and sat, dragging Jess's right arm with him. 'Let's see if we can discover how long it might last.'

Jess's heart sank. She'd only replaced the battery the day before her unexpected trip, and, as ever, had used one of the more expensive, long-lasting brands. Unless anyone else had tried it out since it was stolen from her possessions then it would have an awful lot of life left in it yet.

'Jason.' Lady Tia said no more to the man behind Jess. He'd obviously already been told what to do. Maintaining a steady pressure, he tugged the straps attached to the back of Jess's legs up and out, so the figure of eight shifted position again, scraping her clit and tightening the straps that ran across her buttocks.

Thankful she hadn't been instructed to keep quiet; Jess vented a gust of contained air through her parted lips. Both the physical and mental upper hand was theirs, and she knew it. What was worse, Jess knew they realised it too. Already, even at this early stage of their fun, the best she could do for her reputation was damage limitation. Only one more swipe of pressure between her legs, and she knew she'd come. She wasn't sure if she longed for it to happen, or if she dreaded the consequences of its inevitability.

'Keep the lines at her back rigid, Jason.' Lady Tia, keeping the vibrator running over the base of Jess's large bust, swapped her attention to the other side. 'Perhaps pull a little harder, David. I'd like to give her right tit the attention it deserves.'

Surprised by how physically tired she was already, Jess wondered where Miss Sarah was, and if she was aware of what was happening to her. Wishing she'd been allowed to lean against something for support, she felt her balance began to suffer from her body being drawn in so many different directions at once. She knew she could either focus on staying on her feet or deferring her orgasm for as long as possible, but not on both.

Lady Tia, while running the bullet vibrator over Jess's wobbling breasts, lifted the glass dildo, along with the leather straps she held in the same hand. It caused Jess's arm to move again, and her body to feel as if she would overbalance at any moment. 'You have excellent taste in toys for one so menial.'

Raising the ribbed, gently curved glass cylinder to the light, Lady Tia asked David, 'Front or back? This beauty could plug her safely in either orifice.'

Jess, fighting the temptation to close her eyes, found she was mentally chanting her mantra faster and faster. *Do Fables and yourself proud. Do Fables and yourself proud.*

Lady Tia was now standing so close to Jess that her black, crystal-encrusted basque was adding to the irritating stimulation already caused by the rough rope. As the dominatrix lowered the arm holding the dildo, and thus Jess's arm as well, she forced another gasp of frustrated discomfort from the imprisoned submissive.

'She is making an awful lot of noise; perhaps the dildo should go in her mouth?' David shuffled his chair a few inches nearer to the now swaying Jess, and pulled her arm lower so that her hand had no choice but to land over his trouser-encased cock.

'True.' Lady Tia's voice was laced with sarcasm. 'You would expect, after the high level of training she received, that we'd be guaranteed silence. I mean, Jason isn't making a sound, is he?'

He isn't trussed like something out of a Hammer horror movie, though, is he? Jess thought to herself, as she took advantage of David placing her hand where it could work him off to support some of her weight.

Lady Tia drove the vibrator deeper against Jess's globe, making the submissive yearn for her to shift it up and over her tenderly stiff nipples, 'I am quite enjoying the grunting coming from Miss Sanders. She sounds not unlike one of the three little pigs waiting for their house to be blown down.'

First fairy tales, now a bloody nursery story.

Round blotches were being left on the undersides of Jess's tits as Lady Tia pressed the vibe so hard that the head couldn't properly rotate. For a moment, Jess dared to hope the battery had already run low. But then Lady Tia eased the toy away for a second, and its motor whined out as loudly as before.

The sound of a zip came as no surprise to Jess, as her hand was taken via its lead and replaced over David's now freed dick. Grasping it firmly, she was gratified to hear a small wince from Proctor as she pinched him.

Pride prevented him from admitting she'd caused him pain. Instead he snapped out, 'Wedge the vibrator in the harness. Time to see how much Mrs Peters' dream submissive can really take.'

Dots of perspiration on Jess's forehead graduated to drips of sweat as Lady Tia hauled at the hoop of rope around her right breast. By pushing the sensitive flesh of Jess's abused tit, while pulling at the hemp, the dominatrix wriggled the short pink vibe between the two.

The rope harness cut against her shoulders as the juddering dildo was trapped in place. It misshaped Jess's tit as the plastic thrummed relentlessly against it; vibrations continued to shudder through her hypersensitive flesh.

Jess's breathing came in short, sharp bursts as the harness was pulled harder still. She couldn't have called out for the climax she had to have even if she'd wanted to.

'Looking good, Miss Sanders.' David levered the piece of leather that operated Jess's left wrist, so that her exhausted arm had no choice but to move up and down his length.

Jess tried to grab him, to move her hand of her own free will over his cock, knowing that would feel better for him, and give her at least a modicum of control. Proctor, however, was relishing treating Jess as if she was a rag doll too much to relinquish any power to her, and continued to flap her palm on and off his straining tip in teasingly haphazard fashion.

The pressure from the leads attached to the back of Jess had remained so constant that she'd temporarily forgotten about Jason's role in Proctor's game. A situation Lady Tia remedied with her next instruction.

'I require a climax, Master Richards. Come here. Do not let go of the straps.'

Jess told herself sternly that her extreme craving for an orgasm was ridiculous. The only sexual contact she'd had was an occasional touch of David's dick, and a lump of jumping plastic. Although she could not deny that lump of plastic was sending a constant current of rippling lust through her swollen chest.

It was the helplessness of her situation that was causing her juice to pour from her pussy as if she'd sprung a leak. The idea that this group of sex-hungry voyeurs could take any part of her and do anything they liked to it aroused her far more than it frightened her, and once again Jess knew there was no way she could live any other life than that of a submissive.

Her need to rest her aching arms and legs, which might as well have been shackled with chains such was her inability to move them, was rising as fast as her desire to come. She watched with helpless envy as Jason, still with a strap in each hand, knelt to remove the panties Lady Tia wore. As he knelt, Jess's legs had no choice but to shuffle with him, her lower limbs echoing his stripping of the older woman.

Then, on an unspoken instruction from Lady Tia, Jason shot his hands forward to his mistress's ankles.

Jess screamed.

The act of thrusting his hands in that direction had levered the figure of eight around Jess's crotch, so that the knot tilted roughly over her clit. With the vibrator's wobble relentless in her chest, her nipples were desperate for attention. Jess couldn't help but strain against the hold of the leather straps, fighting to be able to touch her tits as her orgasm spasmed up from her numb toes to the top of her head.

'Feisty, isn't she?' David's tone was more amused than cross that Jess had come without his permission. 'I must commend you, Lady Tia. This is a fascinating experiment. I've never seen a harness used in this way before.'

Her voice a trifle huskier than it had been, as Jason continued to lick her out, Lady Tia replied, 'Thank you, David. I often employed the harness and strap suit in this way when I was working in London. I generally attached my guest to a table, a bedpost, or some other handy upright structure. But I wanted to keep this creature suspended, and yet keep her on the ground helpless, with no choice but to have as many or as few climaxes as we see fit ...' Lady Tia adjusted her own position, giving Jason greater access to her pussy. 'I think this may be a technique we should refine and repeat.'

'Agreed.' David, who hadn't stopped moving the leather strap attached to Jess's wrist, keeping up his insubstantial handjob, added, 'Although, as we can see from Miss Sanders, it is evidently a demanding challenge. We've hardly touched her, and she's a mess. Look at the shake in her knees!'

Jess, dividing her concentration between trying not to listen to the delicious sound of another woman being tongued, and making sure her fast-weakening legs didn't give way, grunted with the effort of staying on her feet.

With a barely detectable jolt, Lady Tia puffed out an efficient climax, before saying calmly, 'Enough, Jason. Excellent technique.'

Rounding on Jess, she added, 'That, Miss Sanders, is as much fuss as I will tolerate from the staff of The Retreat. Please take note of that for the future. The noise and drama you create really isn't professional.'

With no spare energy, and far too much common sense to allow Lady Tia's comment to goad her, Jess closed her eyes. She wasn't sure if she was allowed to or not, but at that moment she didn't care. Chances were her companions wouldn't even notice, as her head was still bent, her hair shading her glazed eyes. She needed the dark, the chance to focus on anything but the hot darts pulsing through her chest as the wedged vibrator powered on and on. Whatever game they were playing wasn't over yet. She glanced up to see Lady Tia was holding her glass dildo.

Jess hadn't heard Jason return to his place behind her, but the haul of the straps as the now sodden mass of rope at her clit scraped her again told her this had to be the case. As irritating as it was rousing, the mini shot of a second climax rippled up through her, and sent her crashing to her knees.

She had expected an outcry as her hand was ripped

away from David's cock and the other leapt from Lady Tia's clutches, the heaviness of the fall tearing the leather from their grasp. With a yell, Jess landed awkwardly, the drag at her chest increasing.

She was sore and panting with tension, but the vibrator finally felt as if it was beginning to lose a little momentum. With her head cradled in her arms, and her knees resting against the floor, their width still restricted, Jess only just managed to prevent herself from collapsing completely to the flagstones.

Blood thudded in her ears, wrists, and neck. Every nerve, every pressure point, every blood vessel in her body felt alive and on edge. Her whole being was poised. But Jess wasn't sure what it was poised for. More pleasure? More torture? Or was this really an experimental session, and The Retreat staff were making it up as they went along, with her playing the part of their guinea pig?

The wait didn't last long. Abruptly a feeling of lightness engulfed Jess as all the straps were dropped at once; but there was to be no rest for the submissive. David was already at her head, pushing Jess onto her hands and knees, his hands gripping either side of her face. 'Open.'

As his cock slid inside her mouth, Jess was more relieved than dismayed by its presence, its precome bringing some welcome lubrication to her dehydrated lips and throat.

Moving himself back and forth at the hips, David signalled to Lady Tia. 'Now!' In one co-ordinated move, her inch-thick glass dildo was thrust into her slick channel, while the firm hand of Lady Tia pushed the hemp knot firmly over Jess's clit. With the vibrator more whimpering than buzzing, still imprisoned at her right tit, Jess felt as if her entire being had been hotwired. Her cries of agonised bliss morphed into sobs as David shot his seed down her throat. A swell of unstoppable fatigue washing over her, Jess slid, unhindered, to the floor.

Chapter Sixteen

THE FIRST THING Jess noticed was that she wasn't in the room she'd been sharing with Miss Sarah. The second was the throb of her chest, the nerves of which hummed as if the vibrator remained in place.

Easing herself up onto her side, she registered that she was lying on the camp bed mattress that had been previously placed at the foot of Miss Sarah's bed. Jess's eyes took in the floor to ceiling maroon velvet curtains, the small desk and chair, and the curve of the walls. She was back in the turret, exactly where she'd started.

Clutching the blanket that had been thrown over her naked body, Jess headed to the curtain that hid the huge circular mirror, so she could assess the extent of the damage.

With a sweep of the drape, she exhaled the breath she'd been holding in. The mirror was gone. Not envying whoever had been tasked with removing the vast piece of polished glass, Jess didn't want to think why it was missing, but assumed it had something to do with the forthcoming party.

Ducking through the low doorway into the tiny en suite, Jess squinted against the brightness of the modern lighting after days of being accustomed to the semi-dimness of the castle. The small, square mirror over the sink revealed to her in glorious Technicolor the fast yellowing bruises that surrounded each breast, wrist, and the tops of her legs. These marks, although dark, were of the type that Jess knew would fade in a few hours. They were also completely insignificant when compared to the rectangular bruise on the lower portion of her right tit, which had captured the precise contours of her pocket sex toy.

A little shaky, Jess guided herself into the shower. As steam filled the shower cubicle, she tried to take stock of the situation. She could remember sinking to her knees and being double fucked by David and her dildo courtesy of Lady Tia, but after that it was a blur. Jess had vague memories of being picked up, but she couldn't recall being carried here. Closing her eyes against the water, letting it run through her hair and across her face, she tried to get a grasp on time.

She'd been in the kitchen, baking dozens of ginger twist finger biscuits for Alisha, when the call had come for her to go to the hallway. That had been at almost five o'clock yesterday afternoon. So how long was I with them in the rope suit, she wondered. Have I really slept all night and into the next day?

It hit Jess with a jolt that the party was today. Tonight! How on earth could she cope with the prospect of entertaining multiple guests so soon after what they'd put her through?

'Of course,' she muttered to herself, 'that's the point, isn't it? Lady Tia would love for the Fables girls to fail in the eyes of the Fairtasia delegates.' Squaring her shoulders, Jess immediately winced as her muscles cracked. 'Well, Wicked Queen, I think you'll find Miss Sarah and I don't give in that easily!'

Wondering again where Miss Sarah was, hoping she was employed in helping to arrange events, and not being put through her own brand of torture, Jess switched off the shower and wrapped herself in a towel.

Looking around the turret more carefully, she saw that

a tray holding a flask of tea and some scones had been left for her. Her holdall had been placed by the door, and her boots, and yesterday's clothing was heaped next to it. But Jess couldn't see any written instructions on the desk, and no note had been popped under the door.

Taking a welcome gulp of tea and a mouthful of scone, Jess dressed with care. Avoiding wearing a bra, and picking a thong rather than knickers, whose hem would only irritate the bruises on her thighs, she covered herself in the oversized T-shirt, a chunky jumper, and loose fit denims. Taking a deep breath, she approached the door.

It was locked.

Knowing there was a good chance that she was being watched, Jess sat herself back on the edge of the camp bed. Talking to herself, she stood up again. 'First, assuming that I am now to live here, I'll sort out my clothes, and then I'll make the most of my confinement and rest. I have a feeling I'm going to need as much as I can get.'

Nibbling a scone as she moved, Jess carried her fallen boots to the side of the desk. As she placed the right boot on the floor, her eye caught sight of an item inside.

Instinct telling her that this was something she was supposed to see, but that anyone who might be observing her on the webcam should not, Jess pulled out the desk chair and sat down. Then, taking a tissue from the box on the desk, she lifted the right boot up as if to polish it with the paper cloth. Holding the boot so the top was hidden beneath the desk top, Jess eased out the paper and slipped it, unseen, into her pocket. Continuing to buff the footwear with her makeshift cloth, Jess drank the remainder of her tea and lifted her holdall to the bed. Unable to hang on any longer, she headed to the bathroom, and shut the door behind her.

Furtively, Jess unfolded the crisp piece of cream paper, apprehension making her fingers tremble. Her heart pounded as she read.

Dear Miss Sanders,

Your fears were well founded. Unless Alisha impresses at the party, they intend to keep you here.

They will tell you Mrs Peters doesn't want you back. It is a lie.

Whatever happens – now more than ever – do not trust them.

I have placed a book with your clothing. Read it.

I look forward to us being back at Fables where we will improve our exercise routine and refine the pin the tail on the donkey game.

Miss Sarah.

Reading the note through for a second time, Jess's mind raced. She knew this was as near as she'd ever get to a declaration of closeness from Miss Sarah. Jess hated the fact that she was going to have to destroy it. However, her delight at receiving this written statement of semi-caring from her dominatrix was diluted by the fact that David Proctor really had been trying to trick her.

Ripping the paper into tiny pieces, Jess flushed it down the toilet. Then, heading back to her holdall, she hunted through her bag. Hidden at the very bottom, Jess's hand came to a slim volume. *'Hansel and Gretel'?*

Lying upon the meagre mattress, Jess opened the book. She recognised it as one of the many Grimm's fairy tales she'd seen when exercising against the bookshelves. Knowing Miss Sarah never did anything without a good reason, and that if she thought Jess would benefit by reading the book, then she should, she found the first page, and began to read.

Jess awoke with a start. David was towering over her, the borrowed book in one hand, and a bulky parcel in the other. 'This book belongs in the library bedroom.'

Taking a second to catch up on events, Jess sat up. She must have fallen asleep reading.

'Yes, it does. I borrowed it. I wasn't going to take it home.' Knowing she was blustering, Jess stopped talking.

'As it happens, that won't be a problem. You'll have plenty of time to read as much of the library stock as you like.'

Remembering Miss Sarah's warning note, Jess frowned. 'Forgive me, but Miss Sarah and I are due back at Fables soon.'

'Miss Sarah is packing for her return journey as we speak. She will be heading back to England very soon. You, however, are required for a little longer.'

Forgetting herself, Jess swung her legs around, and stood inches from David. 'What?'

'You heard me, Miss Sanders. I would advise you to moderate your tone.'

Nausea rose in Jess's gullet. Surely they wouldn't send Miss Sarah home without her? The note had said to trust nothing she was told. There was every chance this could be a lie.

Holding out his hand, David said, 'I'll take the book, please. How far did you get?'

Wishing she hadn't fallen asleep, knowing that she'd only reached the middle of the tale, when it had probably been the finale Miss Sarah had intended her to read, Jess spoke honestly. 'To where they lay out the breadcrumbs.'

A cruel smile flashed across Proctor's face. 'The ending is the best bit.' His words neither confirmed nor denied whether the end of the story was different to the version Jess knew.

'I didn't reach the end.'

'Perhaps that is just as well.' Slipping the book into his jacket pocket, David sat on the wooden chair to the side of the bed. 'Some things in life are better when they are a surprise, don't you agree?'

'Some things.'

'I don't think I've ever seen you looking so distrustful,

Miss Sanders.'

'Sorry, David.' Jess hung her head, feeling far less deferential than she appeared. Determined not to let herself or Miss Sarah down, she forced herself to sound contrite. 'I was simply shaken by the news of Miss Sarah's imminent departure.'

'We no longer require her training services. She has tutored Alisha for several days. If the girl cannot satisfy my clients tonight then Miss Sarah is clearly not good enough to stay on my staff, and if Alisha does make the grade, then Miss Sarah's skills will not be required further.'

'I'm sure Alisha will not disappoint you.'

'I commend your loyalty to both Miss Sarah and Fables.' David leafed through the book in his lap. 'However, I'm afraid I have to tell you that they don't think as highly of you as you do of them.'

'David?' Even though, thanks to Miss Sarah's letter, she already knew what Proctor was about to say, Jess felt unease steal over her body.

'I have been in discussions with Mrs Peters.' David sighed as if what he was saying was giving him no pleasure, although the spark in his eyes gave him away. 'And, as per our agreement, should Alisha not perform to the standard I expect from my staff, then you will remain at The Retreat in her place.'

Jess's head jerked up. Despite the warning from her mistress, hearing David say the words, each one dripping with sincerity and sounding disturbingly plausible, sent a chill to her heart. 'But sir – David, I mean – I belong at Fables.'

'Only if Mrs Peters says that you do. And as submissives are not hard to find, then I'm sure Laura will already have a girl lined up to train.' David stared at the book on his lap. 'That is probably why Miss Sarah is required to go home with such haste after the event tonight, to take over from Laura as the new girl's dominatrix.'

Opening and closing her mouth like a stunned goldfish, Jess gulped. This had to be a lie. 'Is there is a new girl?'

'With Mrs Peters, there is *always* a new girl.' Shutting the book with a bang, David stood up.

'But if submissives are easy to come by, can't you replace Alisha with someone else? I don't want ...' She hadn't meant to plead, but couldn't help herself.

'Miss Sanders!' David thrust the package he'd brought with him into her hands. 'You are a sub. What you want does not come into it. Nor is it your place to tell me what I should or shouldn't do!'

Lowering his voice from his burst of anger to its usual, treacle-smooth tone, David said, 'You will be collected from this room at six o'clock this evening. Jason will bring you some lunch in one hour, and a small meal at four. Eat, rest, and dress in the garments in the package. They should fit you well. Miss Sarah gave the measurements, and I suspect she knows your shape down to the tiniest degree.' David reached the door in one giant stride. His parting words provided a further splinter of thought to niggle away inside Jess's brain. 'I wonder how long it will take her to get to know the anatomy of your replacement so well?'

Jess didn't open the parcel David had brought her until half past five. As she placed it on the bed, a rectangle of white card fell out of its meagre folds, blank side up. Staring at it, Jess's nerves, which she had been doing her best to deny access to her brain all day, raced to the surface. She decided not to flip the card over and read what it said until she absolutely had to. Breathing slowly, she took off her clothes, ignored the new garment, and returned to the shower.

As she went through the routine of making sure her body was clean and fresh, Jess prayed with every fibre of her being that Alisha would perform as well as David hoped. But she couldn't shift the feeling that no matter how well the cook did, Proctor would make an excuse to keep her on his staff anyway.

Dry, Jess brushed her hair in methodical strokes. She couldn't put off the moment any longer. It was time to dress.

If there had ever been any doubt about the theme of the party, it vanished now, as Jess turned over the crisp white card, and saw why Miss Sarah had slipped that particular story into her luggage.

Written in the centre of the invitation, in a clear, gothic script, was

The Retreat
Gretel

Surely Gretel would never have looked like this, Jess thought as she cursed herself for falling asleep and not finishing reading the story. In the version she knew, the Wicked Witch had been consumed by the oven. Her thoughts flew back to the sight of Lady Tia and Miss Sarah stretched over the range. Is that how it had to end this time? Did she have to get The Retreat's resident Wicked Witch into the kitchen, and force her against the ancient oven?

She picked up the oak brown basque, which had been cut to keep her chest on show, and secured the garment with a set of hooks and eyes. Having pulled on a miniskirt that was little more than a four-inch wide band of stiff leather, Jess slipped on some knee-high cream socks, and a pair of brown canvas shoes.

There was no time to look at her appearance, for there was a knock on the door.

Kane, a calculating expression on his face, passed Jess a brown cloak. 'Put this on.'

Jess covered her cold shoulders gratefully, but said nothing as she waited for his instructions, conscious of the racing blood in her veins.

'Do you have your invitation?'

'Yes, sir.'

'Then follow me. Mr Proctor tells me that it is time to put you in place.'

Following Kane's silent footfall, Jess could feel the promise of sex vibrate off every wall. Her head filled with images of all the erotic encounters that must have happened within the castle in the hundreds of years since it had been built. Had noble Scottish kings screwed their wives and mistresses here? Had lusty courtiers fucked in the stairwells, had cooks been rogered by amorous stewards in the servants' quarters? The prospect of adding to the building's rich sexual history sent crackles of erotic electricity through the soles of Jess's thin shoes, dampened her crotch, and stiffened her exposed nipples.

I have no need to be nervous, she told herself as she got closer to the entrance hall. I have survived so much as a submissive – and ultimately enjoyed it. This is just one more task.

This time, though, Jess knew she had to make sure it was a task she lost.

However well or badly Alisha performed, Jess had to make sure she did worse, but without making it look obvious that she was failing on purpose.

As she reached a decision to perform as badly as the coming circumstances would allow, Jess and her taciturn escort arrived at The Retreat's entrance hall.

Chapter Seventeen

STANDING QUIETLY BY a large rectangular table, Dr Ewen was dressed in a white PVC sleeveless catsuit, which highlighted every asset she had; assets which the many zips placed at salient points could reveal at will. Her hands and lower arms, however, were covered in long red satin gloves. The contrast was stark, and Jess was immediately reminded of the superstition that declared it was bad luck to wear red and white together, as it represented blood on a white sheet. Telling herself that this was not a bad omen; Jess switched her gaze from Dr Ewen to the table she was setting up.

Covered in a scarlet tablecloth that matched the shade of the manageress's gloves, it held five white cards similar to Jess's own, declaring themselves to belong to *Hansel, Prince Charming, The Wicked Witch, The Fairy Godmother,* and *The White Witch.* She presumed the first two cards to refer to Alisha and Jason, and the fifth to Dr Ewen herself, as the lack of wings on her costume ruled out her being the fairy godmother. Jess lay down her own invite, not wanting to consider how the role of Wicked Witch would be adapted by Lady Tia. Surely she would have that role, which would make Miss Sarah the fairy godmother. But whose fairy godmother – hers or Alisha's?

She was running her eyes over the other items on the table when she heard movement behind her, and Dr Ewen's voice broke the expectant silence. 'Now we are all here, let me describe the evening ahead.'

Jess scanned the room for Miss Sarah, Alisha, Jason and Lady Tia. She couldn't see any of them. Only she, Dr Ewen, Kane, and now David were there, which she certainly didn't count as all of them. Her already fragile confidence began to disintegrate; a fact she failed to hide in her uneasy expression.

Amusement evident in her voice, Dr Ewen said, 'Don't worry, Miss Sanders, you're not about to face the entire Fairtasia delegation alone. Your colleagues have already received their briefing, and are in place. We require everyone's assistance; but not all at the same point during the evening.'

Her fear that she wouldn't be working where she could see Alisha, and therefore wouldn't know how much or how little to do herself to make sure the Scottish lass won, had been realised. The mantra that had kept her going over the past few days came back to Jess's head – *Do Fables and yourself proud* – and suddenly she knew she'd been kidding herself.

Even if her future depended on it, if she proved to everyone at The Retreat that she was far from the perfect submissive she'd been billed as, when – if – she did make it back to Fables, Jess would never be able to face Mrs Peters, or worse, Miss Sarah, and explain her poor performance. Containing the sigh that was building in her chest, she continued to listen.

'So, as you can see from the table –' Dr Ewen pointed to a large bowl of condoms, and several rows of handcuffs, short pieces of rope, blindfolds, butt-plugs, dildos, and clamps '– as each delegate arrives they will place their invitation here, and then be given the choice of one of these implements to enhance their experience. Condoms are compulsory, of course, but whether they take a toy or not is up to them. These things are very much a personal choice, don't you think?'

Not knowing if she was supposed to give an audible response or not, Jess opted for an inclination of her head in agreement, as Dr Ewen elaborated further. 'As I hope you have worked out by now, Miss Sanders, Fairtasia is not only a vital contact for David's future business plans but, should they be content with our work here tonight, they are keen to adopt The Retreat as the main base for future adult entertainment events; and perhaps even as a place out of which a few of them could be permanently based. But *only* if we impress this evening.'

Jess listened carefully. The first part she'd worked out, the second was news to her, but she kept her mouth shut as the hours ahead of her were outlined.

'Fairtasia produce some of the best quality adult comic books in the world, largely in the Japanese manga style. And when I say adult, I am talking of a brilliant interweaving of dark fantasy, horror, and erotica. They are a multi-million dollar concern, and it is a great honour to David Proctor's standing in the business world that they have chosen to come to him to improve their marketing strategies further; and to us as a means to do so.' Dr Ewen picked up a pair of handcuffs and dangled them temptingly off the ends of her fingers. 'I regret that your time here has been so short, Miss Sanders. I would like to have had time to see you in action a little more myself.'

David, who'd remained quiet until now, chipped in. 'I am sure you will witness a great deal of Miss Sanders' skill in operation tonight, Elena, and for many nights to come.'

Dr Ewen's previously concealed distrust of her employer was now plainly evident as she attempted to contradict him. 'Unless Miss Alisha performs as well as I think she will, in which case, Miss Sanders *will* be going home.'

'We will see.' David left the words hanging in the air, before taking charge of the conversation.

'It seemed fitting, considering Fairtasia's area of interest, to theme tonight around fairy tales. Naturally we cannot follow each story to the letter, but as you'll have learnt during your time at The Retreat, fairy tales are open to some pleasing adaptation.

'Lady Tia is already with Alisha, making sure she is in position ready for our guests, and Miss Sarah is awaiting her call to action.'

Jess's eyes fell back to the two white cards on the table that said *Wicked Witch* and *Fairy Godmother*. She had the sinking feeling that, as much as this was about Proctor securing a lucrative contract, for the mistresses this was a fight for superiority between Fables and The Retreat.

'There will be three different shows set up, plus a finale to round off the evening. Each of these mini-theatres will go on simultaneously for the majority of the evening, and our guests can visit each one at their leisure, although each is linked, as you will discover.

'Jason will take the lead in one of the three in the conference room, which is also where we've provided a buffet and liquid refreshment for our guests.' David came forward and pulled open Jess's cloak. Slowly, he appraised her with greedy eyes. 'Most acceptable. I see that Miss Sarah does indeed know your contours well.'

David let go of her, and Jess immediately wrapped the cloak over her bare tits, making the so far silent Kane snort with derision behind her, as he went on, 'Alisha, as is fitting for her status, is ready to fulfil her role in the second tableau in the kitchen. This is particularly pertinent as she is to take on the role of Hansel who, you will recall from reading the tale, is imprisoned by the Wicked Witch.

'So that we don't lose visitors in the maze of the castle layout, we've blocked off most of the corridors, meaning the only way to get from here to the kitchen is via the conference room. As they progress through the castle, our guests can choose whether to take a voyeuristic stance, or take a more hands on approach to the evening. They are also at liberty to enjoy our facilities between themselves, independent of The Retreat staff. Your task, Miss Sanders, will begin here in the entrance hall. Once all our visitors have arrived, you will, in accordance with the story, follow the breadcrumbs.'

Follow the breadcrumbs? Jess knew that Hansel and Gretel had laid a trail of breadcrumbs to follow in order to find their way out of the forest. But that escape had been thwarted, as the bread had been eaten by woodland birds. Was this David's way of telling her that she was trapped here whatever happened? 'Please, David, could you explain what you mean? Follow the breadcrumbs, and then what would you like me to do?'

'You are an intelligent woman, I'm sure you can work it out. You've read most of the book, after all.' He fired his unfriendly smile directly into Jess's pale green eyes. 'As long as you remember your primary objective, which is to impress and please the Fairtasia staff at all costs, then I have no doubt all will turn out for the best.'

Taking a step back, David waved an expansive arm in Kane's direction. 'I think it's time I introduced you two properly. Miss Jess Sanders, I'd like you to meet Mr Kane Shyland, the managing director of Fairtasia's UK operation.'

So he wasn't David's chauffeur and right-hand man, then. 'I ... I'm pleased to meet you, sir.' Jess didn't know what else to say as she considered how she, Miss Sarah, or Alisha were supposed to impress a man who'd declared himself utterly unimpressable by all three of them on each previous encounter.

Adding no further information about Kane and his undercover observations, David took her arm. 'That's enough talk for now. I will take you to your stage.'

Dropping the cloak from Jess's shoulders and passing it to Dr Ewen, who stashed it beneath the table, Jess found herself hand in hand with David. He led her to the archway that marked the passage from the entrance hall to the corridor which continued to the staff quarters. Now, however, it was blocked with the massive circular mirror from the turret room.

It wasn't the sight of the mirror, or the memory of Miss Sarah's naked form smeared against it, that caused the blood in Jess's veins to chill, but the ropes that had been tied around the two stone posts either side of the archway she stood beneath.

'You see now why it was so important for us to test your stamina within the harness and strap suit last night. I wanted to be sure you could remain relatively motionless with your arms outstretched for a long period of time.'

'Yes, David, I see.' Jess's throat suddenly felt as if it was lined with sand as she waited to hear what he'd say next.

'Our first guests are due shortly. If you were hoping to see their arrival in the mirror's reflection, I have to confess you will be disappointed. I have had fun in positioning its angle so that anyone's approach will come as a surprise to you until the last moment. I thought it would be fun for you to see yourself in action.'

As David positioned Jess so she faced not out into the hall, but towards the circular glass, she realised she was to be the first available port of call for any guest who wanted to take advantage of her captive state. She was the aperitif. Her barely concealed arse and reflected chest were to be the initial temptations on offer at The Retreat. She really wished the idea of her situation didn't enflame her body so much.

'If you have any questions, Miss Sanders, then now is the time to ask. Once I open the doors to The Retreat, you'll not have the chance to talk for some time.' Lifting Jess's right arm as he spoke, David tied it not at the unbending right angle she'd feared, but so it was just

209

suspended out at her sides, preventing her from moving from the archway.

Taking advantage of the invitation to speak, Jess said, 'If I am to follow the story as I understand it, then I have to save Hansel from the witch. I really don't know how you want me to do that.' Her voice was pleading, not because of her submissive status, but because she couldn't see how, if she was tied in place here, she could get to "Hansel". 'If I am to reach Alisha, I have to be free.'

David took up her left wrist, securing it with a second loop of leather. 'As you have already worked out what you need to do, I am sure it won't be long before you work out a way to achieve that goal. After all, you have time on your side – for now at least.'

Finding she could flex her arms a little, but not enough to completely twist her body, Jess felt a modicum of relief that at least her feet hadn't been secured, so she could stand comfortably. That relief faded as David produced a thin black leather collar. 'Do you know about the tradition of collaring, Miss Sanders?'

The expression on his face as he cradled the collar made Jess's body go cold. Her replay came out as a stutter. 'It's when a submissive is … owned by one master or mistress … It is a token – *willingly* worn – and …'

'Broadly speaking, yes. But sometimes a collar can be used in another capacity. To ensure a promise is kept, perhaps.'

'What promise?'

'If you succeed you will find out.' As David held the collar aloft, Jess flinched as if she was being shown something terrifying. 'Beautiful, isn't it?'

The slim strip of leather was secured at the front by a tiny silver padlock. Two small silver hoops hung from the left and the right sides. Hoops, Jess guessed, that were wide enough to thread a thin cord through, so a lead could be attached, and she could be walked like a dog. At the centre of the collar's back, the initials *TR* had been picked out in fine silver thread.

David held it to Jess's throat, and she backed away as much as her arm holds would allow. 'I wonder, Miss Sanders, if Mrs Peters asked you to wear this, to prove you belonged to her, would you wear it?'

Biting her teeth together, feeling tears gathering inside her tear ducts – tears she'd be damned if she'd let him see – Jess said nothing.

'Perhaps if Miss Sarah asked you to wear it? Maybe then you'd take it gladly.'

Jess refrained from comment, but she knew the flash of colour in her eyes had betrayed her.

'As I thought. How might Mrs Peters react to the knowledge that you have more loyalty to her second in command than to her? Not well, I suspect.'

He went to secure the collar for a second time, and again Jess dodged his move, but she knew this wasn't a game she could keep up for long.

'Do I really have to ask Kane to come and help me do this? I am sure he would take immense pleasure in holding you by the hair so that I can claim you for The Retreat.'

'I do not belong here. I do *not*.' Jess, knowing there would be consequences for her stubbornness, stood still. She could not stop him, but as soon as she was free, she resolved to cut it off, and if he really did intend to keep her there against her will, she'd take the first chance she got to escape.

Circling her neck, David brought the ends of the collar together and fastened it with a tiny silver key. Placing the key in his wallet, he watched as Jess gagged against the leather's stranglehold. There was no way this collar could be cut off without being in danger of slicing her skin in the process.

'Truly beautiful.' David walked around Jess's bound body, admiring his collar from all angles.

She continued to struggle to swallow, gulping against the tight choker. 'I suggest you relax, Miss Sanders. Your throat will adjust faster if you untense your muscles. Now, look in the mirror and see how well it suits you.'

Not wanting to see, Jess did as she was told and peered into the mirror she'd been trying to avoid eye contact with. He was right. The collar suited her. Jess hated that it did. She hated what it meant, and felt defeat hit her like a solid lump of concrete.

'You belong to me now.' David ran a finger around the collar, savouring the thump of Jess's pulse as it beat beneath the leather's hold, before walking away and sprinkling a trail of tiny bits of white upon the floor that looked like a trail of breadcrumbs.

Jess wanted to scream "No!" at the top of her voice. She wanted to thrash about and tug at the ropes, wanted her hands to be free so she could claw at the bond around her neck, not caring how much it would hurt to rip it from her skin. She did none of those things. The sense of failure was settling on her with speed. All she could think was why didn't Miss Sarah warn me about this? Maybe she didn't know? Or maybe she did? Perhaps her note was the lie, and Mrs Peters really has agreed to keep me here …

Closing her eyes to her reflection, not wanting to see any part of her outfit, let alone the collar, and consumed in a feeling of abandonment, Jess didn't notice the growing hum of conversation as the Fairtasia delegates gathered behind her in the main part of the entrance hall. While the voice of common sense at the back of her mind tried to battle with the self-pity that had gripped her tethered body, she barely reacted when a pair of hands took hold of her buttocks. If they hadn't squeezed her so hard, she wasn't sure she'd have noticed them at all.

It was the cast of a shadow over her face when a figure arrived directly in front of her that caused Jess to open her eyes again.

The unknown woman wore a more sophisticated, but equally sexy, version of the Red Riding Hood outfit Alisha had worn on the plane from London to Scotland. Her hood up, her scantily clad body protected from the chill of the castle by her cloak, she folded up Jess's leather skirt so that her bare pussy was exposed to anyone who wished to see it, and thanks to the mirror, they could see it from whichever angle they stood around her. Then, with bright blue eyes blazing from the depths of the hood, the woman licked the ends of two of her fingers, and placed their wet tips over Jess's nipples.

The effect was instant. Jess's dormant frame was shocked into life as the delegate rotated her fingers over the top of each nipple. In the second it took for her brain to register that she was probably supposed to be withholding her climax, the stranger slapped a hand against the newly exposed mound and, unable to prevent herself, Jess came on the spot.

Believing that such an early mistake was the final straw, she felt all hope of getting out of The Retreat evaporate. Wiping away thoughts of how to escape, Jess sagged against her bindings, letting them take her weight as another pair of hands found her buttocks, then another, and more, and more, and ...

Losing count of the number of digits that ran over her breasts and backside, and the fingers that found her channel, her anus, her mouth and every section of exposed skin, Jess shuddered and shook against the combined touch of a variety of mismatched fairy tale characters.

Dildos were pushed inside her pussy, and then taken out, so her juices could be used as lubrication for the guests. Jess could see in the reverse show the mirror was affording her that her sap was being used to help satisfy a great many of the individual women and couples who were now swarming around her.

Lips kissed her neck around the collar; voices admired

her outfit, and the curve of her chest. Teeth bit at her tits, and ate at her pussy, and time and time again Jess spasmed and trembled in her rope tethers. Making no effort to stop the multitude of orgasms swimming in her gut, the defeat that had started to simmer from the moment David had secured the collar twisted in Jess's mind.

She was just resigning herself to her failure to live up to Mrs Peters' expectations of her, when Jess was suddenly aware of Dr Ewen's voice close to her ear.

'I'm disappointed in you, Miss Sanders. I thought you were stronger than this. When I watched the recordings of you working with Mrs Peters at Fables I saw unwavering determination in your eyes. Prove to me I wasn't mistaken. Prove to the holders of the 150 invitations who have walked through The Retreat's doorway why Mrs Peters refers to you as her perfect submissive. Only that is going to get you home now. Use the collar to your advantage. Think. Miss Sarah tells me you're clever. Show me she's right. Show me I can trust your mistress more than I can trust David Proctor.'

Chapter Eighteen

JESS'S HEAD JERKED up, and for a brief moment she was eye to eye with Dr Ewen. From the moment she and Miss Sarah had arrived at The Retreat, she had been unsure if the manageress wanted her to remain within her castle or not. Now, in the blunt shine of the woman's grey gaze, she saw that whatever agenda Dr Ewen had, it did not involve Jess failing herself, Fables, or The Retreat.

With the blessed arrival of clarity, Jess gave herself a mental shake. She'd already wasted time. Heaven knew how Alisha was holding up. She had to think, and fast.

Watching Dr Ewen's wafer-thin figure disappear into a throng of assorted fairy tale characters, Jess blanked out all the activity around her. How could she use the collar to her advantage? It was a visible symbol of being something she didn't want to be. There wasn't even enough leeway between it and her neck to wriggle a little finger between the leather and her skin, and only David had a key for the padlock, so how could …

Jess stood up straight. No one had told her she had to remain silent, although until then she had hardly uttered more than a moan. With shame she realised how close she'd come to giving up. She'd put her consciousness somewhere safe while hand after hand and tongue after tongue explored and exploited her body. She hadn't even registered the pleasing bloom of the climaxes she couldn't be bothered to fight off. It was as if with the application of

215

the collar, Jess's purpose had been sapped from her.

With the warming knowledge that Miss Sarah had told Dr Ewen she thought her to be clever, Jess swept away the doubts she'd had about her mistress's loyalty. Pulling her shoulders back, she stuck out her chest, much to the delight of the kingly gentleman before her, who'd been about to suckle upon her left side.

Jess ran her eyes over the gathering of partygoers before her. The group was smaller than it had been. Many people had moved on into the conference room to visit Jason, get a drink, some food, and continue their business chatter and orgy-based activities. There were still a few who lingered, however. Some held handcuffs and butt-plugs; some used the toys between themselves while others held them in readiness for the best opportunity to employ them. Gritting her teeth against the tantalizing sensations the talented man at her torso was causing, Jess spotted that he was holding exactly what she was looking for.

'Sire?'

He didn't look up, so Jess took a gamble. 'Sire, your majesty?'

The short, overweight man who, although dressed as a king was as far from regal as it was possible to get, teased her right nipple out as far as it would go before dropping it and peering up at her.

'Please, sire, that feels so good. Why not release me so you can do more? I see you chose a cord from the table. If you used it as a lead, you could take me with you. You'll be ready to move to the next room soon, and – well, I don't want to be left here all alone when I could have your mouth upon me.'

The man surveyed the dwindling number of guests behind him, all of whom were now intent upon each other and not the suspended girl. Speaking as if he was taking the role of the father of a princess very seriously, he responded eagerly, 'Verily, my Lord Proctor did say we could do anything we wanted. So yes, in return for being able to explore you better, I'll escort you, young woman.'

As he threaded the cord through the small hoop at the right of her collar, Jess could see the bulge of his wood swell beneath the peacock blue tights of his ill-fitting costume. She felt a familiar tingle of emptiness between her legs. Although she'd been invaded by a host of fingers and dildos she had not, so far that evening, felt the thrust of a real dick between her legs.

'Thank you, sire.'

The fake king hurriedly untied her hands, and Jess flexed her arms before her new companion seized her right hand and pushed it against his stiffening length. Tugging her via the neck, Jess groaned as he didn't tow her towards the conference room, but to an armchair at the side of the room.

'You're missing the fun, sire; the conference room is the next stop.'

'On the contrary, my Gretel.' Undoing his hose, keeping the lead wrapped around his arm, he donned one of the many condoms he'd stuffed into his waistcoat pocket. Sitting at the edge of the chair, he pulled Jess onto his lap. 'We can have fun right here.'

His moan was almost guttural as he thrust his dick into her. Holding his prize by her tits, the king levered Jess up and down. As fast as she could, she matched his rhythm, hammering onto his lap with a desire that was more concerned with getting to the kitchen than with coming.

Feeling the stiffening of his cock that indicated the man was close, Jess slipped one hand to his balls, and slid a finger from the other between his gasping lips. She let him suck her digit as she took him to orgasm with a grunt of heady pleasure. Taking advantage of the brief moment of disorientation ejaculation always brings, Jess extracted the lead from his hand, and ran.

Ignoring the seeping of her own juices down her bare legs, she prepared herself to think fairy tale, and as Gretel she fled towards the conference room. It was time to follow the few fake breadcrumbs that hadn't been scuffed away by the Fairtasia delegation, and find Hansel.

She took advantage of being just another face in the crowd while she could. The semi-naked state afforded by her costume did not make Jess stand out amongst the equally minimally dressed throng of Sleeping Beauties and huge profusion of woodcutters as she crept through the delegates. Only now did she see how few male roles there were in fairy tales. The thought was immediately overtaken by a less pleasant one. The majority of the bad guys were women. An image of how Lady Tia might soon be treating her loomed menacingly in Jess's head.

A regiment of buffet tables lined the wall. Jess saw that amongst those delegates taking advantage of the opportunity to indulge in sexual excess, there were many small groups of people deep in conversation, discussing business plans, The Retreat, and the future of Fairtasia. As Jess surreptitiously picked a red and white striped sugar candy cane from the nearest table, nibbling at it to keep up her strength, she saw the starkly white figure of Dr Ewen in such a discussion with a couple of equally unusually dressed guests.

Moving on slowly, she admired the impressive culinary spread on offer. The table was laden with cupcakes, gateaux, ginger biscuits, and bowl after bowl of sweets, apples, clear squares of sugar glass, marshmallows, syrup twists, and gallons of milk and honey. Every food you'd ever read about in the pages of a fairy tale was laid out on that table; a testament to Alisha's skill as a cook. In the centre of the table sat the focal point of the display; a gingerbread cottage, complete with white iced doors and windows. Jess wouldn't have been surprised if David had insisted that Alisha bake an edible oven to place inside …

The oven. How on earth, she wondered, am I going to lure Lady Tia towards the oven? Presumably when I've done that, it's over? Surely I won't actually to have to shove Lady Tia inside – she'd never fit for a start! Jess shook herself. Don't be ridiculous, this is a twisted, adult interpretation of a fairy tale, not a carbon copy. Focus!

Unlike the entrance hall, which had just had its furniture moved back and the mirror used to block a corridor, the conference room was a riot of scenery. It was as if David had gone mad in a pantomime props supplier's warehouse. Huge cardboard cut-outs of magical castles, Jack's beanstalk, and the entrance to the Seven Dwarves' mine were placed here and there. Roll after roll of velvet and chiffon fabric in rich, shimmering colours were draped across the ceiling and around the granite pillars. The whole feel of the place was of opulent fairy tale confusion.

Hidden at the back of the people crowding around the food tables, Jess stood on tiptoe to survey the hall in search of Jason. It was obvious from the cluster of bodies by the huge picture windows facing out on to the loch that whatever was happening to Jason in phrase two of Kane and David's plan was over there.

'There you are!'

Jess jumped. In her quest to get to the kitchen, and hopefully bypass Jason entirely, she had forgotten about her promise to the far from regal king. 'Forgive me, sire, but I have a quest. A girl's future depends upon it!'

Taking a firm hold of the lead that hung from Jess's collar, he bowed low. 'Then let me escort you, Gretel, as you promised I could, to wherever you need to go.'

'Thank you, sire.'

'But you will make it worth my while.' This time the edge of chivalry to his voice was replaced with steel.

'Of course, sire.' Bobbing a quick curtsey, Jess hurriedly added, 'But first I must reach the kitchen without being noticed.'

Conscious of the fact that she didn't actually know where David was, a fact that made her uneasy, she allowed herself to be led towards the door at the opposite end of the room. Wondering what reward would be asked of her by her mock-royal companion, but grateful that at least they were moving through the conference room at a faster pace than she'd dared hope, Jess felt a few of her muscles unknot.

Reaching the edge of the crowd, the king stopped and craned his neck to see what was happening by the window. Jess's heart sank. 'Please, sire, I must go on.' She wrenched at her lead, making herself cough as the collar constricted around her neck. Too late she saw her mistake in speaking so near the centre of action as David's voice hit her ears.

'Miss Gretel. Thank you for honouring us with your presence.'

David and Kane, standing out from the people around them as the only ones not wearing fancy dress, stepped from behind the cardboard cut-out of Jack's beanstalk. Kane turned to her companion. 'How has she performed so far, Simon?'

The makeshift king pulled his shoulders back, tucked in his stomach, and abandoned the "happy ever after" crap as he spoke to his boss. 'Very well, Mr Shyland. I was wary from your initial reports, but my observations of her work were most rewarding. And I must confess it was extremely difficult to observe her for as long as I did without stepping forward and sampling her skills for myself.'

The hold on the lead at Jess's neck increased as Simon went on, 'I am also pleased to report that I did not have to drop any hints to Gretel suggesting I fasten my lead to her collar. She asked me for freedom herself without prompting.'

Kane solemnly nodded. A slight sheen of sweat across

his forehead showed Jess that perhaps, at last, the heated erotic atmosphere surrounding them had pierced his armour. 'That is excellent.'

As the toweringly tall, dark man smiled, Jess felt her blood chill to ice as the penny finally dropped. He'd never thought she was no good at her job. He'd always been impressed; he just hadn't wanted her to know. He'd played her to get what he wanted; just like he'd played David.

'Your insight into the workings of the minds of The Retreat and Fables staff never ceases to amaze me, David. Let's hope –' Kane took the lead from his colleague, and dragged Jess, her big breasts bobbing against the top of her basque, towards Jason '– that Gretel can complete this stage of the challenge and make it to Hansel in time.'

Jess wanted to ask "in time for what?", but she didn't dare.

Whatever had been happening to Jason had clearly been going on for at least as long as she'd been in the entrance hall, if not longer. Dressed as the archetypal Prince Charming, Jason had been gagged with a small, round, rosy red apple.

Accessing the situation quickly, Jess realised she'd temporarily left *Hansel and Gretel* behind, and had walked onto the set of a corrupted version of *Snow White*. Everything had been flipped on its head. It was not the sleeping princess who lay in the glass coffin after biting the poisoned apple, but the prince.

She gasped as she was clumsily shoved closer to Jason, her way hampered by the hands of various onlookers, who took her uncovered backside and free breasts as an invitation to touch, pinch, and generally feel her up.

Propped at an angle that made him visible to the widest possible audience, Jason lay in an oversized, see-through coffin. The lower edge of the box was missing, offering easier access to the young man within. Not made of glass as Jess had first presumed, the three sides of the coffin had been created from boiled and set sugar, like the windows of the witch's house in both the original Hansel and Gretel story, and its miniature copy on the dining room table.

As well as the apple in his mouth, Jason had been blindfolded with one of the masks Jess had spotted on the table in the entrance hall, but she wasn't sure if David had ordered it to be there, or if it had been added by a delegate for their own amusement. Jason's hands were secured with a pair of short-chained handcuffs in front of his torso. The medieval-style hose he wore on his legs had been cut so that a pertinent square of material was missing, exposing his groin. Judging by the distended state of his balls, and the rigid nature of his shaft, he'd received a lot of attention in the early stages of the party, but no relief.

'Looks as if this is where Snow White saves the Prince?' David stared at Jess.

'But I'm not ...' As she spoke, he produced a blue cape and fastened it around her throat beneath the leather collar, making sure he drew his statement of ownership to Kane's attention as he did so.

'While you are in this room you are Snow White.'

The babble of conversation around them, and the steady drumbeat of spanks and resulting cries, died away. All eyes were now on Jess, Jason, and the sticky, open-ended coffin.

Kane and Simon moved to stand behind Jason's head, ensuring they would miss nothing of the show to follow. As Jess looked around her, desperately searching for clues as to how to proceed, she heard David mutter to Kane, 'Doesn't she look exquisite in that collar? As time goes on, and she has accepted her submissive status at The Retreat, I will make it an inch longer, so she doesn't gag so often.'

Jess did her best to block her ears and blank her eyes to the smirking men. How long ago had the collar been made for her? In the last few days? Or before she'd even set foot on the plane to Scotland?

She was aware that David was still talking, but she wasn't sure if it was to her or a member of the delegation. She didn't care. She had a job to do, and that job was to get home. Home to Fables. Away from here, and back working with Mrs Peters, Sam, Lee, and Miss Sarah. Where was Miss Sarah? Jess shook away the thought. There was no time to worry about her mistress now. The party couldn't last for ever, and whatever odd plan David and Kane were working to, Jess knew she was a pivotal part of it, whether she liked it or not.

Proctor had said Prince Charming needed rescuing. How had Snow White been rescued in the original story? With a kiss, of course. But she couldn't kiss Jason on the lips; his mouth was full. She'd have to kiss him somewhere else.

Her eyes fell upon the cock she had longed to suck the first time she'd seen it in the boathouse; the cock that had filled her so satisfyingly during Alisha's first training session. Surely it couldn't be as simple as that? Could it?

Alisha took a long, drawn-out breath. Every part of her ached with the smarting throb that came from having skilled fingers dance across your chest over and over again. Everyone in the kitchen seemed fascinated with her tits, but had no interest at all in providing her with any level of fulfilment. Dressed as the boy Hansel, she wore a rough brown tunic, which was open at the front to reveal her breasts. A thick strap-on protruded from a pair of leather trousers which hid the clench of her sodden pussy.

The cook had been laid upon the table, which was more used to being covered in her culinary miracles than her body. Her arms had been stretched up and were raised above her head. Both Alisha's wrists were secured in the place by the weight of Lady Tia, whose palms pressed down upon them as she watched every trace of emotion that appeared on the trainee submissive's face.

Adorned in a fitted bottle green and black velvet dress which was embroidered with fine silver spider webs, Lady Tia's demeanour was as witchlike as her outfit. Her eyes shone devilment from her frowning face. Her hair was piled on top of her head, and her face was made up with vivid green lipstick and eye shadow; her fingernails were painted with a patent emerald varnish to match. So far all she'd done was silently watch, and direct the amount of attention the imprisoned Hansel had received.

From the moment Alisha had been ordered onto the table, a queue of guests had begun to form at her feet. With a quiet menace, Lady Tia had invited each of the guests in turn to come forward and sample the goods. But as soon as they got close to making Alisha come, they had to make way for the next delegate.

As they waited, the impatient customers spent their time amusing each other in a way that did nothing to help Alisha's simmering arousal.

At last, having lost count of all the bodies that had passed by, Alisha noticed that the queue was finally diminishing. The kitchen air was ripe with an infusion of wet cunt and spent come. As the penultimate woman in the line of horny visitors climbed up beside her, Alisha's eyes ached from being forced to hold the dominatrix's gaze, for she'd been forbidden from looking away.

Fastening her lips around his dick, Jess sucked Jason off with every fellatio skill that she had. Manipulating him between her lips and tongue, she pushed at the sides of the casket with the flat of her hands. The crack of sugar as it splintered apart was painful to the ears, and Jess hoped whoever had moulded it would understand her necessary vandalism.

Jess was about to tell Jason to sit up so she could reposition her mouth and finish bringing him off when she heard Kane muttering to Simon. 'If Miss Sanders thinks that's all an audience expects from a show, she hasn't watched enough theatre.'

Thinking fast, Jess remembered what David had said to her when they were in the boathouse about Jason wanting cock as much as he yearned for pussy. If it's a show they want, she told herself, that's what they'll get.

Grabbing hold of his tethered wrists, Jess undid the bindings, and pulled him to his knees. Kicking the shattered sugar away to clear some space around them, she whispered to Jason to get onto his hands and knees. The square cut from the front of his hose had been copied around the back, and his handsome arse was on display for all to see.

Overstepping the bounds of accepted submissive behaviour in her quest to get to the kitchen as fast as possible, Jess fixed her eyes on Proctor. 'David, would you like to? I don't see why you should miss out on all the fun. This is, after all, your party.'

Proctor's eyes narrowed. 'You forget your place, Miss Sanders.'

'My place at the moment is to be Snow White for you. And Snow White was a forthright, brave woman, who I'm sure would do whatever she could to rescue her prince. That is what I am doing.'

Running her hands over Jason's buttocks, Jess trailed a finger to his anus, making him wince and groan into the jaw-aching apple.

The outline of David's trousers made it clear that he was more than capable of obliging Jason's need to be buggered, but he deferred to Kane. 'I think it would be fitting if you performed the honours.'

'And I –' Kane spoke with his usual economy of words '– owe Simon a favour.' He gestured to the mock royal. 'My lord king, if you would be so kind.'

Simon, adopting a suitable air of regal haughtiness, stepped forward. His cock strained beneath his hose, evidently already recovered from his servicing of Jess. Taking the semi-sucked candy cane from Jess's hand he brought it to her lips and told her to suck it. Then, using her spittle as lube, he spread Jason's butt cheeks with one hand and laughed as the anus before him puckered, readily sucking up the red and white striped sweet.

Jess watched in fascination as Jason's body pushed back, hungry for the attention of the cane as it was eased in and out of him. Remembering that she wasn't supposed to be just watching, but providing the best show she could in order to get to the kitchen, she crashed to her knees. Instantly more comfortable in her usual subservient role, she lay upon her back, and threaded an arm beneath Jason. Her job was made a little easier as Simon slackened his hold on her lead so he could grasp Jason's right hip as well, allowing her neck to settle in a more comfortable position.

Wrapping her palm around Jason's length, she kept her eyes on Simon, judging the moment to start working the male submissive off.

With a dramatic cry of, 'I hope you're ready, my prince,' King Simon thrust his newly sheathed cock into Jason's back passage.

As Jason's grunts were muffled into squeaks by the apple, his body responded in relief at having some proper attention, rather than all the tantalizing touches that had gone before. Jess gripped him harder, giving him a handjob that was as fast paced as Simon's rutting of his arse.

Working on autopilot, she tried to work out how best to get from where she was now, right under the noses of The Retreat's and Fairtasia's elite, to Alisha, and presumably Lady Tia.

Until now, Jess had not allowed herself to think about what Lady Tia might be doing to the cook, or indeed what she would do to her once she reached the kitchen. She closed her eyes. Images of Miss Sarah filled her head. Where was she? What would she do if she was here?

Bringing her free hand to her neck, trying to ease the growing strain caused by the collar and lead, Jess felt the quietening of Jason's body, indicating that he was about to come. Then, suddenly, the hold on the lead slackened again, and Jess opened her eyes.

Rather than finding herself staring directly into the eyes of Simon, she saw Miss Sarah looking at her. Jess gasped, overjoyed that she wasn't going to have to face the last stage of this challenge alone.

As Jason let go, crying out his discharge in time to Simon's animalistic rasps, Miss Sarah said, 'Come with me, Miss Gretel.'

Rising unsteadily to her feet, feeling much better now Miss Sarah was in charge of the lead, and she wouldn't have to repeat her brief show of bravado, Jess stood meekly next to her mistress. The outfit that had been prepared for the dominatrix glittered in the light. Made of leaf after tiny leaf of silver, gold, and bronze material, it hugged her chest like a second skin, before puffing out at the waist into a waterfall of net skirt, which moved with distinguished elegance at her every step. From the centre of Miss Sarah's back two gossamer wings protruded, and in her hand was the strangest magic wand any Fairy Godmother had ever held. Topped with a silver star, there was no disguising the fact that it was, in reality, a suitably fashioned dildo.

Removing Snow White's blue cape from around Jess's shoulders, Miss Sarah addressed Kane and David, looking through Simon as if he wasn't there. 'I think you gentleman will agree that Miss Gretel has performed her task admirably. As her fairy godmother it is time for me to take her where she needs to be to free Master Hansel.'

Her sapphire eyes daring anyone to oppose her, Miss Sarah led Jess away from the panting Simon, with David,

Kane, and several of their followers close behind them.

As they moved, from the corner of her mouth Miss Sarah muttered into Jess's ear, 'I am sorry I took so long. Kane instructed one of his assistants to keep me locked in my room, but Dr Ewen found me and we've had a long chat. Things are not as we've been led to believe. You found my note?'

'Yes, ma'am.'

'Good. You are going to have to be strong now, Miss Sanders. Very strong. The fact you have been collared is not good news. Whatever happens, I am on your side. Don't forget that.'

Miss Sarah gave her a look which was stacked with emotion. Like the note, it told Jess more about the way Miss Sarah felt towards her submissive than she'd ever be able to say out loud. It disappeared the moment they crossed the threshold into the kitchen.

Chapter Nineteen

'CONGRATULATIONS, GRETEL, YOU made it to the kitchen.' Lady Tia's words dripped with sarcasm, as befitted her role as the Wicked Witch. Jess was sure she'd only spoken at all to keep the action going for delegates who'd formed an audience along one side of the kitchen table, each neck straining to get the best view of the stricken Hansel.

Led forward by Miss Sarah, Jess didn't look at the audience for long. All her attention was focused on Alisha. Until that point, she hadn't considered the implication of Hansel being a boy. She'd assumed that, as with a pantomime, the role of a boy would be played by a girl with no questions asked beyond the requirements of the audience's imagination. Now she saw David hadn't been content to let things be that straightforward, and had provided Alisha with a thick, cumbersome strap-on, which stuck proudly up from the table, ever ready for action.

Alisha lay with her back to the pine table, her wrists pulled at a sharp angle above her head and held firmly in place by Lady Tia's green-clawed hands. Jess could see that her face was red with effort and exhaustion. The despair in her eyes as she rolled her head to face Jess told her quite clearly, that like Jason, Alisha had been brought to the edge of pleasure many times, but had been denied the final plunge into personal gratification.

Unhooking the lead from Jess's collar, every inch the

fairy godmother, Miss Sarah spoke to the room at large, but addressed Jess directly. 'Gretel, to complete tonight's quest, you must free Hansel and get the evil crone to the oven.'

Noting the relish with which Miss Sarah charged the phrase "evil crone", Jess felt the invisible daggers of resentment fly between the dominatrices as the silver of Miss Sarah's costume shone and glittered, its mirror-like quality reflecting back the figure-hugging jet of Lady Tia's outfit.

The audience hushed, holding its collective breath. Every person in the kitchen felt the rise in tension as the Fairy Godmother, at one end of the table, locked eyes with the Wicked Witch at the other. Alisha, as Hansel, stuck helplessly between them, could only stare at Jess.

Knowing Alisha had done well so far, and hoping she could hang on a bit longer, Jess tried to watch all three of the other players in the game at the same time. She was aware she should also be keeping a track on where David and Kane were, but simply did not have enough senses to cover every angle. She knew what she had to do, and was convinced that Miss Sarah was going to try to do something to help her – but how to proceed in the meantime …? She had to do something to break the stalemate.

The only thing Jess was sure of was that Alisha's body was ready to explode, and somehow she was the one who had to trigger that orgasm; and the sooner the better. Not only could she feel the desperation flowing from Alisha like gamma rays, but now her own body had recovered from its earlier climaxes, her renewed desire was rising fast.

Jess wasn't worried that in the story Hansel and Gretel had been brother and sister. Let's face it, she thought as she respectfully took her lead from Miss Sarah's unresisting hand, there's no Fairy Godmother, Snow

White, or Prince Charming in the story, and I'm damn sure there was absolutely no sex.

The audience behind them was swelling in number as those who'd been in the entrance and conference room had all sauntered into the kitchen after Jess in search of fresh voyeuristic action. She took no notice of the continuing pats and slaps to her rump as she stood next to her mistress. Flashing her eyes at Miss Sarah, she hoped she'd guessed what she was about to do as she climbed up onto the scrubbed wooden table.

Kneeling next to Alisha, Jess was about to plead with Lady Tia to allow her to give Hansel the release "he" needed, when Miss Sarah moved with a speed that cut a swath through the watching delegates. They opened up a space before her as if she really was casting a magic spell upon the room.

Jess didn't pause. If this had been in David's script, then the surprised look on Lady Tia's face as Miss Sarah's hand came to her throat, the wand pressed hard into her right breast, made it plain that The Retreat's dominatrix had not been told about it.

Gently taking hold of Alisha's wrists, Jess slowly lowered her arms so that the muscles loosened and her joints cracked back into place. Bringing her face to Alisha's, Jess whispered, 'Don't move your head. I know you want to see what they're doing, but if you don't witness it, then whatever is about to happen can't be your fault.'

Hoping the cook didn't think her cruel for stopping her seeing the action behind her, Jess spoke urgently. 'This is important. After all you've gone through, do you still want this life? '

Breathless, her tattered wits a heady mix of the hands that had agitated her chest, the tongues that had licked her nipples, the pussies that had engulfed her fake phallus, the men who had invaded her throat, treating her mouth as though it was her channel, Alisha was having a massive battle with herself not to sit up, unstrap the toy, and thrust it inside herself right now. She panted out her reply. 'Yes, yes, I do.'

'Good.' As Jess worked off the harness of Alisha's strap-on, the crowd continued to spread from one side of the kitchen to all around the table. Some were so close that the first row was now pressed up against the table's wooden sides, their digits assisting with the continued stimulation of Hansel and Gretel. Jess, her hands fumbling, found her eyes fixing on Miss Sarah's silver varnish-tipped fingers, still at the throat of the much bigger woman.

Straining to hear, she couldn't make out what her mistress was saying to Lady Tia, but the thunderous expression on the larger woman's face told Jess clearly that she didn't like it.

With the strap-on now free, Jess did not take her eyes from the two fantasy incarnations of good and evil as she undid Alisha's trousers, and peeled the sweat and pussy juice-soaked leather down.

'She wants you to push it inside her.' David's voice behind Jess made her jump. While her attention had been elsewhere, he'd barged his way through the crowd, which now appeared to include every one of the 150 invited delegates. Even when the range belted out its extreme heat, the kitchen had never felt so hot and sticky. 'I don't want you to do that, Miss Gretel. In fact, I don't want Hansel filled at all.'

The frustrated whimper from Alisha, her head now lifted off the table, her weight resting back on her elbows, told Jess that she'd heard David's words too.

'She may have one climax. One. No more. And not via penetration.' David, whose eyes didn't once stray to Lady Tia or Miss Sarah, watched hungrily as Alisha's bare pussy twitched before his eyes.

232

The onlookers' fingers continued to stray onto Jess and Alisha, and the murmur of impatience began to mount. Restless mutterings from the crowd morphed into a chant. "Fuck, fuck, fuck …" bounced around the kitchen, as if the delegates were youths egging on two groups of fighters, goading them on to knock the life out of each other.

Then everything happened all at once.

Miss Sarah, her hand at Lady Tia's throat, spun on her heels.

The momentum behind the unexpected move sent Lady Tia staggering backwards. In less than a second, the Wicked Witch was repositioned so that her back was upon the table where she'd held Alisha captive. Miss Sarah ordered someone in the audience to give her a pair of handcuffs, which she quickly fastened around Lady Tia's wrists.

Spurred on by the sight of one stunning woman overcoming another, the chant from the crowd built in a deafening crescendo. With greedy hands still trying to shove themselves beneath Jess's arse, upping her already high state of arousal, she knew she'd have to give into the hunger and come soon. Scrambling onto all fours, her body over Alisha's, Jess grabbed the arm of a man dressed as the Big Bad Wolf. She pointed to Alisha, saying, 'Bring her off. Do not enter her.'

The relief that gushed from Alisha's lips told her the wolf had taken on his task with some relish. Consumed with sympathetic jealousy, Jess shoved Hansel's discarded strap-on dildo into the hands of a woman dressed as Cinderella, shouting, 'Please fuck me, miss.' Then she brought her mouth to Alisha's, smothering her lips with frantic kisses, while keeping her eyes fixed upon Miss Sarah and the top of Lady Tia's head.

As she was fucked by the Cinderella-girl with a gusto born of her own frustration, Jess felt butterflies in her stomach as a climax spilled out of her pent-up body. The strength of her coming coursed onwards from her swaying chest into the digits of the men and women who were rubbing her tits to distraction, before flowing on into Alisha. It caused the cook to howl into Jess's mouth and let go of her own orgasm without any of the problems she'd experienced before Miss Sarah had taken over her training.

Only 120 seconds had passed since Lady Tia's body had crashed on the table, and as Jess's pacified body cooled after her much-needed pleasure rush, Miss Sarah passed Lady Tia's hands up to her.

Trapping the dominatrix's wrists under her palm, Jess shuffled forward on her knees, lowering her breasts over Alisha's face. The girl quickly took the chance to live out her dream of inhaling one of her companion's large nipples.

Feeling the effort Lady Tia was making to try and regain control, and end her humiliation in front of the entire Fairtasia delegation, Miss Sarah flourished her phallus-shaped magic wand at the now jeering crowd, before guiding it between the cursing woman's teeth.

As yet another new hand started to spank her arse, Jess watched Miss Sarah slide off Lady Tia's chest, and stand before her.

Jess's pulse thudded louder than ever in her throat. Positive this was her cue as Gretel to grab hold of the Wicked Witch and thrust her towards the range, she was about to leap when Kane abruptly elbowed his way through the throng, and passed Miss Sarah a pair of shining golden scissors.

Jess froze as if she'd been zapped by the stare of Medusa. Her eyes, like every other pair in the kitchen, fixed upon the shining blades.

Unable to speak, Lady Tia frantically shook her head from side to side, as she too became mesmerised by the scissors. The story of Rapunzel filled Jess's head, and she was sure the Wicked Witch was afraid her dark curls were about to be removed from her head. Miss Sarah had plainly been given different instructions, however, for in one expert swipe she lifted the hem of Lady Tia's beautiful velvet dress, and sliced it from top to bottom, so that it fell away, leaving the dark-skinned woman naked and exposed.

The air was laced with a heavy expectancy. Even the delegates who hadn't been able to see the other end of the table properly sensed the need for quiet.

Kane said nothing as he stared into the furious yet undeniably sexed-up eyes of Lady Tia. His expression spoke volumes about his feelings towards her; his erection shouted even louder.

Miss Sarah was right. Jess recalled her mistress describing the way Kane looked at Lady Tia during her test of endurance over the lit range. There was, or had been, something between those two. Jess couldn't begin to guess which of them had the upper hand – if either of them did – but she was damn sure she didn't want to get in the middle of whatever it was.

Miss Sarah put out a restraining arm to Jess, her face clearly showing that she'd known this was going to happen, making the submissive wonder if Kane and her mistress had been working together. And if they had, then for how long? Just tonight, or from the moment they'd set foot in The Retreat?

Leaning towards Alisha, Miss Sarah twisted her head forcibly toward the action at the other end of the table, 'Sometimes we have to see that our monsters are human underneath.'

The cook's eyes hit the voluptuous curves of Lady Tia's flesh; flesh she'd longed to bury herself in time and time again.

Kane levered the naked body to its feet. Balancing with a wobble on her killer heels, Lady Tia snarled through her gag, but she had no choice but to allow herself to be walked to the range.

Feeling the urgency in the air, Jess broke protocol and spoke to Miss Sarah without permission. 'If Kane gets the witch to the range I can't complete the task. It has to be Gretel who gets her there. I …' With an overwhelming sense that time was slipping through her fingers, Jess seized Alisha's hand, and together they jumped from the table, only to have David bar their way.

'Astute as ever, Miss Sanders.' He nodded over Jess's shoulder.

No longer dressed as Prince Charming, but now in a chauffeur's uniform, Jason stepped smartly forward.

'You forget this is a Fairtasia fairy tale,' David went on. 'Even the Brothers Grimm could have learnt from this lot. I would have thought you'd realised by now that within these walls the storybook characters make their own endings.'

Jess's eyes were drawn to Jason's hand. He was holding Miss Sarah's suitcase. '*No*! No, you can't, that's cheating that's …' Her pleas were cut short by a sharp slap across her breasts from Miss Sarah's cane; a slap that brought her swiftly to her senses.

'He can, and he will. Don't forget what Mrs Peters told you.' Then, allowing herself to be led from the room, Miss Sarah shouted out for all to hear, 'I will see you very soon, Miss Sanders.'

The sensation of being alone crept over Jess. It was a feeling far more painful than the sting of the cane lashing her chest. How on earth was she going to get out of here without Miss Sarah's support? Her arms hung at her sides as her head filled with the sound of Proctor's mocking laughter.

Alisha, however, had her eyes trained on Lady Tia and Kane. Understanding that, for a moment at least, Jess needed her guidance more than she required Jess's, she took her wrist, and marched the dazed redhead towards the range.

Kane had taken the wand-style dildo from Lady Tia's mouth. His suit was off, and he stood, naked and unashamed, before his workforce, his chocolate body toned, his cock taunting the woman who once again lay upon the range. This time, however, the heat was off, and the dominatrix faced upwards so all the spectators could see her pendulous tits rise and fall, and her handcuffed wrists rest over her crotch.

Towing her fairy tale sister in her wake, Alisha dived between Lady Tia and Kane. The potentially rash move woke Jess up to events. She grabbed the Wicked Witch's wrists, and held onto Lady Tia for all she was worth. As Alisha swung open the range door, Jess manoeuvred the dominatrix's hands into the oven. The move could be no more than symbolic. No way could anyone have fitted in the cramped, square cooking space, but the act brought a roar of anger from Kane as his fuck was interrupted, and a shout from David, who roughly grabbed hold of Alisha, yanking her away from Lady Tia, the oven, and Jess.

This was not how the men had planned this session to end. They had evidently meant for both women to fail, so everything rested upon the finale. Jess knew she had just caused herself a heap of trouble, but such was her anger at having Miss Sarah taken away from her she couldn't stop the words that poured from her throat. 'You can't change some endings. You can't. The story of Hansel and Gretel ends with the witch entering the oven. Some endings are how they are. Fairtasia or not, you can't mess with them.'

No one moved.

David gripped Alisha's upper arms even harder. Jess saw the pressure of his thumbs against the cook's flesh, and the erection imprisoned within his suit trousers grow more urgent.

At last, she saw the reason why he had forbidden her to

use the strap-on on Alisha. It was all blindingly clear. Kane had been going to screw Lady Tia, and David had been going to take Alisha, and she'd probably have had to watch – or would have been sent out into the crowd for a final mass fumble.

David wants Alisha for himself, she realised. This had never been about training her as the submissive for the whole of The Retreat. Proctor lusted after the young blonde. Just for himself, and no one else. Jess wondered if Proctor could read her mind as well as Mrs Peters could as she tried to wipe from her head the thought that, in bringing herself and Miss Sarah to The Retreat to train the object of his affections, David had ruined his chances of keeping Alisha to himself for ever. One man would never be enough for Alisha now, however much she cared for him.

'Clear some space!' Proctor's menacing shout echoed round the room, and the crowd drew back as if scolded.

Kane, still naked and angry, spun towards Jess. Catching hold of her hair, he threw her to David's feet, before gently unlocking Lady Tia's handcuffs.

As the dominatrix, Kane, and David surrounded the cowering Alisha and Jess, Dr Ewen, clad in her startlingly white catsuit, magically appeared at their side, as if she really was the White Witch.

She had a determined and dissatisfied look on her face that matched those of her counterparts. And in her red silk-gloved fingers she held a long, thin ginger twist biscuit …

Chapter Twenty

THERE WAS NO doubt who was in charge now.

With the arrival of Dr Ewen the whole dynamic of the group changed in a split second.

Jess and Alisha were efficiently snapped in place, standing back to back in the middle of an expanding circle of delegates with the remaining Retreat staff around them.

Dr Ewen stepped into the centre of the circle, and called for quiet. 'Ladies and gentlemen!' The few guests who'd continued to indulge their own appetites at the back of the gathering stopped moving, and all necks once again craned towards the makeshift stage, to see what would happen to the hapless Hansel and Gretel. 'I'd like to thank you very much for coming.'

Jess couldn't believe what she was hearing. Surely this wasn't the time for a speech of thanks?

Dr Ewen, however, evidently thought differently. 'I think you'll agree that David Proctor and my staff here at The Retreat have put on an excellent show for you this evening, and I am hopeful that Mr Kane Shyland –' she gestured her scarlet-gloved fingers in the Fairtasia boss's direction '– will decide to work with us on a permanent basis, and therefore allow you all to use the facilities here on many occasions in the future.'

The crowd, high on the scent of sex, their own physical exertions, and too much sugar from Alisha's sickly-sweet repast, roared with approval. Suddenly Jess understood why Dr Ewen was giving this speech. There was no way Kane couldn't sign on the dotted line now; his staff would never forgive him. Jess didn't dare glance at the men to see their expressions as Dr Ewen went on.

'So far this evening, we've had the chance to savour the flesh of Gretel before her inspired escape from the entrance hall.' Jess felt herself blush as all eyes fixed on her. The memory of so many fingers upon her skin served to stiffen her nipples again as she felt the leather of Alisha's jacket, and the warmth of her bare butt against her back.

'We have feasted upon a banquet that wouldn't look out of place in any fairy princess's palace, and we have revelled in the frustration of our very own Prince Charming, and his unorthodox rescue by Snow White.'

Again Jess felt her cheeks darken as the collective stares of the audience bore into her. None of them, however, was as hard or cold as the stare directed towards her from Lady Tia.

'Let us also not forget the plots, plans, and dreams we've all shared between the visual entertainments. And may I add, on a personal note, how honoured I am to have been chosen by David to act as hostess for the recreational side of his interests – which I am now confident will include Fairtasia.'

Another cheer went up. Jess reached behind her and grasped Alisha's hands for mutual reassurance as Dr Ewen continued to back either David or Kane into a corner – she wasn't sure which.

'And of course –' Dr Ewen undid some of the zips that adorned her skin-tight outfit '– I don't think any of us will ever forget the endurance of our Hansel, who has artificially fucked so many of you via her strap-on this evening, not to forget all the blowjobs she has given, and last but not least, the food she so expertly cooked.'

Slipping a hand into a space that would have been far

too small to act as a pocket for anyone who had even an inch of fat on their bones, Dr Ewen pulled out a neatly folded document. With everyone focusing on the zips, hoping that more than paperwork would soon be on show, the White Witch unzipped another pocket and produced a pen. 'So, with the battle to get the Wicked Witch to the range won, which as our brave Gretel rightly proclaimed is precisely how the tale is supposed to end, we have almost reached the conclusion of our proceedings.'

The audience's cheers turned to cries of "Encore!"

Elena Ewen held up her hands, complete with paperwork, as if to appeal for calm. 'However, as with all good acts of theatre, I am delighted to inform you that we still have the evening's finale to come!'

This time the cheer was accompanied by a gale of clapping hands and stamping feet that Jess and Alisha felt reverberate up through their legs and into their chests.

'But before our gorgeous Hansel and Gretel close tonight's fairy tale fest, I think now would be a fitting moment for your very own Kane Shyland to sign on the dotted line, ensuring The Retreat's involvement in the future of Fairtasia!'

David moved first, ripping the document from Dr Ewen's hand. He scanned it with suspicious eyes, 'You bitch, you ...' He turned to Kane. 'How could you? I've provided so much, I ...'

Kane's emotionless gaze met Proctor's. 'It was a failsafe, nothing more. A private agreement directly with Dr Ewen, not unlike the one you have with Mrs Peters. You own the establishment, so you haven't lost out completely – just your seat on our board.'

Taking the document from David's sweaty fingers, Kane rotated Lady Tia away from him, so he could lean upon her back to sign the document. He passed it back to Dr Ewen, who zipped it back into place. Then he smiled, showing off his dazzlingly white teeth. 'You have indeed put on an excellent show, doctor. Your staff are a credit to you, but then –' Kane turned Lady Tia back to face him '– how could they not be with this incredible specimen in control of the whip hand?'

Jess didn't know where to look. The uncertainties she'd had, everything that hadn't rung true about this place, made some sense for a second, only to be replaced by another set of new, even more pressing problems. How would David take being hoodwinked out on her body, and if she was being regarded by the watching delegates as part of The Retreat staff, how was she ever going to get home? Her fingers came to her collar, and her thoughts jumped to Miss Sarah. Was she really on a plane home now? Or was this just another trick? Whatever the truth, she was convinced without doubt that Kane, Miss Sarah, and Dr Ewen had been planning this outcome together.

The audience was getting restless. Jess could feel tension bunching in Alisha's muscles behind her as the gap between them and the guests began to close.

David opened his mouth to protest further, but Kane was ahead of him. 'I've made my decision. The Retreat is excellent, and I love your set-up here, but beyond that, well – you don't appear to be entirely trustworthy. If you can prove to me I'm wrong in the future, I may have a rethink.'

Far from mollified, David nodded tersely, aware that every single member of the UK staff of Fairtasia had witnessed his unprofessional outburst.

Not allowing more time to be wasted, satisfied she had steered things to her advantage, Elena stretched her arms out wide, and strode around the internal edge of the circle. 'Many thanks for your patience, ladies and gentlemen. I am sure each and every one of you understands the need to address business before pleasure!'

There was a ripple of laughter, as the expectant crowd hung on Dr Ewen's every word.

'If I could ask you to take five steps backwards – our performers require a little more room. You can, of course, climb upon the counter, tables, and chairs if you wish to secure a more aerial view, although I would caution that you do so at your own risk. I will not be liable for any accidental falls you may have during the forthcoming show due to spontaneous outbreaks of lust!'

There was more laughter, but this time it was undercut with a hunger that showed exactly why these men and women spent their working lives steeped in the world of dark fairy tale fantasies, where happy endings were far from guaranteed. There was a mad scramble of arms and legs as those guests beyond the first two rows of the circle clamoured to get the best view possible.

Coming between Jess and Alisha, Dr Ewen took one of their hands each, and continued to verbally back Proctor into a corner. 'Let me introduce you formally to our subjects this evening. First we have The Retreat's very own submissive, Miss Alisha, who has manfully played Hansel for us tonight. She is only a trainee, but I think you'll agree …'

The rest of Dr Ewen's sentence was lost on Alisha as she looked from Jess to David for confirmation of what the manageress was proclaiming. Was she the official submissive now?

David leant forward and whispered into Alisha's ear, 'Whatever you may think, you're still my trainee, and have much to prove.'

Alisha nodded, glowing with a mixture of terror and hope. David hadn't contradicted what Dr Ewen had said. With a determination to do the best she could in the final challenge of the night, the blonde tucked her curls behind her ears, pushed her shoulders back in the way she'd seen Jess do so many times, and prayed for their task to begin as soon as possible.

Unlike her counterpart, Jess was listening to every

word Dr Ewen was saying. 'Which brings me to Miss Jess Sanders, a well-trained and very experienced submissive who has kindly been loaned to us by my one-time colleague from England, Mrs Laura Peters.'

Colleague? Loaned to her? Surely I was loaned to Proctor? Just when Jess thought there was no further way events at The Retreat could confuse her, she had been proved wrong. If she was on loan, surely that meant she would be going home soon after all? Had Proctor got a contract with Fairtasia or not? What the hell was going on?

Her musings were cut short by the continuation of Dr Ewen's monologue, 'So I suggest you make the most of Miss Sanders' last evening with us here at The Retreat, ladies and gentleman, and enjoy the spectacle to come.'

This time it was Jess's turn to twist sharply and look from Proctor, to Kane, to Lady Tia. Proctor was obviously struggling not to show his fury, Kane was looking smug, but Lady Tia looked merciless.

The crowd roared in response, its state becoming more bacchanal by the moment.

Kane's looming presence in the circle sent Jess and Alisha's hearts racing a little faster. They each tried to adjust their perceptions as to how the evening was turning out, sure that Alisha had to win this final test, but neither sure how that was to be accomplished yet. Their employer called out, 'Miss Sanders, Miss Alisha, strip!'

To a cacophony of catcalls from the onlookers, the girls nervously removed their remaining garments.

'On your hands and knees, your feet touching. Now.' Kane spoke with the same level of command Jess was used to hearing from Mrs Peters. It was a tone that demanded unquestioning obedience; a tone David had never quite managed to master.

With a nod of reassurance she didn't feel toward Alisha, Jess dropped to the floor. Facing away from her companion, she soon felt the back of Alisha's feet against her own.

'This will be a test of stamina, strength, and endurance.'

Jess could see the jet-black heels of the otherwise naked Lady Tia walk past her hanging head, and wondered exactly how the Wicked Witch would gain revenge for her humiliation on the submissives before her. There was no doubt that was what she wanted to do. But would Kane let her?

'Dr Ewen –' Kane addressed the room, though his words were aimed directly at the submissives '– has brought with her from the dining table a number of items for use in this finale. The first you have already seen.' Holding up the extra-long ginger biscuit twist to the crowd, Kane flashed it in front of Jess's eyes before showing it to Alisha. 'Hansel, Gretel, I require you to rock your butts back towards each other.'

As he handed the cylindrical biscuit to Lady Tia, Jess braced herself.

The dominatrix's sharp fingernails spared no consideration for the fact they were scratching the most sensitive flesh on the two submissives. Steering one end of the ginger twist into Alisha's sopping channel, Lady Tia manoeuvred Jess's arse forward, then abruptly backwards, rocking her as if she was merely an awkward item of furniture. She positioned the other end of the biscuit in Jess's pussy, connecting the two women.

Gasping with the gratification of being filled, albeit insubstantially, Jess had to concentrate on what Kane was saying as the delicate heat of the ginger caressed the inside of her climax-addicted body. 'Both of you shuffle back. I don't want to be able to see any of the cookie cylinder.'

Alisha moved slowly, fearful that any move might accidentally expel the biscuit. She rested her forearms on the floor, pushed her arse back and felt the sugary twist slip deeper within her, as her butt was kissed by Jess's similarly positioned backside.

Nether submissive dared move, as they waited for Kane's next pronouncement.

'The challenge is not, as you might have assumed, ladies and gentlemen, to see which of our submissives can endure the most without coming. It is in fact, to see which of them can last the longest without sinking to the ground. The more climaxes they have before sheer exhaustion overtakes them will count in their favour rather than against them.'

Jess felt rather than heard the groan that escaped from Alisha's mouth; it echoed through her body and quivered through the makeshift dildo that connected them. She also felt troubled. If the contest had been to see who could last the longest without an orgasm, Alisha could easily have won – but this situation was weighted in Jess's favour.

'In the interests of fairness, I will ask Lady Tia to administer to Miss Sanders for ten minutes, while Dr Ewen assists Miss Alisha, then the mistresses will swap sides for the next ten, and so on, for as long as necessary. David will keep score of the climaxes, and I will referee to ensure fair play. Begin!'

Crouching in front of Jess, Lady Tia cranked her head up via the chin. Trying to block out the look of hate in the dominatrix's eyes, she thought instead of Miss Sarah and all the things she might do in such a scenario.

The kiss took Jess by surprise. She'd expected slaps and pinches, bites and bruises, but what she was getting was a full-on snogging session from the nude dominatrix, while claw-like fingers raked through her hair. It was so passionate that Jess couldn't help but savour the plump lips against hers, before she realised what Lady Tia was actually doing. Her fingers twined in Jess's hair, she was driving the submissive's head downwards with all her weight, attempting to make her collapse to the floor before even the first ten minutes was up.

With her mouth unable to escape the lock of Lady Tia's lips, Jess's shoulders began to quake. Her neck strained at its unaccustomed angle as submissive and dominatrix became locked in conflict; one determined to remain on her arms and knees, the other to push her victim to the floor.

It was Alisha's cry of climax, and the shudder that accompanied it, setting the ginger biscuit juddering inside both girls' channels, that made Lady Tia draw back without either her or Jess winning the fight.

'One climax goes to Alisha.' David called out, his anger at being publicly slapped down diminishing, as he watched his submissive take an early lead.

Changing tactic, Lady Tia crawled beneath Jess, only to find Dr Ewen had had the same idea and was beneath Alisha. As one, they sucked greedily at their subjects' nipples in a race to see which submissive would have the next orgasm propelled out of her.

Closing her eyes, not wanting to see the audience's solo or shared masturbation as she fought the swelling of her own desire, Jess flexed her knees so her hips moved back and forth. Her backside bumped against Alisha's, allowing her to feel the edible dildo sliding around within her.

Quickly catching on to what Jess was doing, the cook began to sway too, and soon it was clear to all that the submissives were working themselves off against each other. David was about to complain, but Kane held up a hand to stop him. This was all about entertainment and impressing the audience.

Jess knew she was close. As Lady Tia's sucking developed into biting, she couldn't prevent herself from jacking against the body behind her, triggering off not only her climax, but a second from Alisha.

'Two to Alisha, one to Miss Sanders,' David duly proclaimed.

Still determined to lose, but knowing it was too early

for her to collapse to the floor without it looking as if she was throwing the contest and incurring more of Proctor's wrath, Jess was relieved when Kane announced, 'Time to swap sides.'

Dr Ewen sat before Jess's face, just as Lady Tia had done, but her technique was a million miles away from that of the dominatrix she employed, and far more effective. 'Watch this, Miss Sanders.'

Lifting her head as best she could, Jess saw Dr Ewen slowly unzip each of the PVC panels that covered her chest. The whoops of the crowd told Jess how much they appreciated the sight of the bare tits as Elena softly said, 'Suckle the left one.'

Holding her breast out to the submissive's dry lips, she smiled as Jess inhaled her nipple with eagerness.

Tasting of clean skin and rubber, the rough yet velvety texture of Elena's areola against her tongue sent Jess's imagination into overload. Visions of Alisha crowded her head. Alisha attached to her with nothing but a long, cylindrical biscuit. Her temptingly freckled chest. The spanking she was receiving that echoed through their connected rumps. These pictures were chased away by images of herself suckling Miss Sarah's tits, and Miss Sarah licking her in return, and a second orgasm overtook Jess before her brain had even registered it was on its way.

'Two all!' David called. 'Both contestants are looking unsteady on their arms and legs. Who do you think will hit the deck first, ladies and gentlemen?'

Chapter Twenty-one

ONLY PRIDE WAS keeping Jess's shaking limbs in place now. Pride and her decision to make sure of Alisha's victory by hanging on long enough for The Retreat's submissive to have one more climax. Jess didn't want David, Kane, or Lady Tia to be able to argue about the outcome. Kane would never want a failed submissive to stay at The Retreat. Jess knew she had to hold back every one of her hypersensitive nerves until Alisha had come again. Then she would hit the deck.

Dr Ewen's hands had come to Jess's backside, smoothing over her rump as if she was polishing it, before tucking her fingers over the seal which held the ginger biscuit in place. Again, Jess felt Alisha tense, then she discovered why. Lady Tia's fingers had joined Dr Ewen's.

As the mistresses' hands combined in a strange tango on the submissives' butts, and fingertips trailed across their stimulated, yet somehow neglected clits, Jess felt herself begin to shake.

Suddenly everything she'd been through in the last 24 hours crowded through her head. She'd been strung up in a harness and turned into a puppet, tied and used as a sex toy by the Fairtasia delegates, felt up in every possible way, given Jason a handjob, watched her unofficial lover being taken away from her, been collared by a man she distrusted, and helped metaphorically defeat the Wicked Witch by shoving her "into" an oven. Until that point, Jess had managed to keep exhaustion at bay, adrenalin and her will to get home spurring her on. But now she could feel her muscles failing, and Jess knew if the quivering from behind her was anything to go by, Alisha was having the same problem.

A sharp clap from Kane made Jess jump, and told her that he'd also sensed the end was nigh as he called for hush. 'If you please, ladies!'

Jess and Alisha peered around at each other, not sure if it was them or Lady Tia and Dr Ewen who were being addressed. Understanding the glazed sheen in each other's eyes, both submissives knew they were equally tired. It was now a case of who hit the deck first.

Their telepathic exchange was cut short as Lady Tia and Dr Ewen snapped satin masks over the girls' eyes, followed by ear mufflers.

Plunged into a claustrophobic, darkened deafness, Jess and Alisha could feel the vibration of unheard conversations resonate through their hands and feet. Their combined pulses raced, knocking against each other as they fought to stay on their feet long enough to discover what Kane planned next.

Jess, knowing she should fall to the floor now so that Alisha could win, found she couldn't. Despite her tiredness, something deep inside her had to see how far her body could be pushed this time, to see what new limit she could reach. Then, she told herself, then I'll go down for sure and Alisha can win.

The abrupt rearing up of Alisha's butt took Jess by surprise. A pair of male hands had grabbed her hips, making sure the girls didn't lose their precarious biscuit connection. Although she couldn't hear it, Jess was convinced from the stiffening of the previously wobbly legs that were now entwined with her own that Alisha was making a fair amount of noise.

In the next moment, Jess found out why.

The hands at her hips disappeared, presumably to hold on to Alisha, and the unmistakably pointed fingernails of Lady Tia prised apart the rim of Jess's anus. Gasping, her whole being fixated on staying as statuesque as possible, Jess fought every instinct to stiffen up her muscles, and attempted to relax.

A sudden invasion of intense cold made her jump. The snowman touch of ice cream was confirmed as the sweet aroma of vanilla hit Jess's nostrils. A digit, covered in frozen dessert, was eased in and out of her back passage, lubricating her with chilled ease.

Jess shook with the shock of having something so cold creaming her anus, wishing she'd not been so stupid as to want to see what would happen next. She hoped that Alisha was holding firm as the icy finger was removed, and a new, slim object was inserted in its place.

Her guts churned as the unknown item was pushed deep within her. She kept expecting its girth to widen, but it remained only a centimetre or so thick, making her suspect it was another ginger twist.

Denied their eyes and ears, all Alisha and Jess had for their senses to focus on was the pressure of their edible dildo, the presence of each other's rear ends, the play of their toes as they wrapped around each other, and the heady scent of sex.

No one was touching Jess now but, rather than relax, she became tenser than ever. If no one was doing anything to her, it meant they were all just watching them. *Why?*

Sixty seconds later, Jess found out. The warmth of the unusual anal plug had been nice at first after the cold of the cream, but now it began to heighten into a richer heat. Unnoticeable at first, it slowly started to smoulder inside the crouched women.

Jess could feel Alisha's breathing rapidly increase. Whatever had been inserted into each of their butts was so heavily sprinkled with ginger powder that it was making them sweat from the inside out.

She screwed up her watering eyes beneath the blindfold, convinced only Alisha's rookie status had stopped it being raw ginger root that invaded them, and cupped her hands into fists. Guessing what was coming, she locked her legs more firmly around Alisha's, more to help keep her comrade upright than herself.

Before her next thought had time to form, the earmuffs and masks were removed, and she saw the whip-welding arm of Dr Ewen being raised. A scream and accompanying leap from behind her informed Jess that Lady Tia had already struck Alisha. As the weapon landed on her butt, making the plug within her glow with an even more intense heat, Jess let her own scream fly from her lips.

There was no time to take in the encouraging noises from the audience. No concentration left to hear the words coming from David as he shouted. There was only the spank of the cane and the heat of the plug. Only the underlying presence of the biscuit twist at each pussy, and the cold air of neglect that teased their chests, as the two submissives entered a world where surviving long enough for the reward of orgasm was all that mattered.

It was the firm application of a finger to her clit that brought Jess back to reality. She could feel the stripes of Dr Ewen's whip on her arse, almost as hot as the ginger cane within her. But that was nothing compared to the friction burns that were being caused as Alisha's backside banged and thudded against her, each move feeling more and more as if someone was swiping sandpaper over her tender flesh.

Alisha's cries were as much laced with gratitude for what The Retreat staff were doing to her as pleading for it to stop, but Jess knew there was no way the trainee sub would hold out much longer.

The anonymous thumb on her nub circled the tiny peak in time to the strikes of her arse, and suddenly the choice to hit the ground before Alisha did was purely academic. As the supercharged rod in Jess's butt was rapidly pumped in and out, each move sending a zip of fire to every nerve in her body, her arms buckled, and her head and shoulders crashed to the floor. With her legs caught up in her comrade's, Jess couldn't help but bring Alisha down with her.

As both submissives yelped out their climaxes of delicious defeat, the biscuit that had connected their cunts dissolved, coming away in soggy lumps, freeing their frames from each other. The ginger sticks were extracted from their butts before the burning climbed any further up the temperature scale. To the rapturous applause of the Fairtasia delegation, the exhausted Hansel and Gretel curled into each other's arms, and closed their eyes.

The crowd had gone.

Jess kept her eyes shut as they left, not wanting to give Kane or David the opportunity to ask any more of her or Alisha that evening. At some point someone had placed a thick, red cloak over them. Dazed and sore, Jess had enjoyed its weight as she cradled the sleeping Alisha.

Eventually, the rustle of the cloak made Jess raise her eyelids, and she found herself looking straight into Alisha's green gaze. Putting a finger to her lips to tell the cook to remain quiet, Jess silently mouthed, 'Are you OK?'

Nodding in reply, Alisha smiled. Her body bore the hallmarks of their experience, but Jess recognised the new shine to the girl's eyes. It closely resembled that of her own. Whatever happened to them next, there would be no going back for Alisha now.

Proctor's voice, booming out in frustrated anger, made them close their eyes again, feigning sleep. 'You tricked me, you bitch! You grabbed Fairtasia's business for The Retreat without allowing me to secure my place on their board. I confided in you! I told you what I truly wished for myself and the girl and you betrayed me! And you've backed me into a corner over Miss Sanders. How the hell can I keep the Fables girl here now?'

'She was never yours to keep.' Dr Ewen's reply was as controlled as ever. 'The power of the whip is one thing, David, but you would be wise never to underestimate the power of words. Now if you'll excuse me, I think it's time that these young women were escorted to their private rooms, and we all got a good night's sleep. Goodnight, Mr Proctor.'

Despite being tired to the bone, Jess couldn't sleep. Pacing the turret room, she felt confusion swamp her. Had she earned her release? Had what Dr Ewen said in front of Kane and the Fairtasia workforce made any difference? She couldn't see Proctor letting her go back to Fables so easily, especially after he'd been humiliated in public. Jess clawed at the collar around her neck. Why am I wearing this? she wondered. Surely it should be Alisha's by right. She has not only earned it, but she wants it. Perhaps once David has calmed down he'll see he has a brilliant client for The Retreat, even if it didn't come with the power he wanted, and Alisha has been trained up, so …

Still trapped in thought, deciding another shower would help her think straight, Jess did her best to keep her neck out of the hot water, as it made the choker around her neck feel tighter than ever.

She spoke to herself beneath the jets of steam. 'Right, first I have to get out of here, which means packing up as much of my stuff as I can carry, leaving the rest, and reaching the door without being spotted.'

Despite her words, her determination disappeared. Although Jess knew the turret room door hadn't been locked, the main castle doors probably would be, and even if she found a key, what would she do then? She had no idea where she was, no mobile phone, and no money.

Wrapping a towel around her body, drying herself with care so she didn't irritate the bruises on her backside, Jess refused to let herself panic. She had to do something, she had to try.

Having dressed in her most comfortable clothes, Jess stuffed her things into her holdall, zipped it shut, and headed for the entrance hall. If she could get into Dr Ewen's study, then she could phone Fables. Mrs Peters would know what to do, and Jess could at least find out if Miss Sarah had got home safely. There might even be some money she could borrow for the journey.

The sound of her heart beating thudded in her ears as she crept down the narrow stairway, and stole quietly along the corridor towards the entrance hall. Her ears straining, Jess listened out for anybody who might be up, clearing away the detritus of the party. She heard the familiar grunting sound of David in the throes of climax before she saw him.

About to scuttle back to her room, she was stopped in her tracks as Proctor twisted on his feet. 'Miss Sanders! Here, now!'

Jess obeyed, her eyes widening as she saw Alisha bending over the table which had been used to lay out the evening's invitations. The cook's backside was flushed with the signs of fresh spanking.

Reading Jess's thoughts, David said, 'I was denied the fuck I most wanted during the party.' He glanced covetously at Alisha's bare back. 'And so I took it afterwards.'

Swallowing carefully, knowing she had nothing to lose as it was blatantly obvious she'd been attempting to escape, Jess replied, 'And you took what you wanted, despite Alisha being utterly exhausted.'

'She wanted me to.'

'Did you?' Even as she asked the question, she knew

the answer, and couldn't help but give a wry smile as the cook meekly replied.

'I did. Yes.'

'I assume Kane and Lady Tia are off somewhere making up for lost time as well.'

'Being amongst the Fairtasia staff appears to make you cheeky, Miss Sanders!'

Swallowing back her instincts, she ignored the barbed comment and asked, 'Does this mean I can leave now? I did all you asked of me, and you plainly no longer need an additional female submissive here.'

David took a step closer, his hand coming to Jess's throat. 'While you wear this collar, you belong to me.'

Fighting her natural instinct to reply, 'Yes, David,' Jess said, 'But it should belong to Alisha now.'

'And so it shall. Eventually –' David smiled, and Jess felt her insides roll over. 'First you have to get home.'

'I am sure Mrs Peters will pay my air fare.'

'I have no doubt she would. But if you call her, that collar is not coming off. There is only one key and I have it. And before you think it can be cut off, it can't be done. Not without hurting you. Anyway, if you did get it cut off, you'd have failed, and part of you would always remain mine. I can't see Mrs Peters liking that very much; can you?'

Jess averted her gaze from Proctor's face to Alisha's backside, so she didn't have to witness his sneering victory. She spoke quietly. 'What do I have to do so you'll take it off?'

David sat on one of the repositioned armchairs. 'I suggest you sit down and listen. Alisha, go and fetch Miss Sanders a drink and some food. She has a long journey ahead of her.'

'A long journey? I'm going home after all?'

'You, Miss Sanders –' Proctor fished a sealed envelope out of his pocket '– are going on a quest.'

Taking the envelope from him with shaking hands, Jess opened it, and produced a list of five different addresses. 'What are these?'

'They are the locations you will visit on your journey south. At each one you will be given enough resources to get you to the next stop. Once the fifth and final address has been reached, then I will be in touch.'

Jess suddenly felt foolish. 'You planned this, didn't you; whether you got the Fairtasia contract or not? You've had this list on you the whole time.'

'Of course.' David leant back and pulled a tiny silver key from his other pocket, dangling it in front of her eyes. 'I always plan everything. Although I confess this time my plans haven't gone precisely as I'd hoped. This list was merely a back-up if Alisha did succeed in becoming The Retreat's sub, despite my hopes to the contrary.'

'You wanted her to fail?' Jess nodded to herself. 'I suspected you wanted her to serve just you, and keep me for everyone else to play with.'

'Miss Sarah warned me you were clever.' David stood and stretched as the naked Alisha reappeared with a tray of sandwiches and a flask of coffee. 'And now it's time for some sleep.'

'But Alisha isn't just yours now – Kane wants her at The Retreat. What will you do?'

'Make a new plan, of course.' He took Alisha by the elbow, about to lead her away. 'A car will be here for you in one hour,' he added. 'In the meantime I suggest you eat, drink, and rest.'

Jess looked at the envelope suspiciously. 'What am I to do at these places?'

'You will find out soon enough. I wish you a safe trip Miss Sanders. I will be in touch ...'

Epilogue

MRS PETERS LOOKED up from where she had her lover blindfolded and handcuffed to her desk. Her paddle-wielding arm froze in the air as her dominatrix walked in. 'Miss Sarah!'

'I apologise for interrupting.' Miss Sarah curtseyed and inclined her head towards an incapacitated Sam. 'I had no chance to find a telephone to warn of my premature return.'

Accepting this, Mrs Peters simply said, 'Where is Miss Sanders?'

'He has kept her.'

The paddle was slammed down on Sam's rump, before Laura quickly freed her partner of the blindfold and ordered him to sit. The artist, his cock sticking out incongruously towards both women, sat on the desk. The look on Laura's face did not make any of the "I told you so" comments that were clearly forming on his lips wise to utter.

'If you would be so kind as to finish off here for me, Miss Sarah –' Mrs Peters pointed to Sam's dick '– I have a call to make.'

Snatching up the phone as Miss Sarah's mouth obediently engulfed Sam's shaft, Mrs Peters spoke sharply into the speaker. 'Get me Dr Ewen at The Retreat. Now.'

The silence in the room, punctuated only by the industrious licks of Miss Sarah's tongue, hung heavy. At last, Mrs Peters spoke into the receiver. 'Elena, what the hell is going on? You promised you'd look after my girls for me. I need not remind you that we had a deal.'

Miss Sarah's eyes narrowed as she worked. She should have known Mrs Peters had been in league with Dr Ewen all along; after all, things were never what they seemed with her boss.

There was a pause while Laura listened to her counterpart in Scotland. 'You did what? You robbed David of his contract? Still practising deviousness and underhand behaviour then! But at the cost of my submissive, I ...'

The next pause lasted longer.

Thunderclouds gathered across Mrs Peters' face, exploding into a tempest of anger, and she jumped to her feet, yelling down the line, 'How the hell could you be so reckless with the wellbeing of a member of my staff! We both know the score with Proctor! Rule one – you do not trust the man. There is no rule two!'

Miss Sarah, her throat full of dick, tried and failed not to worry about what might be happening to Jess. Mrs Peters spoke with deadly calm down the phone. 'Elena Ewen, you will get my submissive back home right now. Right now, do I make myself clear ...?

'What do you mean she's gone? Miss Sanders has gone?

Gone where?'

The Third Book in *The Perfect Submissive Trilogy*
Knowing Her Place

With her head full of unanswered questions, exhausted from her fairytale experience at the hands of Dr Ewen, Lady Tia, and the staff of the adult entertainment service provided by The Retreat, Jess Sanders is desperate to leave Scotland, and return to her usual submissive position at the exclusive Fables Hotel in Oxford.

Having been thwarted in his plans to keep Jess at The Retreat permanently, its owner David Proctor isn't willing to let Jess go back to her dominatrix, Miss Sarah, and her employer, Mrs Peters, without sending her on one final mission. Only if she succeeds in her task, will Proctor remove the collar of servitude he has locked around Jess's neck.

With a list of five unknown addresses in her hand, Jess Sanders is placed in a car and driven from The Retreat towards England. With no idea what or who awaits her at the first stop, all Jess can hope for is that her journey will eventually take her back to where she belongs. To the Fables Hotel, where Jess Sanders truly knows her place.

Lightning Source UK Ltd.
Milton Keynes UK
UKOW04f0330101213

222675UK00001B/4/P